A Parachute in the Lime Tree

Annemarie Neary

The History Press Ireland

For my son Rory

First published 2012

The History Press Ireland
119 Lower Baggot Street
Dublin 2
Ireland
www.thehistorypress.ie

British Library Cataloguing in Publication Data.
A catalogue record for this book is available from the British Library.

ISBN 978 1 84588 732 2

Typesetting and origination by The History Press
Printed in Great Britain

Contents

Oskar

The Fall

Oskar had never been afraid of falling. He'd always loved the abandonment of the jump and the feeling of reprieve when the parachute did its job. This time, though, he screamed his way down. Once the parachute jolted in, he was a puppet in the dark.

He didn't see the tree. It tossed him this way and that as he bumped down through its layers. He felt a sharp twist to his knee, and was stationary at last, slung upside down among the branches. Then the rain began, coming at him from all angles and pelting the earth beyond the tree. He released his harness: tugged at the ropes, swung on them. The canopy of the tree released a shower of raindrops but the parachute wouldn't shift. The moon slid out from behind the clouds like a searchlight, and made it stubbornly visible.

He'd dreaded the jump but he was through the hatch before the others had time to tackle him. Willy was the only one who was quick enough but he couldn't hold his grip. As he plunged free of the plane, and the cold air whistled in his ears, Oskar was suddenly unreachable. Now, though, the parachute flapping overhead seemed like a bad omen.

It was only when he'd clambered painfully down that he saw the house. His first instinct was to head off in the opposite direction, until he realised the overgrown garden gave the only shelter for miles. Here and there, a small tree clawed at the lightening sky but there were no woods, no natural hiding places at all.

He skirted the right flank of the house, limped his way past an old bathtub invaded by weeds and scrawny daffodils, and headed for the densest growth. He was desperate to find somewhere to stop, think, gather himself. He pissed into a clump of nettles, and a cat sped out from under a bush and scrambled onto a wall, eyeing him suspiciously. Down here, there were traces of an old vegetable patch and a rotting shed that was barely distinguishable from the growth around it. Inside, it smelt of damp earth and rot, and the only window was green with slime. It might have been a summerhouse, though he doubted it had ever seen much sun. When he lifted a cushion, a trail of small black mice squealed out the door. There were jars of dark viscous liquids, a jumble of brushes and pencils in an old tin can; scraps of faded diagrams were pinned to the window frame.

He could hardly remember the last time he'd been alone. Before Vannes, there was the training school at Köthen: before that, the endless hikes with the Hitler Jugend. There had always been someone to tell him what to do next. Now, he didn't even know where exactly he was.

Later, when the sky was bright, there were voices and the scrape of something along a path but soon the sounds faded again. By now his knee had swollen; he forced himself to stand on it and used an old rag that smelt of linseed to bind it up but it wouldn't take him far. He fell into a fitful sleep. Joachim was there, playing his clarinet in some late-night bar with three elderly women in *dirndl*; there was the Jew with the bloodied face on the ground outside the Cafe Weissner, and Reinhard in his black uniform, drinking plundered French cognac with Vati. Elsa hardly featured but that's the way with dreams.

He awoke to the sound of an engine, and unsheathed his knife. After a while, he heard the vehicle drive off again. He remained on his guard, though, certain that by now someone would have seen the parachute. Hours passed and no one came, and fear turned to boredom. He found a tin of boiled sweets on the shelf, crunched on them two at a time, pooling the saliva in his mouth to try and quench his thirst. Afterwards, his mouth tasted of metal and he was thirstier than ever.

By nightfall, his tongue was dry against the roof of his mouth and his whole body felt battered. He opened the door of the shed just wide enough, then hobbled his way to the edge of the undergrowth. In front of the house was a grassy area, more field than lawn, then a gravelled stretch. Overhead, there was an ocean of stars so vast it took his breath away. He had forgotten a sky could be so silent. Once, with Elsa, back in Berlin in the old days, they had each chosen a star. Elsa wasn't interested in spring skies and winter skies and all the technical stuff.

'I'll just take the one above my head, Oskar. What does it matter which star is mine? A star is a star.'

But it mattered. And when the night sorties began, he became superstitious about catching sight of it. He would crouch in the gondola beneath the black belly of the plane like a grub in a cocoon, sickened by the smell of fuel, legs frozen, certain he'd be the one to catch the first hit. As he flew through clear, star-scattered skies to light the targets for the bombers who would follow, he always kept his eyes down.

He watched the house for signs of life. A dim light burned in a downstairs window. When the light died, he waited. Then, he took off his boots to cross the gravelled path that separated the house from the garden and crept in through an unlocked door. He drank in splutters from the tap, filled his can with water. In the pantry, he tore a hunk off a rough loaf, found some hard cheese under a china dome. He cracked an egg into a cup, then, holding his nose, he gulped it down. The clanging of a clock startled him. The sound was identical to his own family's hall clock, the one his father had threatened to throw in the Spree, and for an instant he was back home in Zweibrückenstrasse with his sister, Emmi.

'Forget her, Oskar. She's not coming back.'

The House Next Door

They struggled through a blizzard for most of the way but it was in the wilds of Brandenburg that the snow finally forced the train to a halt. For a while it looked as though Oskar's leave would be spent out there in the wilderness, but in the end they sent a snowplough out to clear the tracks and the train made it to Berlin after all. By the time he reached Zweibrückenstrasse, he was exhausted. As he walked up the path, he turned his head away from the Frankels' house, determined to start things on a positive note. Inside, with the *Eintopf* on the hob and the log fire burning, he felt reassured; it still smelt like home. His mother kissed him gingerly; his father clapped him on the back. When he asked where Emmi was, Vati seemed taken aback, as if it wasn't an obvious question.

'Married,' Mutti glanced at him nervously, 'to Reinhard. How long ago, Gert?'

'Oh, it must be a month or so.'

They used to joke about Reinhard, always strutting about with those friends of his. Oskar was barely in the door but already he felt the house close in on him. 'Nobody wrote. Why didn't Emmi—'

'Let's get you something to drink, Oskar. Some hot milk with cinnamon, maybe, something to warm you up,' said Vati.

'There was no church ceremony, nothing like that.' Mutti was brushing invisible crumbs from the lap of her skirt. 'It was just a Party affair. We weren't even there ourselves, darling.' When he opened his mouth to speak, she cut in, 'Emmi made her own bed.'

It was too soon for a row. Oskar went upstairs to change, even though there was no need. Mutti had kept all his old uniforms, right back to Hitler Jugend days, and they hung in size order in the closet, each lie bigger than the next. He turned his back on them, and went over to the window. It looked like the Frankels' garden had been cleared, and lights shone out onto the snow from a downstairs room. For a moment it was as though none of it had happened at all. He raced down the stairs and almost knocked into Vati, who was crossing the hallway with a tray of drinks.

'When did they get back?'

'Nobody came back. We have new neighbours now.' Vati raised his tray a little, but Oskar shook his head and made for the door without even bothering with a jacket. The Frankels' house looked freshly painted and the torn curtain was gone. The snow had stopped, and now that he was outside he felt his head begin to clear. He couldn't bring himself to go back in, so he just kept on walking. People passed in flurries, the phosphorous buttons on their outer clothing darting about like fireflies. He didn't go anywhere in particular, just walked around in circles, clapping his arms to keep the blood moving. It was hard to believe the war was happening at all; there was so little sign of it here. So far, the English had only managed a graze or two and the city remained confident, out of reach.

Next morning, no one mentioned his disappearance the night before.

'I've saved the *Eintopf*,' Mutti said. 'We won't bother with a big party. Just Frau Auger, of course, and Sophie.'

Oskar wondered what made Frau Auger such essential company; he wasn't even sure he could place her. He'd no idea who Sophie was.

'Oh Oskar, you remember: Emmi's friend, from the choir. Emmi had such high hopes for you two.'

When he saw Frau Auger, he recognised her right away. She was one of the women Elsa had been fearful of; some incident he couldn't recall now involving Herr Goldmann. As he sat down opposite her, he noted the little blue and white motherhood bow pinned to her lapel. He was surprised Mutti had any time for the likes of Frau Auger. 'I'm as much in favour of a glorious Fatherland as the next woman,' she used to say, 'but is there any need to be so unpleasant about it?'

Sophie spoke incessantly about a boyfriend who had some cushy number doing research flights with Telefunken. Frau Auger didn't say much but Oskar felt her dissect him like the meat on her plate. Once he'd had a glass or two of wine, he decided to take her on. 'I see they gave someone the Frankels' house,' he said. 'When did that happen?'

'Oh, Oskar, dear,' Mutti fumbled. 'It's hard to put a date on these things. People are always coming and going. Late summer? Not long after you left, I suppose.' She turned to Frau Auger, 'You know, the berries this year really were the best in years. We've had so many jams and jellies and compotes.'

Frau Auger chewed slowly, glancing up at Oskar from time to time.

'Where are the Frankels' things?' he asked.

'Long gone,' Frau Auger said. 'Sold or dumped.' She tilted her head to one side, awaiting his reaction.

'Stolen?'

'Confiscated.'

'Oskar, why don't you tell us about Brittany, darling. Is it as beautiful as they say? And does it rain all the time?' Mutti knocked over a glass of white wine with her elbow and began dabbing at it with her handkerchief. She looked like she might cry. Frau Auger crossed her knife and fork, and straightened herself in her chair.

'Go on,' she told Oskar, as she patted Mutti's hand maternally.

When Oskar looked up from the mesmerising whiteness of the dinner plate, all four faces were fixed on him. 'There is no point,' he murmured finally.

Frau Auger gave a small smile. 'Precisely,' she said. 'What's gone is gone.'

By the time Oskar got up the next morning, the house was empty. He walked through each floor, trawling it for some tiny sign of change. But even Emmi's room was exactly as it had always been, with her pink eiderdown folded neatly down and her collection of carved animals still on her dressing table. On the attic landing, a jag of sunlight blinded him a moment as he turned to mount the final flight of stairs.

Mutti's attic was a place of crates and packing cases and infallible order. It was a source of pride to her that she could put her hand on anything at all. Items were stored according to the frequency of their use, so that the Christmas decorations, used annually, were kept nearer the door than the schoolbooks that would probably never be read again. When he opened the door, he was astonished to find the place in chaos. There were papers strewn all over the floor, a string of glass beads, a fur collar, a jumble of scarves. Most of the paper seemed to belong to an academic dissertation of some sort, but there were other things, too: bills and general correspondence, even a handwritten score. He knelt down in the middle of it all and began to read.

Dear Herr Frankel,

I do of course remember you. Our meeting was very fine: a true meeting of minds. In relation to your enquiry, however, about the availability of a position in our institution, I regret to inform you that I am unable to assist you in this regard.

Then another:

Dear Frankel,

I am in receipt of yours of 29 April. We hope that one day you will come and speak in Cambridge on your chosen subject. I cannot believe myself that war is likely. I am sorry to hear of your ill fortune with regard to your position in Berlin and sincerely hope that matters improve.

Further in, the attic was as orderly as before. There were boxes labelled in his mother's neat hand: linens, underclothing, neck ties. One was full of piano music, in a house where nobody played. He began tearing them open, rifling through clothing for something of Elsa's. The paintings stacked against the wall were Professor Frankel's. He recognised the black contours, the bold colours now deemed degenerate. He came across a canvas that was much cruder than the others, daubed unevenly with bright red paint as if to cover up some image underneath. It puzzled him, and he took it over to the window to look at it in the light. He could see there was something there: a figure, perhaps. He traced the outline with his finger but the red paint was so thick he couldn't make it out.

He had almost given up hope of finding anything of Elsa when he spotted her handwriting in a stack of papers piled on top of one of the boxes. He raced to read it, then made himself slow down and read it again, measuring each sentence before moving on to the next one.

Dear Oskar,

They say there will be a war soon. But then, you probably know more about that than we do. I didn't get a reply to my earlier letter, so I suppose you've forgotten me by now. My parents are still in Amsterdam but hoping to join me here in Ireland. Papa has someone he thinks may be able to get them a visa, but he

has spent so much time outside embassies that I can't help but
feel it will be the same old story. Do you ever go to the woods
now? Has anything stayed the same?

Your Elsa

Mutti must have intercepted the letter, written almost
two years ago. He struggled to keep control of his anger as
he held the flimsy sheet of paper to his cheek. He tried to
imagine Elsa in Ireland but he had no mental picture of the
place, knew little about it except for black beer and cattle.
A teacher at school claimed once that Irish monks had civi-
lised Germany and everybody laughed. He must have reread
the letter a dozen times, hoping to find something more in it,
before it hit him that Elsa had given no address and was as far
away as ever.

He looked around him at the piles of neatly labelled boxes,
at the jumble of things on the floor. He remembered the
night, soon after the Frankels had left, that he and Vati went
next door to tie back a broken shutter that had banged and
clanked for hours the night before. Perhaps that had been the
start of it.

The brass number on the Frankels' door was so tarnished
it was barely legible but the key was still where they'd always
kept it. It shouldn't have taken long to deal with the shutter
but Vati was upstairs for ages, opening cupboards, sliding out
drawers. Meanwhile, Oskar stood at Elsa's piano. He touched
it lightly with his fingertips, not daring to press down the keys.
As he waited at the bottom of the stairs, he noticed a photograph lying flat on the hall table. It looked like a family portrait;
he wondered why it had been left behind. In the centre of a
group of young men sat a small, elderly couple. The woman
was compact and pigeon-chested. She wore an elaborate hat
covered in flowers and feathers. The little man stared straight at

him, with eyes that were too much like Elsa's. The resemblance disconcerted him, so he turned the image face down.

The thought of Vati rifling through Elsa's things made him feel sick. He refolded her letter and stuffed it into the pocket of his shirt, reclaiming her. He went to the little window in the roof and opened it to get some air. As he looked out on a city that didn't feel his any more, the idea hit him. He could hardly get down the stairs quick enough, almost tripping over himself in his haste to reach the front door.

The tramcar was full, mainly women and girls. It rattled around street corners and when it reached the Tiergarten, Oskar got out. Diplomatic missions were housed in every other building, and he walked up and down Tiergartenstrasse, peering at the nameplates until he found the one he wanted.

The woman who answered the door of the Irish Legation looked about the same age as his mother. She was German, not Irish, though he couldn't place the accent. She looked him up and down before letting him in, but he was sure the uniform would do the trick, and it did. Once inside, he came straight to the point 'I'm hoping to trace a friend. Someone granted permission to enter Ireland. A refugee, if that's the word.'

The woman's nose twitched. 'What kind of refugee?'

'A family from Berlin. Frankel is the name.' He watched her absorb this information blankly.

'And your interest in them?'

'I'd like to correspond.'

She started to snigger. 'Jewish penpals? You're pulling my leg.'

He tried to laugh along with her but found he couldn't.

'Don't go taking offence, Officer.' She was scrutinising him now, her eyes flickering over his uniform, scanning his face. 'Maybe they've not gone at all. Is that what you're thinking? Maybe they're lying low in some cellar, with their diamonds and their fox furs.' She leaned towards him, 'The last man we had here used to give their people back in Dublin all kinds of grief about the Jews. "How am I supposed to cope? It's a tidal wave. I'm inundated." To hear him, you'd think half the Jews in Europe were heading for Ireland. He put the wind up them, all right. He's gone now, more's the pity.' She whispered conspiratorially, 'The Foreign Ministry loved him but he wasn't neutral enough for the Irish. Neutral? With thousands of them fighting for Britain? Don't make me laugh. Anyhow, we've a young gentleman now. Came from Ireland last summer.' She lowered her voice and mouthed the words, 'Out of his depth ... But sit yourself down and I'll see if he'll talk to you.'

She led Oskar into a waiting room, then disappeared through a set of double doors. She came back a moment later and beckoned him in.

The official stood up when Oskar entered the room, which seemed odd until Oskar realised that he was standing for the uniform and not for him.

'All our records are confidential,' he started, 'There is no possibility of my being able to help you. None at all.' The man rubbed his eyes, then felt for his chair and sat down. He took a crumpled handkerchief from his drawer and caught a sneeze in it.

The uniform was no longer an asset, Oskar could tell. Though not invited to, he sat down as well, slid the jacket off and placed it over his lap. The man was watching him from over the top of the handkerchief, his eyes pale and shrewd as he swiped it back and forward on his nose, then rolled it into a ball and shoved it back in his desk.

'Let me show you something,' Oskar said, and handed over Elsa's letter. The man made no comment at first, even though it couldn't have taken long to read.

'You see? I'm not here looking for trouble. I'm not here to cause problems for anyone, least of all the Frankels. I am simply trying to contact an old friend.'

'I'm sorry,' he said, his voice softer now. 'But if your friend is in Ireland at all, she's in the six counties.' The man reached into the drawer again for the handkerchief to stifle another sneeze. 'Just before war broke out, the British let in some children and young people. A few ended up in Belfast. Needless to say, we sat on our hands until it was too late.'

'But if there was a visa application, surely you'd have some record?'

'My predecessor wasn't keen on records.'

The woman reappeared on the landing. She waited until he'd reached her level and then she came so close he could smell violets on her breath.

'Those Jews you're looking for. They won't have been short of a bob or two. Some of them bury it in the garden, you know. My husband told me. Often you will find a Jewish garden is full of loot. I hate to ask, but these people pay next to nothing.'

It took Oskar a moment to realise that she was asking him for money. He found something in one of his pockets and hoped that would be enough.

She smoothed the crumpled note front and back before pocketing it. 'I'll see what I can find,' she said.

The woman was gone half an hour at least. He was beginning to think she might not return at all when she beckoned him into a small side room packed with files. She pointed to a ledger entry, made the year before in looping blue ink, and gave him a scrap of paper on which to write. In the margin, a note had been made in large black letters. 'TAKE NO ACTION.' As far as he could see, the same message was repeated right down the length of the page.

Peter Israel Frankel, aged fifty-one years, Rosl Sara Frankel, aged forty-four years. Formerly of Berlin. Currently resident at 77 Roote Weg, Amsterdam, care of Mr Rudi Wittmeyer.

Representations made to the Taoiseach, Mr Eamon de Valera, by Miss Esther Alexander of Whitecrest, County Wicklow. Copy to the Legation at Den Haag. Only daughter, Elsa Sara Frankel, aged eighteen years, formerly resident in Belfast, now living in the State. Supported by members of the Jewish community. Sponsors available for parents. Employment offered in Miss Alexander's establishment.

After leaving the Legation, Oskar could easily have got home in time for dinner but he couldn't face it. He walked the length of Unter den Linden looking for somewhere quiet to have a beer, then passed through Franz Josef Platz, where, years before, he'd witnessed the first of the Nazi book burnings. Eventually, he found a place in a side street, took a corner table, and ordered two beers in quick succession as he read and reread the details he'd managed to scribble down.

Next morning, he slept late again. When he came downstairs, Frau Auger was already there. She sat slightly in front of Mutti and greeted him over the rim of a coffee cup. Vati, it seemed, had taken yet another walk.

'Almost time to leave us?' she asked.

He ignored her, and turned to his mother. 'I went up to the attic yesterday. There are letters, books, so many things.' His voice tailed off.

Mutti took the coffee pot into the kitchen. He followed her and closed the door behind him. Neither of them said anything right away. Then, she took a small package from her apron pocket. He was in no mood to take anything from her but when he started to tell her that, she put her finger to her lips. 'Take it, Oskar.'

On his way out the gate, Oskar almost collided with one of the next door's new occupants. She was thin, a little shabby, with a wispy plait wound round on the back of her head. She smiled up at him, her hand outstretched in greeting. He looked at the hand, then straight into the watery blue eyes that brightened as she prepared to introduce herself. And then he turned away. Walking off, he realised his protest would have no effect whatsoever; the woman would simply think him rude, deranged even. So, he turned back towards the house. The woman was about to unlock the door. She dropped her key when she spotted him coming up the path. She was still scrabbling around for it when he told her this was Elsa Frankel's house, that it would never really be hers.

At first, she seemed unsure how to react, but once she got the measure of him she gathered herself and squared up to him. 'And who the hell are you?' she said. 'It's our place now. All legal, fair and square. We've got the papers to prove it, contracts, everything. So why don't you go and take a hike.'

Afraid of losing control altogether, he left without another word. As he made off, his own words reverberated in his ears. Each time he heard them they sounded weaker, more pathetic. He strode off in the direction of the station, his heart banging against the wall of his chest. As he reached the Tiergarten, the Charlottenburger Chaussee lay dappled before him, the weak sun dripping through the lines of green and brown burlap threaded through the camouflage netting overhead. A voice in his head jeered him. Once again, he'd achieved nothing. His protest had been pointless. 'You didn't want to know once they made her wear the star,' the voice said. 'Oh, you sneaked around, sure. You met her in places no one would see you. Took her to the woods, to the shady side of the lake. But you were a coward, really. You hadn't the balls to hold her hand in public, so what's the use in crying now?'

When he got to the station it was full of men in uniform. On the train, he sat for a long time looking at nothing at all. They had moved well beyond the city before he could bring himself to open Mutti's package. He waited until the other men had fallen asleep or started another game of *skat*. He turned it over and over in his hands, then tore off the brown paper. It was a beautiful thing, covered in the finest buffed pigskin. Tucked inside, there must have been half a dozen letters in Elsa's ringlety script, tied together with a neat ribbon. He swept his palm over the smooth surface of the page, then wrote the first thing that came into his head.

> *Elsa Elsa in the wood*
> *I would love you if I could*

He hadn't used a pen in such a long time, it felt awkward. He flexed his hand and scratched at the paper with the nib.

> *Love is falling from the sky*
> *Fire and light and dragonfly*

He never was much of a poet. Elsa would laugh her head off at him. But his heart was in it and he didn't care if it was doggerel. Suddenly, his predicament seemed to have one, simple solution. He considered the dangers. He might not even manage to get out; he might hesitate, or catch someone's eye at the crucial moment. He could be drowned or dashed on rocks, captured or shot on sight. And even if he avoided all those things, he still might not find her.

Fraternity

The final leg of the long journey back to Vannes was by plane. He looked from one man to the next, and thought to himself how impossible it would be to jump from a transport. On a Heinkel, though, with each man intent on his own job, it might just work. They flew over recent combat fields, miles and miles of ruined buildings, then across the stonewalled fields of Normandy, before setting down on the high plateau at Meucon. Once the planes were rolled into the paddocks and camouflaged, they drove into Vannes.

By the time he reached his billet at the Hotel Moderne, the idea of jumping seemed ridiculous. Even if he managed to bail out before his comrades stopped him, how could he hope to reach Ireland from a burning English city? He was trapped in the C-station of a Heinkel just as surely as he'd been in Zweibrückenstrasse.

Madame Pouliquen was sitting at the little reception desk in the foyer. A new gold tooth glinted at him as he approached. 'All gone,' she said. 'Forecast's so bad they've cancelled everything tonight. They're down at the Deux Pigeons. Perish the thought they'd hang around here.'

Out of the corner of his eye he could see Delphine watching him from behind the beaded curtain that cut off the reception desk from the Pouliquen quarters. He turned to face her as he walked back across the foyer. Her reddened mouth was like a wound on her pale face, and he felt a sudden rage at himself for living on dreams when real life was there for the taking. He smiled at her and she returned it. He nodded and she returned that too. And sure enough, when he left the hotel on the way to the Deux Pigeons, there she was in the alleyway, waiting for him.

He'd made love to so many girls since Elsa went, desperate to find her in a mouth, a strand of hair. These encounters always followed the same sequence: hope, desire, relief, disgust. But it never seemed to stop him. He closed his eyes tight as she fumbled at his buttons. He felt himself harden as she guided him inside her. Elsa was there, as she always was, running ahead of him all the way to the top of the hill. He had almost reached her when she dipped over the other side and the sun caught him and he was blinded a moment. He opened his eyes and Elsa disappeared. He bashed his hand against the rough wall behind Delphine's head. When he pulled away from her, her mouth was still open, her eyes blurred. She rearranged herself, clutching at her blouse, pulling down her skirt. She said nothing when he pressed the money into her hand, turned away when he reached out to smooth down her hair. His anger frightened him, the desolation when he opened his eyes and she was still not Elsa. He tried to say something to make amends but she was already gone.

As he opened the door of the Deux Pigeons there was the familiar waft of hair oil and cigarette smoke. The crew were sitting together, as they always did. Joachim called out to him and by now the idea of jumping seemed like treachery. The others told tales of the idiots they'd had to put up with while Oskar and Joachim were away. Everyone laughed, even Werner, who was never known for merriment. Oskar rocked back on the frail café chair and let the men's voices wash over him. Next thing, Joachim was in his face, clicking his fingers to demand his attention. 'Come on, Oskar, stay with us.' He turned back to the others, and continued his story. 'She was a peach, and her sister was even lovelier. Next thing I knew, I was walking through the centre of Dresden with one on each arm. I tell you, back home, this uniform works like a charm. What do you say, Oskar?'

'Oh, I'd give Herr Göring the credit, Joachim, wouldn't you?'

'You know they say he can't get it up any more,' Joachim said. 'It takes three at a time to blow that whistle.'

Werner's face reddened. He muttered something about morale.

'Who cares, Werner,' said Joachim, 'Relax, will you?'

Werner was looking nervously over his shoulder, but Joachim wasn't fazed. 'He let the English get their breath back when he could have finished them off. He's a disaster. Besides–' Joachim gulped back his schnapps, 'all he really cares is feathering his own nest. And what a nest!'

'So he's got somewhere he likes to go to wind down,' said Werner. 'What's wrong with that?'

'A dozen Old Masters on the bathroom wall, Werner. Just to watch him piss.'

Oskar's attention began to wander. There was a new girl behind the bar. She looked like she had sealed herself off from her surroundings. Now and then, her eyes darted to the table where Joachim and the others were sitting. When Joachim flashed his brilliant smile at her she ignored him.

Oskar walked over to the bar on the pretext of examining the bottles ranged behind it. He could see Joachim in the mirror, making drunken gestures at him while the others laughed into their beers.

'The seats at the bar are reserved for regulars,' the barmaid said, looking over his shoulder at the crew, 'but I suppose you lot will do as you wish.' The expression of loathing on her face fascinated him. Most people pretended to find them tolerable, whatever they really thought.

'They might be a bit loud, but they don't mean any harm. They're just trying to let off a bit of steam.'

'My heart bleeds. And who might you be? Their nursemaid? You sound like you think you're in a different league.'

For a moment, he considered sharing his dilemma with her. He hadn't felt proud of anything he'd done for a very long time. He'd let himself be thwarted when it came to Elsa. Always caving in, letting them win. Jumping would be brave, he was sure of that. But was it honourable, or just insane? If the barmaid respected him for it – someone like her, who hated Germans no matter what they did – then maybe it was worthwhile. He ordered a small cognac and drank it down in one. He realised then that he'd made his decision without her. When he went back to the others, they had long since lost interest in his progress with the girl behind the bar. Joachim and Willy had just begun dancing a tango when Oskar left.

The smell of planes seemed to linger at the Hotel Moderne. Perhaps that was why nobody seemed to want to drink there. The bar was a staging post between one sortie and the next; a place that never seemed to warm up. Even the crews only frequented it when they were back too late to find anywhere else. On those nights, anywhere would do: follow the beam, light the targets and leave.

The others arrived back at the billet soon enough, with some of the girls from the Deux Pigeons. Joachim spread himself over three rickety chairs, smoking luxuriously, his yellow scarf knotted at his throat. When he spotted Madame, still at her accounts, he sprang to his feet and dragged Oskar with him into the foyer. He gave a little bow. When she continued to ignore him, he rang the brass bell on her desk.

'One moment, please.' She continued writing, licking the end of her pencil as she finished a fresh column of numbers. 'Yes?'

'The mural, Madame. That German paradise we're going to paint for you.'

Madame shrugged and went back to her sums.

'Every airman this side of Quiberon will come here for a glimpse of home: mountains, pretty forests, houses from fairytales.' He lent towards her in a stage whisper. 'And not a swastika in sight.'

She shook her head, still engrossed in the numbers on the page.

'Oh come on, Madame. Oskar here will do the hard bits. I'll stick to the sky. Consider it a fraternal gesture to the Hotel Moderne.'

Madame Pouliquen waved her hand in the air. 'Go ahead, if you must. But no mess.'

He reached out to take her hand but she snatched it away.

They began the mural the next day. Joachim knew someone in ordnance and had managed to get hold of some surplus paint: military green (dark green and black green), two shades of grey (ash and cinder), black, white, maroon and a little dribble of bright red.

They were usually too exhausted after a mission to do anything much. Joachim used to sit at the window of their room with his feet up on the metal balcony, playing his clarinet until Madame Pouliquen arrived in her hairnet to hammer at their door. Now, Oskar and Joachim would go straight to work on the mural. By that time, dawn would be upon them and its thin light seemed to suit the colours they had at their disposal. No matter how tired, they got a second wind, daubing at the uneven surface of the wall. Joachim used to say it made him feel a little better, to have made something for a change.

When they started, they didn't have a plan for this paradise of theirs. Oskar wanted a lake and with a lake went mountains. Joachim described the hotel by the Bodensee where he had met Gisela, his girl back home, and Oskar painted that too. Then, he added his grandmother's house in Schwetzingen and a small church on a hill. One night they came back to find that someone had painted a little party flag onto the filigree balcony that Oskar had spent the previous night perfecting. The red paint was still tacky. Joachim smeared it off with his thumb and wiped it on the leg of his flying suit, before using some cinder grey to cancel it out completely. Normally, they'd enjoy a bit of banter and wear themselves out enough to be able to sleep. The flag made them both despondent. It reminded them that, whatever they might like to pretend, there was no longer any Germany without it: that even the fairytale they painted was rotten now. The next night, Oskar used the last drops of red paint for a row of geraniums in the window of his grandmother's house and threw away the can.

Joachim had been right about the mural's popularity. Once it was finished, the bar was full of German airmen. Madame was suddenly excessively friendly, and keen to offer them a reward. 'I know what will cheer you up,' she said. The tooth glinted. 'You've not been out in the bay yet, have you? There's an island for each day of the year out there. I'll arrange for someone to take you out on a little fishing trip when the weather improves. Out to the Île aux Moines, perhaps. The Île d'Arz? Catch some sardines, oysters.'

Madame Pouliquen kept her promise about the fishing. A week or so later, her nephew took a group on weekend leave out to the Golfe du Morbihan. Fish, camp, drink. Joachim said he didn't need another break so soon. He'd stay behind. He agreed to do a training flight instead, a favour for someone.

The nephew was surly, and Oskar felt they were no more than tolerated. They went out under sail on the outgoing tide, the boy navigating in silence. They hit a school of mackerel after a couple of hours and pulled in at one of the islands to light a fire to cook lunch. When the time came to return, they were warmed by spring sunshine and a bellyful of fish, and the nephew was almost friendly.

It wasn't until they got back to the billet that they realised anything was wrong. For once, Delphine came out from behind her curtain. She rushed towards Oskar, hesitated a moment, then reached out to touch his arm. Madame Pouliquen stood at her desk, a black scarf at her throat.

It had been raining heavily in Vannes that day, though it seemed the rain had nothing to do with it. Oskar tried to visualise Joachim's plane as it set off, shortly before dawn: rolling in driving rain from the paddock to the take-off point, taking its position on the starting grid, with the faint illumination of the kerosene lamps, then roaring down the track. Something went wrong shortly after take off. Everyone had his theory. The trimming wheel, perhaps. Some freak obstruction. Maybe they'd jammed the sprocket, rolled over a border lamp when taxiing. With only the instruments for a guide, how soon would Joachim have noticed that the rate of climb was excessive? They'd have struggled with all their might to keep the nose down.

Oskar found it impossible to sleep. He kept imagining he could hear Joachim's clarinet, those jazz tunes he used to belt out to annoy the Prussians. They hadn't yet reallocated Joachim's bed, so he turned on the light and, for the first time since arriving back in Vannes, he took out the journal he kept outside on the windowsill, tucked behind the flower box. One by one, he read through Elsa's letters. He tried to visualise the grey city she described, where it rained all the time. He tried to imagine the torment it would be for her to be so far from home without anyone to speak to in German, unless somehow her parents had made it to Ireland after all. Now that Joachim was gone, it became Oskar's habit to write in the journal most nights after returning from a mission. It gave him hope that there was something beyond the war, and gradually his thoughts began to turn again to escape.

10 April 1941
Overheard Werner speaking to someone from another crew. It was a while before I realised it was Joachim they were talking about. The other guy said he'd heard Joachim was

a cocky bastard who thought he was infallible. Thought he didn't have to prove his loyalty, either. One of those aristocrats who think they can look into their own hearts and see the Fatherland: so full of shit, they don't seem to realise they're yesterday's men.

Then Werner started. Probably lucky for his family he went down when he did. Might have found their Schloss a little harder to hold on to if he kept shooting his mouth off like that.

I didn't realise that's how he thought of Joachim. It shocked me, the words he used. The balance of his mind was disturbed: that's how he put it. I wonder if that's what they'll say about me.

11 April 1941
No news from Berlin since I was home on leave. Willy was in back there last week. He'd promised to look in on Zweibrückenstrasse but when he returned he said he couldn't find the place. I began to think of all kinds of dreadful reasons why he mightn't have been able to find it. I worried that there were raids on Berlin they weren't telling us about. Turns out he didn't even look. Got lucky with some girl and didn't bother his head.

12 April 1941
Today we were over a place code-named 'Speisekammer'. Caught in a searchlight and survived that only to find ourselves in the midst of concentrated flak a little way on. Weather better but forecasts still not very reliable. The beams are intercepted whenever possible by the British. Dummies everywhere, too. They set fires themselves to throw the bombers off course. There's always some idiot who ends up bombing the hell out of a little patch of countryside someone has mocked up to look worthwhile. Some Easter.

13 April 1941

All I can think of now is escape. I never mentioned Elsa to Joachim. I suppose I wasn't sure how he would have reacted. The Jewish question was not something we'd ever discussed. Maybe I was afraid to find out what his views were. He was no Nazi but he'd never have dreamed of betraying his comrades by leaving them one short on the home run. He would despise me for it. He would tell me my duty was to Germany. These people won't last, he'd say. We do our duty for Germany, not for them. He liked to say that Hitler would wind up Bürgermeister back in Linz, if someone didn't bump him off first.

One of the higher-ups took me aside today. They have their eye on me. They tell me they're worried about my state of mind since Joachim died. This kind of emotionalism can affect the rest of a crew, they said. I don't know where they get their infor- mation. Werner? I've been thinking about that chap who just disappeared last month when he fell to pieces and took to weep- ing into his drink. Nobody ever found out where they took him.

14 April 1941

Today my luck changed. At the preflight briefing, they told us that tonight's target is the Etappe. Belfast. An industrial city, it seems, a port. Apparently, the other Irish have daubed their independence in large white letters on clifftops all along their coast, to warn us to keep out. But if we have enough fuel left, Rolf will fly back along it anyway, to avoid crossing England a second time.

So that's what war has done for me: made me ecstatic to be bombing the place where Elsa's been given refuge. Madness. Yet for the first time there is also hope.

Nobody felt comfortable flying without Joachim. It didn't help that the new boy had fallen asleep on the home run the very first time they'd flown together. Besides, they'd all become so superstitious now, clinging on to their own personal mascots. They'd become just like the old Norway hands, determined to do everything exactly as they'd done it the day before. Before the flight, Oskar off-loaded as much standard-issue kit as he could. Rations, maps, even his beloved *traubenzucker*. Instead, he stuffed his pockets with her letters, his journal and Joachim's yellow scarf, folded to no bigger than a pack of cards. He left his Luftwaffe watch behind and brought Grandpapa's pocket watch in its place. As always, in the moments before take off, each man was immersed in his own most intimate thoughts. Oskar thought of Mutti and how she would feel when the word came back that he'd deserted the Reich. Maybe they'd just write him off as a casualty. For her sake, he hoped so.

Rolf took the plane up over the tip of Cornwall and north of the Isle of Man. He skirted the coast of the neutral place they call Éire until they reached the inverted V of Belfast Lough. The mission had seemed straightforward enough, with most of the targets clustered together, but the weather conditions were much worse than had been expected. Cloud cover was 9/10. The crew were tense, focused. Werner was stretched out on the mattress, peering through the glass nose, scanning for cloud breaks through which to drop the incendiaries. Willy fretted about the fuel supply as they circled over the targets. They were all furious that the weather forecast had been so inaccurate.

As for Oskar, he crouched down in his glass pod, jerking the gun this way and that to keep alert for tracer fire. He hoped they would get it over quickly. He was more rattled than usual, sickened by the smell of kerosene and the knowledge that there was only one way out. When the time came he would have to make for the hatch and push his way through it so fast they couldn't stop him. His only hope was that Rolf would decide to fly home over Éire. A good chance, he thought, provided the fuel would hold out. It wouldn't be like Rolf to risk a run down the English coast if there was a safer way of getting home. But they were spending far longer than usual trying to find targets, battling against the dense blanket of cirrocumulus that stretched underneath them. He was painfully aware that each minute was eating away at his chances of escape, until at last the plane scythed up and away from the burning city. They left the coast behind them and veered west. He knew then they were taking the long way home. His heart tightened when he realised he would get his chance.

Kitty

This Parachute Business

The parachute hung like a cloud over one of the lime trees at the end of the garden. Still half asleep, Kitty watched the magpies fussing over it like a clatter of nuns. They could fuss away, but it was clear that whoever had come down with it was well gone. Was he lying in a ditch somewhere, his face burned off him, his cries carried onto the bog? She opened the window and listened. Nothing. Maybe this was just the start of it. Maybe this fellow had given the game away and there were dozens of others, all along the coast from Killary Harbour to Roonagh Quay. Those men, hiding the evidence, slipping in like the flu. Most girls would be frightened, she thought. Most girls would be beside themselves at the very thought. She felt a hop in her guts all right but she didn't think it was fright.

Mother wouldn't have spotted it yet. Since the funeral, she slept on half the morning. Later, they sat together at the kitchen table and waited for the tea to draw while Mother pasted her bread with bright yellow butter. More than once, Kitty opened her mouth to mention the parachute but the moment never felt right. After breakfast, Mother disappeared into the parlour with *The White Feather* under her arm.

'I'll just cock the feet a while,' she announced, leaving Kitty to the clearing up.

Kitty wandered through the hallway. A stream of light lit up the dust particles in the air, flurries of them, like moments piling up into one more day. She took the scarf from around her neck and snapped it across the hall table to stop the moments from congregating. Then she made her way to the lime tree through the new vegetable garden Sean Galligan had planted after Father passed away to replace the old one that the brambles had taken. Sean always said you couldn't eat a peony rose.

By the time she got to the bottom of the garden, the silk of the parachute had ballooned up around the side of the tree like the skin of an onion. Although Easter had been and gone, there was still a nip in the air. Kitty gave a little shiver. If the parachute man was still nearby, he might be watching her, willing her not to call in the Guards, to give him a bit longer to get clear. She smoothed her hair back over her forehead and wondered where the fellow might be.

Back at the house, Mother was sitting bolt upright in the parlour with the wireless tuned to Raidió Éireann. When Kitty opened her mouth to mention the parachute, Mother raised a hand to halt her. She listened attentively until the broadcast came to an end and then she interpreted the news in breathy chunks for Kitty. Hundreds of planes … bombing the daylights out of Belfast … mountains of fire and carnage everywhere … and even the water mains blown up. 'Those poor people, Kitty, blown to bits by the Germans. Nothing but great big cowardly vultures with their night bombing, and the people half starved up there anyway.'

They didn't know anyone in Belfast. Mother was always saying what black-hearted bastards they were. Kitty walked over and set her hand lightly on Mother's shoulder. Her back started to shake even more violently then, as though Kitty had released some terrible, pent-up sorrow that was being spent tonight on Belfast. 'We're hardly off our knees yet and there's people fighting their battles over our heads.'

Kitty wondered how to bring up the matter of the parachute without upsetting her even more. Maybe, she thought, it was best to let it pass; just have Sean cut it down and say no more about it. All the same, she couldn't help wondering if one day she'd say: that was the day the war came to Dunkerin.

Mother put some Chopin on the gramophone and Kitty decided to keep her trap shut. It wasn't the right moment, and anyway, she liked Chopin. It was soothing and it always gave her hope that one day there'd be dancing again. Years ago, Cora Redmond used to give ballet lessons in the old ballroom up at Cloheen. Mother said Cora was always carried and had lost the run of herself altogether when she snared Eric Redmond. 'It's far from the ballet that one was dragged up.'

It was almost a year, now, since Con signed up for the Ulster Rifles and Mrs Redmond shut up the old house and moved across the border. 'To be nearer him in spirit,' she said.

Con had been around during the summer holidays for as long as Kitty could remember. When they were younger, a gang of them would go off together on the bicycles for the whole day, across to Dunkerin Bay where they would fish for crabs in the rock pools and eat sandy doorsteps for lunch. Once he left school, he didn't come home much any more and the little group of friends began to disperse.

Then one day, out of the blue, Con arrived at the door. Kitty hadn't even realised he was home. She invited him into the parlour and they had a glass of lemonade. She couldn't find any biscuits.

'I'm heading over beyond,' he said.

'To fight for King and Country?'

'For the rights of small nations, Kitty. That's my war. I'm fighting for no King.'

She thought it was funny, him coming all the way over to tell her what she would have heard in a few days anyway. She hoped he would stay out of trouble. Mind you, wasn't that what a war was all about? Trouble, then more trouble. Someone had told her that during the Great War there were villages of fellows went off and never came back at all.

'Try to keep to *terra firma*, Con,' she said as he left, giving her one of his strong handshakes. He seemed a little hesitant at the door, as though there was something else to be said, but then he just walked away. She'd like to have seen him in his uniform but Mother said he probably wasn't allowed to wear it around here. 'It wouldn't be wise, anyhow.'

Sean Galligan arrived around mid-morning. By that time, the sun had come out and the parachute was even more noticeable. Sean was chewing on something, looking hard at Kitty.

'That Gerry parachute you have in the lime tree, Miss. There'll have been a fella on the end of that yoke. Have you been on to the Guards?'

She looked at Sean's reflection in the hall mirror. He was raising his eyebrows and pulling a face at the wall. He'd not have done that if Father was still alive. 'You think I should then?'

'God knows what the fella might be up to. Couldn't he be anywhere? Skulking about, waiting till dark.' Sean walked away, shaking his head.

She followed him out into the garden. Sean ignored her; just kept on stabbing at the ground with the hoe.

'I suppose we'd better get Sergeant McCreesh up to have a look,' she said.

'About time.'

After Sean left, Kitty took a turn around the garden, down as far as the old bathtub where the last of the daffodils lay flattened. The grass was an unnatural, electric green; the colour you sometimes get before gales. She lay down on the electric grass and looked right up into the sky. The thing is, there's no beginning to a sky. She'd no idea how high a plane could fly, or what happened if it tried to fly too high. She wondered how small a speck he'd have been when he left the plane. She imagined him hurtling through that sky, all the way down to Dunkerin. She brushed her hand over the blades of grass. A spy more than likely. Bloody useless place for a spy. She clenched her fist around a clump of grass and pulled. The moisture in the grass began to seep into her back and she wondered again whether he was watching her.

Back in the kitchen, she scrambled two eggs and watched as Mother ate them slowly, revolving the mixture loosely in her mouth. 'Lovely, pet. You've a lovely touch with the eggs.'

She didn't ask Kitty if she had eaten. A little later, when Mother had gone off to tend to her geraniums, Kitty stood at the side door in the grey light and waited for Sergeant McCreesh. By mid-afternoon, he still hadn't arrived and she began to wonder just how seriously he was taking this parachute business.

It was almost seven when, from some distance off, she heard a noise like a throat clearing. The light had faded a little but she could still see the motorcar as it wound its way towards the house. Meanwhile, Mother was dozing in the parlour, propped stiffly between two embroidered cushions.

When he climbed out of the car, the sergeant looked past her shoulder at first, as though hoping for someone more important to talk to, until he seemed to remember that there were just women in the Hennessy household now. He had the eyes of a hard case and his remaining hair was oiled down carefully across his scalp. The sergeant captured her hand in both of his. She guessed that she was not in any trouble as far as he was concerned.

'Sean tells me you have a matter to bring to our attention under the Emergency Provisions.'

'The parachute?'

'Indeed so.'

'Sean tells me it's a German parachute, not that it makes much difference.'

For the second time that day she heard how hundreds of German planes had just bombed the bejaysus out of Belfast, how Dev was sending up the fire brigades and weren't we all brothers when it came to the bit.

'Surely to God, Miss Hennessy, that makes a difference. Killary Harbour, Clew Bay.' He looked over his shoulder and hissed at her 'U-boats. Taking their ease in our waters. We'd want to watch we don't swap one master for another.' He chuckled at his own worldliness.

She led him down the garden to where the parachute was snagged. It no longer looked like it was about to be whipped away by the wind but had entered complicated bondage with the tree. The magpies had gone.

The sergeant tucked his thumb in his belt and seemed lost in contemplation. 'There'll be people looking for him, you realise that, Miss Hennessy.' The sergeant nodded earnestly to himself. 'Not to mention our own desperadoes.'

'Who?'

'Surely you know, Miss, there's men in this country still think England's difficulty and that …'

'IRA men?'

'I suppose.'

'I thought you'd them all locked up already.'

'There's always one or two slips through the net.' He looked sharply at her. 'If you come across anything out of the ordinary you're to get in touch right away, like a good girl. Any strange movements in and around the farm; anybody you don't recognise in the vicinity, same thing goes.'

She might have sighed a little because he seemed to think he had worried her after all.

'Don't you fret now, Miss. We'll track him down. The last one over this way, we had him the same day. He'd some class of an attaché case with him that he dropped on the way down. When the lads picked him up, he was in a ditch still looking for his change of clothes. Turned out he hadn't a word of English. I mean to say, Miss Hennessy, what class of an eejit do they think we are?'

The sergeant had hardly left when Mother emerged from

the kitchen, already dressed for bed in her flannelette night-dress. When she'd gone upstairs, Kitty went over to the back door and fiddled with the bolts, top and bottom. The door seemed to have swollen since the last time she'd bothered to bolt it. She tried to kick it flush with the frame but it wouldn't budge, so in the end she let it be. She lit a candle that night for a bit of company. What on Earth did you look out for in a German, she wondered? Years ago, Uncle Malachy had brought back a picture book about the last war from his commercial travels up North. She got it down and had a flick through it until she came across a fierce man with blond hair leaping over the mouth of a trench, about to bayonet a cluster of cowering men on the other side. She pulled the eiderdown up around her neck, swallowing dryly as she ran her finger down the delicate little grooves in her throat.

As she lay there, holding her breath, night sounds began to emerge from the camouflage of day: creaks from the staircase, a dull thud some way down the corridor. From the room next door, she could hear the shallow ripple of her Mother's snore, and on the quarter hour the insistent whirr and clang of the Viennese wall clock Father had brought back from the Alps the time he went for his lungs. All the while, she was aware of the unlocked kitchen door, like a hole in a sock. Eventually, she put on her slippers and walked down the stairs. She brought the candle with her, even though Mother had always told her not to be walking around the house with a candle in her hand. 'It's not like we don't have the electricity, for the love of Mike.'

Cupping her hand around the flame, she fancied she cut a romantic enough figure in her white nightgown. She walked slowly down the stairs, exaggerating her tread in the hope of forewarning any living thing that might be on the move. The candle flame flicked random shadows across ceiling and walls as she listened at the door of each of the ground floor rooms.

She wondered should she try to barricade the back door, slide the old chest across it maybe. She sat on the stairs for a couple of minutes and thought about it, but then she decided the fellow was likely well gone, and went back to bed.

She lay awake and wondered what Father would have done if he was still alive and in the whole of his health. Then she realised that she no longer had any idea what Father would have done about anything. What an end it was for him, laid up for months on end, coughing up bloody gobbets into a jar, then out like a light. She had just left the room to refill his glass of water and when she returned he was gone. She must have screamed, for the next thing she remembered was Mother hobbling in, one heel snapped from its sole in her hurry, a handful of withered blooms in her hand. And so the dying of him smelt of damp earth and spit and geraniums.

The funeral was on an edgy summer's day; not quite secure in its sunshine, not wholly irreverent when it came to the Hennessys' trouble. Now and then, a cloud scuffed at the sun as they lowered him into the ground. Desmond was head of the family now, Mother said, and Kitty resented his easy assumption of the role. Aunt Effie sat in the pew behind them, resplendent in her purple silk, thick black feathers lying sleek over the top of her head. She sang along loudly in her cracked soprano until Mother had enough. 'For the love of God, Effie,' she hissed at her, 'would you ever shut up.'

After the funeral, the rest of summer spun like a dial. Autumn too, until winter settled in on them. They felt the loss of him even more in the winter when they were inside all the time, listening to the clocks he used to wind. At night, Mother took to throwing a handful of his tobacco onto the open fire to give the place, she said, 'a touch of Frank again.' One day, Kitty moved his chair out into the hallway, she was that sick of looking up from a book or a piece of darning and finding it there in front of her. The next morning, she felt guilty for being impatient with his shadow and moved it back in again.

Nine months on, Kitty still wondered where her life in Dublin had gone. She read and re-read Rita's letters, full of gossip and dances and the latest style, while Mother went to bed early with hot milk and bile beans. Now though, with this parachute business, maybe things were on the turn.

Man Trap

The day opened with a flurry and the yard was full of men in uniform; they crouched at corners, levelling sights, covering ground. She heard Mother answer the door to Sergeant McCreesh.

'Just taking a few LDF boys to check the ditches and that … Ah, no bother on me, thanks be to God. Yourself? … Great stuff … Ah no, I'll be off now, Mrs Hennessy. Thanks all the same.'

It was only while Kitty was clearing away the kitchen things that she realised something was not right. The bread bin, open wide like a tinker's hand. And the scullery soap, covered in scum. She closed her eyes to try and catch a change in the air, the way you might stand on a hill and catch thunder. She started at a knock on the door. It was Sergeant McCreesh again.

She shook her head. 'No sign.'

'No matter. We'll find him soon enough. Between the sea and the bog, he'll not go far.'

As he shut the door, she could hear the men hopping up into the truck and the flaps being slid in place.

That morning, word came that her brother, Desmond, would be down for the weekend with Bobby Coyle, a pal of his from Surgeons. Bobby had the gas adapter fitted to his motorcar and they planned to test out the contraption by making the long trip to Dunkerin. They had a tent and billycans and all the rest, for fear the motor wouldn't make it.

Kitty rode down to the village for supplies and Dr Russell saluted her as he passed in the opposite direction on his sturdy bicycle, his little black bag snug as a pet in the front basket. Dr Russell would be Desmond's competition in the medical business, if Des ever managed to get himself qualified. 'Dr Russell's well in,' Mother never tired of reminding him. 'Well in.'

A heavy vehicle shuddered towards her on the next corner and she had to move her bicycle in off the road and climb up onto the verge. The lorry was full of LDF volunteers in their thin green uniforms and as she turned to watch them go, a fellow in the back waved out at her. She watched him say something to the others that had them creasing themselves laughing. She didn't know any of them, and wished they'd go back to wherever they came from and not be clogging up the roads.

She got back on her bicycle. Standing on the pedals to get herself started again, she set off across the expanse of bog that splayed out like a dark damp stain at the foot of Knockree. The earth was scored from turf cutting. There were little brown tepees of peat, and clumps of heather sprouted next to pools of water. Not much of a hiding place. She felt sorry for anyone who hoped to lie low out there. Later that day, Sergeant McCreesh was back, and the parachute was cut down and sent off for examination up in Dublin.

The boys arrived after Kitty had gone to bed and she heard them rattling around downstairs until all hours. At breakfast, she served them warm curranty scones with the last jar of strawberry jam, while the man on the wireless gave news of devastation in London. Five hundred machines coming in continuous waves, bombing anything going: shops, hotels, even hospitals, and street after street of houses. Kitty tried not to think of things that fell from the sky. She sat in silence, peeling carrots, as Desmond dealt to Bobby and himself from a pack of cards. Mother switched off the wireless and went off to her geraniums, and gloom seemed to settle on them all. Eventually, she suggested they take a walk and give Mother some peace and quiet, not that Mother was worried, and her in the parlour nodding over *The White Feather*.

They spent the afternoon skirting the edge of the bog below Knockree. Bobby had short legs and had to move fast to keep up. Kitty was mad for news from Dublin, and even though she knew she was driving Desmond round the bend with all her questions, she couldn't stop herself.

'Bobby's your man if you want the inside track,' said Desmond. 'He's part-time with the LDF now.'

Bobby was out of breath from running, his face shining and his little arms working furiously to propel himself along. 'Friday last I was in Nesbitt's,' he said, 'Met a fellow there, some class of a civil servant, says the German Legation is full of spies. The powers that be are worried sick but sure what can they do? They're stuck between a rock and a hard place. Whatever they do they'll offend somebody so they're doing feck all, as per usual. From what that fellow said, I'd be worried enough about this parachute lark.'

She was wondering when they'd get to the parachute.

'That was a strange thing,' said Desmond. 'Sean mentioned it, right enough. Apparently half the village is out looking for him. It's the most exciting thing to have happened in many's the long day. Fame at last, Kitty.'

'You can mock away,' said Bobby, 'but if the Germans had their way, they'd take over the place and good luck to the rest of us. There's a few German fellows in the National Museum,' he broke into a trot now to keep up with the Hennessys. 'Word is they get up to no good in some hotel down in Wicklow. Uniforms and salutes and God knows what.'

'Still and all,' said Desmond, 'you could worry yourself sick, too. Next thing, you'd be paranoid.'

They walked on a bit in silence. Kitty kept hearing it: paranoid, a real medical word. Maybe that's what happens when you're stuck in the back of beyond; you start thinking you're the centre of things and everything's aimed at you. Maybe that's why she kept seeing traces of the German all over the place: in the kitchen, the pantry, the scullery. Even that old bucket she'd not noticed before, over by the waterbutt.

'One thing's for sure,' said Bobby. 'If the Germans come over here, they'll rule the roost. They'll put some fella with a sour puss on him in charge and the rest of us will be put to work milking cows.'

Kitty began to wish she had been a bit quicker off the mark when it came to the parachute.

'Did Sergeant McCreesh have nothing to say?' asked Desmond.

She shook her head and wished they'd change the subject.

'No advice about bolting the outhouses? Nothing like that?'

They hadn't been the least bit worried about the parachute to start with but now it was like it was the be all and end all. She thought about those poor people in London, blown to kingdom come. Not to mention the ones just up the road in Belfast. Desmond had told her about the long line of people he'd seen at Amiens Street Station: people come South away from the bombs. Poor, pasty-faced people with fright in their eyes. Mary Ryan in the post office had relatives in the North. She'd heard tell of some poor woman who'd just stepped into her bath when the bombing began and who'd been tossed, bath and all, through the roof of the house to land naked and dead in the street. Then there was the big noise in the fire brigade who hid under his desk and wouldn't come out. The poor man had suffered a nervous collapse, they said.

'Kitty?'

She looked up and realised she hadn't answered him.

'Ah, he just said the man'd be well gone. The G2 men will be taking care of it from now on.'

That night, they sat on after dinner. The boys drank whiskey and Kitty had a sweet sherry. Mother sat up for a while, too, and produced package after package of handkerchiefs for Bobby. The only time they had visitors now was when

Desmond had friends for the weekend. Each visitor would head back to Dublin with a parcel containing something bought in Kilcoyne for Father and never opened.

It must have been one in the morning when, flushed with whiskey, Desmond and Bobby decided they should set a trap for the German.

'You know the Fox Gogarty is about,' said Kitty.

'Sure what about him? I've no fear of the Fox,' said Desmond. 'Anyway, we'll not need to venture far. I'd say the German is still within shouting distance.'

Bobby nodded vigorously. 'If he's any sense, Kitty, he'd not wander far from you.'

She glared at him for that and he fell silent, examining the toe of his shoe.

'A man trap's what we need, Bobby,' said Desmond, 'I'll get Sean onto it in the morning.'

'Sean has enough to be doing with the vegetables and the hens and God knows what else without setting traps for some poor eejit who's landed, God help his head, in Dunkerin.' That shut them up, and she took up her knitting, though she couldn't stand knitting and had enough Aran scarves to last a lifetime. The boys slipped away, as if she wouldn't guess they were up to something, and when they came back they were kitted out in deerstalkers and oilskin jackets, and swiping blackthorns all round them. They looked ridiculous and it was only then that she realised they were half cut on the whiskey. They must have woken Mother with all the commotion, because next thing she appeared at the door in her candle-wick dressing gown. 'Lovely night for a walk, lads. The moon's bursting a gut up there.'

When the boys had left, Kitty paced forward and back. She hated waiting, hated more than anything being the one who made the tea and waited. But as she peered out into the blackness, she couldn't bring herself to go outside. She supposed she must hate the dark even more. She closed her eyes and hoped the airman wouldn't be found, then that he would. She hoped that the likes of Bobby Coyle wouldn't have one over on him. But then she thought of Belfast and shuddered to think of it.

She took down a piece of embroidery from on top of the dresser, a cushion cover for Mother's birthday. She began to work on the petal of a large red gerbera, then threw the bit of cloth away in frustration. Who'd have ever imagined that Kitty Hennessy, the spit of Hedy Lamarr, so sharp she'll cut herself, would end up like this; stuck in Dunkerin with the rain and Mother and two eejit boys and their blackthorns. If the airman was still around, she wished that she could be the one to find him. She lifted the meat mallet and stood at the door with the lamp off, though she wasn't sure what she expected to do with it. Catch yourself on, she thought, and she put the mallet down, went into the sitting room and sat in the dark in Mother's chair.

They were gone half an hour or so when she heard the rustle in the kitchen. At first, she wasn't sure. Couldn't it be a mouse, maybe, or one of the cats come in for its milk? Then, there was a low nobbling sound, the sound of wood rolling on wood. She took off her shoes, and placed them to the side so she wouldn't trip over them. Then, very quietly, she crept in stockinged feet into the hall. The sound came in short bursts. She could tell that he was struggling with the top drawer of the dresser, the one that always stuck. The plates rattled. She could have told him there was nothing worth having in there, just bills. Then, a sound she couldn't place. A rubbing, sawing sound. She closed her eyes to hear better. Water now, rushing fast and loud. The sound hollowed out as the water was contained in something. She crossed the hallway, avoiding the one board that squeaked, until she was just outside the cloakroom that led into the kitchen itself.

She was close enough to hear him breathe. She could hear the voices of the boys again now, coming from the direction of the blackberry hedge. She opened her mouth to rehearse silently a scream, should she need it, and reached her hand in for the flashlight where it hung on its hook inside the cloak-room door. His footsteps into the pantry sounded confident; he seemed to know his way. How often had he been there without her knowing, leaving traces even she hadn't noticed? Had she brushed his fingerprints from a loaf of bread before cutting into it, had his lips tasted honey from her spoon? She heard Desmond's voice, then Bobby's. Then the man's footsteps again, back in the kitchen. He was nearer now. For a moment she hesitated, no more that.

Then, she lit him with her lamp. Using both hands, she managed to keep the beam steady but her guts were a tangle of fear and excitement and inexplicable hope. She caught him side on. She could see his hands and there was no gun or knife or anything like that. In fact, he looked like he was trying to sink into the wall, stretched flat as a pancake against it, shoulders high, leaning out of the light. Outside, footsteps crunched on the gravel. He raised a finger to his lips. She opened her mouth to alert the boys, breathed in sharp, then shut it again.

She moved the beam of the flashlight an inch until she'd haloed his head. Again he slid free from it and again she followed him. He lay still against the wall. Then, suddenly, he turned his face into the light. There was sky in his eyes, bluer than the bluest day over Dunkerin Bay. There was a kind of a spring-day excitement in her stomach. Then, she noticed the scarf around his neck. It was a pale primrose colour. Not the kind of colour you'd ever see here on a man. It didn't strike her as a fighting kind of a colour at all. She almost laughed when she saw that yellow scarf, and maybe a smile slipped out, because his shoulders seemed to relax a bit when he saw she wasn't about to scream. She wondered, then, whether she should open her lungs at all. In the distance, the boys' laughter rang out. He glanced nervously over his shoulder. She jerked her head towards the door. 'That pair of eejits? Don't worry your head about them.'

He stayed very still, flat against the wall. She wondered if he understood a word she said. They both seemed to spend an eternity frozen like that. Next thing, she heard the boys' voices from just beyond the house. He looked terrified now, and for a moment she thought he might dive under the table. The German in Uncle Malachy's book flashed across her mind and she almost laughed again. The boys were nearly at the door now. He stepped towards her and instinctively she took a step backwards. He was panting, struggling to catch his breath, almost wheezing. Outside, getting closer, the boys with their sticks. He looked her straight in the eye and she realised then that she couldn't stand the way nothing ever changed. She heard Bobby Coyle and that ridiculous Indian war cry of his. How could she bear for it all to just stay the same? The German was shivering now; waiting for her decision.

'Come on then,' she said, and turned on her heel. When she turned round, he hadn't moved. 'Hurry up, this way.' She opened the cellar door and almost pushed him through. Then she turned the key in the lock and put it in her pocket. She had barely enough time to take her seat at the table before the boys scrambled in through the door.

'What the blazes are you doing sitting in the dark?' Desmond rattled in his pocket for some matches and lit the paraffin lamp. Their faces materialised and she saw Desmond spot the flash-light on the table. 'We were looking for that,' he said. 'Could have done with that, Bobby.'

Bobby grunted. 'Any chance of a cup of tea, Kitty?'

She said nothing but she got up all the same and slid the kettle onto the hob. Desmond went into the pantry and came out with Mother's baking box. 'Bit of a mess in there, Kitty,' he said, like she was Cinderella. She wondered what the German had knocked over. 'Shouldn't leave the bread out, either. The mice'll be on to it in no time.'

'Another go round outside before we turn in?' Bobby asked, lifting the flashlight.

Desmond nodded. 'We'll have a quick check round upstairs first, Kitty, just in case, and then we'll be off.'

She sat at the table with her head in her hands as she heard their heavy feet on the stairs. By the time they came down again the tea was harsh with tannin. There was nothing much left in the baking box. They drank their tea standing up and were soon gone outside again, rubbing their hands together as they went. She could hardly believe that her face hadn't given her away, that she could possibly look the same as she had done that morning, or the day before that, or any other day she'd ever lived for that mattter.

She tiptoed over to the cellar door, nibbling at her knuckles. What if she'd bitten off more than she could chew? She put her ear against the door, felt the key in her pocket. She didn't like leaving him down there but what could she do? It gave her time to think what to do with him. She could hear the faint scrape of his boots on the flagstones as he walked around down there. If he kicked up a racket she'd have her mind made up for her. She almost hoped he would.

She climbed the stairs to go up to bed, but she couldn't settle, she was that worried he'd freeze to death down there. She hoped he wasn't afraid of small spaces. The cellar was no more than a coal hole really, though it was a while since there'd been any coal in it. From the window on the landing she could see the boys' flashlight bobbing down the avenue. Mother had a pile of old blankets she'd left out for the Red Cross when she heard of the business in Belfast. Kitty took her chance, bundled one under her arm and went back downstairs. When she reached the cellar door, she unlocked it as quietly as she could, then flung the blanket into the blackness, closing it again quickly and sliding the bolt across.

A Spy without a Map

Next morning, Kitty was exhausted. She'd been too jittery to sleep much. Instead, she was tossed in and out of a dream where she'd lost the cellar key and had to get Sean Galligan to kick the door in to save the man from starving to death down there. When she came downstairs, Bobby was already up out of bed. He was wearing a paisley-pattern dressing gown that she hoped wasn't Father's. He looked like he must have fallen into a ditch, for one side of his face was badly scratched. She noticed how he tried to turn that cheek away from her as he talked with great gusto about their antics the night before. The fact that they'd risked sharing a ditch with the Fox Gogarty he seemed to find particularly worthy of admiration.

'Sure why would the Fox be bothered playing toy soldiers with you lot?' she said.

'Well there was definitely people round about the place last night,' said Bobby, 'whatever caper they were at.'

'He'll be needing his bayonet then,' she said innocently.

'Oh I doubt he'll have one of those, Kitty,' Bobby replied, all condescending now. 'Sure how could he have a bayonet, coming down in a parachute?'

'The man they caught over Lough Swilly way had a bayonet; took five men to get it off him. They can be terrible fierce when they're cornered, these German types. The Lough Swilly man was jabbing away with it. One of the guards got it in the arm. Nasty old gash. You mind yourself, Bobby.'

Desmond appeared at the door with his hand to his head. She hoped he had a hangover. 'Nine'll be the height of it, Bobby,' he said.

'Well, nine it'll be then.' Bobby was raring to go. He fidgeted constantly as Desmond sipped at his tea, and in the end he just couldn't contain himself. He moved away from the table and began practising his swing.

Kitty was beside herself. Would they never be gone? Finally, the boys slung the golf clubs into the boot of Bobby's car and set off down the drive. She was about to attend to the parachute man when she saw Sean outside. Blast it. She'd forgotten about Sean. She was relieved to see him harnessing up the old gig they'd come across a couple of months ago in one of the barns; Sean had done it up because there was no point in having a motor if there was nothing to put in it. If the gig was out, it meant that Mother was planning a trip to Father's grave.

When Mother appeared at the top of the stairs, she was covered from head to toe in the old black velvet opera cloak she wore all the time now, for reasons Kitty hadn't got to the bottom of yet. As she reached the bottom stair, the cloak gaped to reveal the figured organza underneath. She gave Kitty a dirty look and gathered the cloak back around her.

'You're off to the grave, then?' Kitty asked.

'I'll put in a word on your behalf.'

Kitty stood at the window, watching the gig head down the avenue. Her knuckles were red raw from her gnawing at them. What if he was mad as a bear from being cooped up all night? What if he ambushed her the moment she opened the door? What if he was a spy? She hugged herself with excitement. She'd talk to him through the door. That would be safe. She'd see how the land lay.

When it came to it, she just flung the door open. He was sitting at the bottom of the cellar stairs, his hands clasped between his knees. He flinched as the daylight hit him, and looked away. He made no attempt to rush her. In fact, there was nothing desperate about him this morning. As he climbed the stairs, she noticed the limp for the first time, and thought of the wounded pigeon Desmond had kept for weeks. He seemed almost relaxed, for a man on the run. He was very well mannered, too. He stood back for her at the top of the stairs but she kept her distance all the same.

He waited outside the kitchen door while she tripped over herself, bundling bits and pieces of leftovers onto a plate. When she went to give him his breakfast, he was standing outside, looking off into the distance at Knockree. She wished he'd take that yellow scarf off him. He was like a beacon with that round his neck. She kept an eye on him, pretending to wipe over the kitchen table and dust the jam jars in the pantry, as he sat on a whitewashed rock outside the back door and wolfed down cold mutton pie.

'Where are the others?' she asked when she went back out to him.

He didn't seem to understand what she meant.

'Your friends, comrades, whatever you want to call them. The other fellas in the plane? Where are they?'

'I am the only one.'

'Did you crash or what?'

'I jumped.'

If he was on his own, that could only mean he was here on purpose. And if he was here on purpose, didn't that make him a spy? Sergeant McCreesh would be furious.

'There's no need for you to have any concern,' he said, as if he could read her mind. 'Soon, I will leave for Wicklow.'

Did he not have a map? Sure he was miles from Wicklow. Did they let them on the loose with no preparation at all?

He gave her back the plate and drank a mug full of milk, wiping his lips on his sleeve.

'Do you not even know where you are? There's no way you're walking to Wicklow with that leg on you. Besides, you'd be picked up in ten minutes flat in that get-up.'

'If I could see a map please?'

'Wait there.'

She went to slide across the bolt on the door in case he followed her, then remembered it didn't work anyway. He was like something out of the Keystone Cops, this fellow. No map?

She rushed up into the back bedroom, the one that was once Father's study, and got down the atlas. It smelt peppery and she blew the dust off the top. She'd been brought up to have respect for books but she thought Father would understand the needs of a traveller. She laid the volume on the floor and flicked through the pages until she found Ireland. She made herself tear out the page, though it hurt to do it. Ireland: what was it but a little baby curled up with its back to England and France and Russia and all the other places where things happened?

When she came back downstairs, he was still standing in the same place, waiting for her.

'There you go,' she said, handing him the page. 'Ireland.' Then, when she remembered he didn't have a clue where he was, she showed him Dunkerin. 'You're here, by the way. That little speck over there.'

She couldn't stop herself telling him that Ireland wasn't in the war and didn't want to be, that she'd heard all about Belfast and the terrible things that had happened there and didn't he feel ashamed and why shouldn't she call in the Guards right now and have him locked up. The sergeant had told her there were IRA men, too, looking for the likes of him, thinking what's good for Germany was good for them and she didn't want any of that lot hanging around the place. Mother would have a fit. It was like she hadn't talked to anyone for months.

But he didn't wait for her to finish. He raised his hand, quite politely, and interrupted. 'I do not want to make trouble for you. I will leave as soon as I can.'

He looked at the map. His finger traced the distance from Dunkerin to Wicklow. Then he shook his head and all of a sudden he looked so tired. He looked like he knew all kinds of things that she couldn't even imagine. Hard things. She wished she could prise open his head and sit in there among all his brain cells, watching the pictures in his mind, getting the measure of him. He turned away and tucked the map inside his flying suit, zipping it up. 'Thank you,' he said, calm as you like.

She watched him limp a little crookedly across the path and out of view. She stood there on the doorstep a minute with her arms folded, and then she followed him. It was easy to catch up with him; he was like a human gorse bush in that yellow scarf. He was moving slowly through the tangle of growth that had invaded the old vegetable patch. She knew immediately where he was going, and when she reached Father's old shed she stood outside a moment before plucking up the courage to announce herself. She rapped on the dirty window and just asked him straight out if he was a spy or what.

She could hear him chuckling away to himself in there, and she wondered then whether 'spy' was a rude word in German. Who the hell did he think he was to be laughing, and her after feeding him? The floor of the old shed creaked as he moved towards the door. She pulled at it from the outside to help him push it open.

He stood there in the doorway as though he owned the place. 'The reason I am here has nothing to do with wars. I have left the war.'

He said this rather grandly, but she didn't think wars were things you could just leave, and she wondered did he have a notion of himself. 'So you're a traitor to your cause, then,' she said, not to be outdone, but he didn't understand that so she just said, 'why are you here?' Plain enough for a baby to understand.

'I jumped. I did not know where I would land. Perhaps I jumped too soon but better too soon than too late. I hoped for Éire but I did not know. I am here because I can no longer bear to be up there.' He looked up at the sky then, and she did too. She felt a bit daft, for there was nothing to see but a jumble of leaves. He was so mysterious and sure of himself and so totally unlike anyone else she had ever come across. He must be brave, too, to jump out of the sky.

'Were you one of the ones who bombed Belfast?' she asked. Maybe that was a bit blunt but she had to know.

'I was a lamplighter.'

That sounded a nice thing to be but she knew it couldn't be nice at all. She assumed she should know what that was, so she didn't ask any more.

'I will leave soon. As soon as my leg is strong enough, I will go.'

'If you're gone when I see you next,' she said, 'I'll say nothing.'

When she went back to the house, she couldn't settle to anything. There was the baking to do and the pantry to be done over and the boys' beds to be stripped. Instead, she went up to Mother's dressing table and took out the manicure set with all the sharp little instruments with their pearly handles. She prised out specks of dirt from under her nails, soaked, clipped, filed and buffed them. All the time, she could see his tired face with the blue, blue eyes. She wished there was something she wanted enough to jump out of a plane for it.

She still talked to Father sometimes and she knew he wouldn't like what she'd done to his atlas. No one ever came to his shed uninvited either, but maybe he would like that a traveller was in there. He would be curious, of that she was sure. He was always far more interested in what was happening on the other side of the world than in what went on in Dunkerin. Mother always told him that to succeed in a country practice, you needed to join this and that, pay heed to give a little bit of business to this grocer, a bit to that draper. Father did none of that. He pretended not the slightest interest in either golf or bridge. There were those, of course, who said Dr Hennessy couldn't give a hoot about anything; spent all his day doodling on maps in his consulting room while the queue of patients got longer and more restless. He never bothered about the order of arrivals, either. He would come out and scan the grey faces in the room and form a snap judgement as to who was most in need.

'Every doctor needs a diversion,' Father used to say. His own passion was St Brendan and his voyages. 'First to reach America, not that the rest of the bloody world will give him the credit for it.' All summer long, he'd be at his experiments. He spent months soaking scraps of leather in the old bath he filled with seawater, each one coated in a different substance from the pots he kept in his shed to see which one provided most protection from the brine. He tried tallow, beeswax, cod oil, lanolin, and God knows what else. Finally, he came down in favour of one, though she couldn't remember now which one it was. He had Sean Galligan dig and line a trench that ran all the way down from the henhouse to the gooseberry bushes, which he filled with seawater from Dunkerin Bay. Then, he built himself a model curragh – gunwhale to keel about three feet long – covered it in stretched oxhide, treated it, and set it afloat.

She went to put away the atlas she had defiled earlier. On the map of Europe were hundreds of pinpricks where Father had stuck little flags in different colours, trying to predict where the Germans would go next. She ran her fingers over the pitted surface of Poland and the Low Countries. He was dead before they reached France.

When she went to bring the airman some food, she warned him about the lads.

'Don't worry,' he said.

'It's not me who needs to be worrying.'

He smiled, and suddenly it seemed the right response.

'What's your name?' he asked. He said it back to himself a few times, flicking her name on the tip of his tongue like he was calling the cat. 'Well, Kitty, I might need to be here for a couple of days. After a couple of days they will forget about me and my knee will be stronger.'

She wondered how she could have lost control of things so quickly. She had enjoyed being the ministering angel but he didn't seem to need any of that now.

'The boys go back to Dublin today,' she said. 'The two fellows who scared the living daylights out of you last night.' It gave her some satisfaction to put him back in his place. Before she closed the door, he called after her. 'My name is Oskar Müller.'

She continued to pull the door to, as though she hadn't heard him, but all the way back to the house she was thinking to herself what a lovely name it was, and how she'd never heard of anyone else called that, except for Oscar Wilde.

Elsa

Painting over Elsa

Elsa played Scarlatti. Next door, the windows were flung open, even though it was already September. If Oskar had returned for the holiday, he would hear her play. She would make him hear. Now and then, she wandered over to the window to look for him in the Müller garden.

Frau Müller sat there, as she always did on sunny mornings, her back to the Frankel house, her tea tray arranged as meticulously as the hair that shimmered at her neck. Once, they would take tea together in the garden, Mama and Frau Müller. Once, Oskar would paint with Papa, learning to be bold. They had mingled their blood, Elsa and Oskar, down in the shadiest part of the woods. Oskar couldn't bring himself to cut her, so in the end she'd had to do it herself. They held up their index fingers and closed their eyes and promised each other an ever after. Now, a glassy membrane had settled between their houses. Whilst the Müllers lived in the air, amongst flowers, the Frankels dwelt behind shutters.

For all that, I am still Elsa, she thought. It's not such a great adventure, surely, even today, to run an errand in my own city. To fold back the shutters for once. No one met her eye as she turned the corner of Adlerstrasse. That was good, she thought. No one held his nose as she passed, either. She might, if all was well, make it to Herr Goldmann's shop without catching a spray of spittle on her sleeve.

The blinds were down when she got there, the awning in and the door pulled to. No broken windows, though. Nothing daubed on the front. That was also good, she thought. But no sign of life either. She was about to give up when she heard the creak of a sash somewhere above her head. Inside, the shop smelt of dead things. He stood there, Herr Goldmann, his hands at his sides, palms cast downwards. He said nothing. Not a word. To break the silence and because she was, after all, still Elsa, she elaborated on the adventure, such as it was.

'Some cotton, brown. For stockings. I'm always needing to darn my stockings. Sharp bones like all the Frankels. Aunt Frieda was forever putting her elbows through her cardigans.'

He shook his head and drew in a long wavering breath that seemed to steal something from the room. At the counter, he tugged at a narrow drawer that released itself in a rattle of spools.

Elsa trailed her fingers along the carefully graded colours until she lit on just the right shade of brown. Why not have purple, she thought suddenly, or yellow for that matter? Why pretend anymore that a brown stocking need remain brown when everything else has changed? She gathered up two handfuls of spools, bright as bridesmaids' posies, and shoved them deep into her pockets. Herr Goldmann pushed away the few coins she gave him and asked instead that she bring him some bread, perhaps an egg or two if they had some. She babbled on as prettily as a Scarlatti sonata. 'And jam. I'll bring you jam. Mama still makes some from the berries in the garden.'

'And jam, then,' he said.

Outside, the sun still shone and the city gleamed and the crimson folds cascading from the buildings were almost beautiful. Even so, she hurried her step. Best get home before they welcome their little leader, before they grow glassy-eyed. She fixed her thoughts on the colours with which she would embroider her knees when all the stockings had worn through. That afternoon, she would scatter Scarlatti into the air in the house where no one said much anymore, where Papa sat motionless at his desk with papers strewn around him, as though the changes hadn't happened, as though he was still the Professor.

Elsa could hardly remember the days when he was self-assured and surrounded by friends. Nowadays, he wasn't even permitted to paint.

'Degenerate,' they said, 'that art of yours.' So Papa's life's work was dismissed at a click of the Direktor's fingers. They stuck him at the back of some office where he didn't officially exist and paid him enough to feed the cat.

Elsa turned the corner of Schillerstrasse, where all the flower boxes were red and white. Geraniums. Just red and white. She wondered when they would cultivate a black one to celebrate all that they had ruined. The sun was in her eyes now and for a moment she felt less sure of her way. The crowds out early on the streets today seemed to blur the city's contours.

She almost collided with a man standing in the centre of the pavement, watching his little dog relieve itself against a tree. She kept her eyes down, her fingers rumbling through the spools of thread in her pockets, her shoulders braced away from him. His voice came out of the haze of sunshine high above her,

'Ah, but if it isn't little Miss Frankel.'

She squinted but even as his face took shape, she didn't recognise him. Once upon a time it wouldn't have mattered that the Professor had to introduce himself. After all, she'd only met him a couple of times, when he was a junior lecturer in Papa's faculty and she was young enough to be tweaked under the chin. Nowadays, though, Papa talked constantly of the Professor. For Papa, he was a giant; a man who held the power to crush them all but who had decided instead to show kindness.

Elsa shielded her eyes against the sun as she felt the little dog weave its way around her ankles. He asked about her music, did she still play? And her Mutti, how was she these days? When the questions came to an end, she left a respectful gap, then wished him a good day, such as it was.

'What a fine man your father is,' he said then. She smiled, tried to make herself pleasant. 'People complain so. I mean,

I don't blame the man. He wasn't educated to be a clerk.' He gave a dry little laugh and wiped his lips with a crumpled handkerchief. 'Come and take coffee with me,' he said. 'Such a glorious morning to talk of dear old Papa.'

She didn't drink coffee, so perhaps that was why she hesitated, or maybe it was the gaggle of Austrians in national dress, with their sharp accents, who came a little too close.

'Your father would want you to help him, Fraulein.' He pronounced the word elaborately, extravagantly. It gave her hope and so she went with him. The Professor strode on in front of her, his little dog leading the way, the lead pulled taut.

As she walked, she began to feel a little brighter. Perhaps the Professor had more interesting work for Papa. Some research, perhaps. Anything other than bookkeeping. Then, when they had passed two cafés, she began to wonder why neither would do. He turned around as though he had read her mind but perhaps also to make sure she was still there. 'My rooms are on Genferplatz,' he said.

The Professor stood back and let her climb the narrow staircase ahead of him. As she walked slowly up the stairs, she heard the little dog scramble through a doorway and out the back. The building was hushed, confident. It was the silence of those who speak only when they wish. She would have liked the little dog to stay.

Papa always said it was the key to a man, what he chose to display of himself on his walls. She was astonished by the Professor's walls. They were covered in watery sunsets and bowls of fruit that had never seen a tree. It made her feel at once superior and puzzled that a Professor of Fine Art at the university could have such cautious, uneducated tastes.

He entered the room behind her. As he clicked the door shut, she heard him turn the key. There was no more talk of coffee. He pointed at the couch and indicated where she was to sit. He pulled over a chair that scraped on the polished floor.

He sat opposite her – too close – his legs almost touching hers. For the first time, she had a chance to evaluate further this Professor. She spotted the pin in his lapel. That was only to be expected, she supposed, but all the same it struck her that she'd never before been alone with a man who wore such a pin. She drew her legs in closer. She noted the long creases that joined nose to mouth, the faint milky blue of his eyes.

When she opened her mouth to babble as she always did when others were silent, he raised his hand sharply and a wisp of air passed across her face like the ghost of a blow. She flinched, then ran her fingers across the spools in her pocket, playing them like semiquavers. He could speak first if it mattered that much to him. She understood that, above all else, she must be humble, grateful for whatever he might offer. He was so close she could smell cake on his breath, sweet cream and coffee. Wary now, she covered her knees with her skirt, pulling it tightly, wrapping it under her thighs.

He cleared his throat, lowered his hand as though about to touch her, then drew it back again. Whether his disgust was at himself or at her, she couldn't tell. A filmy moisture had settled on his upper lip and she had already half risen from the couch when he struck her in the face, hard and sharp. The force jerked her head to one side, forced her back onto the couch. Tears sprang to her eyes with the pain and shock of it. Still, he said nothing. When her eyes cleared, he was sitting in the same position, examining his raised hand as if it was something quite separate from the rest of him. As she scrambled up to make for the door, drawing her coat tight around her, he moved quicker still.

'Sit,' he said, as if she were the little dog downstairs. He held her chin tight between index finger and thumb; examined one side of her face then the other. When he started to speak, it was as though he was talking to himself. That was what frightened her most. She tried to shake off his grip but he held her firm. 'He was the devil's own twin when he was in my shoes.

Pull your socks up, Weber. Most irregular, Weber. Most inaccurate. Most out of order. He loved to lord it over me, your old Papa. Even now he forgets himself sometimes. Can you believe that? Even now.'

She wanted to cry but she wouldn't. Wouldn't cry for him.

'You want to know why he's still there, incompetent, pathetic, bumbling over those figures?' She turned away from him, biting her lip. 'Because it gives me pleasure. That's why. Because he is learning humility.'

He was matter-of-fact when it came to undressing her. He stood at arm's length, like a doctor. He took care to undo each button, to avoid ripping anything. At school, she had always hidden from others the birthmark that stained her left breast like a swirl of purple ink, avoided swimming with anyone but Oskar, worn blouses that reached the neck. He could look at that, if it made him merciful. All the same, she couldn't stop her shoulders from curling inward, her knees from clamping together. She tried so hard not to shake, not to be sick, not to show anything of what she felt.

She concentrated on a vase of delphiniums on the table behind him; tucked herself inside the bell of one of the flowers. She managed to stay there a moment but the air from the open window was like another assault and she was too afraid not to watch him, to be prepared. And so she watched. The Professor's mouth was gaping, his eyes slurred, his hand working furiously at his trousers. He didn't seem to notice her move a step or two back from him, and she realised that she had seen that look before. A painting, she thought, one of their saints, someone who believed he'd seen God. He didn't try to touch her. It was as though her shame was enough for him. Sensing he was finished, she dived to find her clothes.

'Not yet.' Seated at his desk, he became the Professor again, his eyes clearer now, his pencil whispering on the paper on front of him. 'Look up.'

Whilst she did raise her head a little, she looked at a sunset, not at him. Then she found the delphinium again as he took what he wanted from her and put it down on the paper.

When he had finished, he got up from the desk and, with his foot, edged the neat pile of clothes in her direction. 'Out.'

She shoved on enough bits and pieces to be decent and bundled the rest into the pockets of her coat. She was almost at the door when he threw her the key.

Somehow she made it home, skirting the walls of the buildings, avoiding the strangers with beer already on their breath. She was desperate for Oskar but they always seemed to think up new ways of keeping him away. She conjured him up and had him kiss her eyes, her neck, the curve of her stomach, but it only made the longing worse. Oskar had always been there. As kids they'd ignored one another; Emmi was the one who used to slip through the connecting gate to share secrets and bonbons. Then, when the hate began to spread and the connecting gate was bricked up, they fell defiantly in love. He couldn't stand the Hitler Jugend; he said it was all bullshit but that he'd do it if it meant they'd leave him alone. He was always so certain it would all blow over. Oskar: so blue-eyed and sure of himself and unafraid of everything. So different from her and careful with her and eager for her. Forever telling her she was the only thing that made it possible for him to live in this shithole of a city. If only she had Oskar, she could bear the rest of it.

In her room, she took out Herr Goldmann's spools, rolling them around on her table until their colours became more real than the memory of the Professor. All afternoon she worked, stabbing fiercely at her clothing with a fine needle; reclaiming it, filling up the moth holes on her grey coat with little scribbles of orange, purple, pink. In the distance, they were playing their music now; strutting too, no doubt, for the little leader.

She thought of the Professor and hoped that what he had taken would be enough. Papa was late that night. Mama busied herself straightening the pictures in the drawing room, wiping away the dust that Beate no longer chose to notice.

Next door, at the Müller house, guests had arrived. Arranged in the garden like new-grown shrubs, they clinked and drank and trilled happily. Of Oskar, there was no sign. It was when the garden was empty again, long after the last of the Party faithful had trailed past the house, some singing, others still bearing their torches, that Elsa heard Papa fumbling at the lock. Once inside, he slumped back against the door, his eyes closed, a package under his arm.

Mama tripped along the corridor like a little duck, her fists out from her sides. She knocked over a photograph from the hall table in her rush to get to him. Soon she had her hands on his waist and was guiding him into the drawing room from behind. He slumped into a chair. Beate appeared at the kitchen door, eyes cast up to her heaven, a shrug on her shoulders. Mama was kneeling at his feet, gently clapping his cheek with one hand as she held him steady with the other. 'What have they done to you? Elsa, a cup of water. Hurry now.'

Elsa held the glass out at arm's length to stop her hand from shaking. He didn't take it, so she laid it on the table beside him. He held his head in his hands so all that could be seen of him was the fragile pink shell of his skull. He placed his hand over Mama's. 'I need to talk to Elsa,' he said.

Mama looked hurt and Elsa could tell she was angry with her already. Even so, she shut the door behind her in her precise, quiet way.

'You know we can't afford to stand out.' He shook his head slowly, laid the package on the table, then nudged it towards her.

The first thing she noticed was the colours. Forbidden colours: a skirl of harsh pink, a scream of green. Even on first sight, Elsa could see that the girl's face was a version of her own.

Older than she remembered it, thinner, with wary eyes. As she tried to make sense of the thick black lines of the girl's body, she heard Papa gulp back his glass of water like a man returned from the desert. This Elsa was naked, her sharp knees set apart and between them something raw, red, secret. Across her concave chest a long purple gash seemed to open up her left breast.

She felt serene, because that wounded ghost of a thing wasn't her. It wasn't Elsa. She tried to tell Papa that the Professor had wanted to crush her but that he hadn't dared. That this was the nearest he could get. That when the time came, none of them would dare. She opened her mouth to start explaining it all to him but he just shook his head. 'No words, Elsa. They don't matter now.'

When he had swallowed the last of the water he looked at her. "'After all, Frankel," he said to me, "it is your kind of thing."'

He sniffed, then wiped his nose with his sleeve. She was ashamed to notice that his fingernails were bitten, his cuff frayed. Her thoughts were like butterflies now, unaccustomed to the freedom she allowed them to find a way to sweep away Papa's hurt.

"'Surely you haven't forgotten," he said, "the merest whiff of turpentine and they'll cart you off. Whatever you people do amongst yourselves, you live in our world now." *You people.* That's how he spoke to me, the Professor.' His voice quavered. "'You say it's not yours, Frankel, that of course you no longer paint, that if you did paint it would be anything but this. But it is your kind of art," he said. "Between the two of us, it is your kind of thing. And it is undoubtedly your daughter, is it not?"'

Papa was rubbing his clenched fist along his leg and then he began to sob. "'Frankel," he said, "teach your daughter to keep her clothes on and her legs closed. You people must live by our rules."'

For an instant, she wondered which was worse for him, his own shame or hers. She bowed her head and felt for the spools that weren't there.

He began to settle himself, with a deep breath he held for an eternity then released in one harsh sigh. He drew himself up higher in his chair, business-like now, more of the old Papa about him. 'All the same, it was kind of the Professor to retrieve it for us, save our blushes. He's a good man, after all. A man who still shows some respect.' He took a crumpled handkerchief from his pocket and laid it over the surface of the painting like a cover on a dead man's face. 'Get some sleep now.'

She took that as a dismissal and so she left the room, leaving a small kiss on his forehead. She stayed just outside the door, though, watching him, as though she had become the parent and he the child. For want of spools, she ran through in her head the pictures in her music book: Schubert – or was it Liszt? – bleeding onto the piano keys; Beethoven with his ear clamped to the floor. Papa propped the painting up on his easel. He surveyed it as if it was something he himself had just completed. Then, he moved out of view. Craning her neck, she could see that he was on his hands and knees in front of one of the cupboards, a tower of papers on either side of him.

She watched him take out some battered biscuit tins. Then, a clatter of brushes on the desk. Colours in tubes and pots. He rolled the pile of brushes back and forth on his desk with the palm of his hand until he found the one he wanted. Thumbed the bristles then laid the chosen one down in front of him like a dessert spoon. He opened a tube of paint and smeared a little on the back of his hand. Another, then another, until at last he had it as he wanted it.

He poised his brush over the canvas and made a series of vertical lines in the air, flicking the tip back as though trying to remember how it was done. Soon, he was smoothing a layer of red onto the girl's naked body. He painted out the birthmark first. When Elsa was younger, Mama used to tell her God had marked her out as special. Papa's brush was more honest. Next her concave chest went, with its small walnut nipples, the thin shoulders and the lower body all disappeared under a layer of red paint. She stayed until it was over and even though he must have known she was watching him, he said nothing. By the time he had finished, a new red dress glowed on the easel.

Papa didn't get up the next morning. Mama made him a tisane and Elsa saw in her eyes that she blamed her. When he did get out of bed a week or so later, he insisted on putting the altered picture on the wall, in that most honoured position over the fruit bowl that he and Mama had bought in Venice on their honeymoon.

'How kind of the Professor to give us all such a charming gift. A most thoughtful farewell.'

Elsa could detect no irony. Mama looked at him with a kind of desperate love.

He threw himself into an orgy of letter writing. In address books, diaries, he underlined everyone who might be of use. Former colleagues, people who got out in the years he'd spent clinging on to the clerk's job, academics who once cited his papers and now didn't even reply to his letters. People in France, England, America. There was something about Madagascar. Just as suddenly, his furious optimism seemed to fizzle out and he went back to bed.

Then came the night Mama had predicted and Papa said would never happen: the synagogue in flames, a fury on those with the wrong names. The glass was shattered and once that went, almost everyone was within their reach: Herr Goldmann for one; the old man gone, his door in splinters, the shop a tangle of coloured yarns like a shredded tapestry.

A whole day passed and still the Frankels remained untouched. Elsa put it down to the painting. She decided that it had absorbed all their hatred. The harm they might do was trapped there in the slashes and stabs of paint that made up the girl's face. For the first time, she understood their fervour for magic images, now that she had one of her own.

All night long, men and boys paraded up and down Zweibrückenstrasse and there was always the chance that the painting would fail them. Elsa watched from the attic window. She knew now that blood or no blood, somewhere Oskar was amongst them.

Next day, Beate walked out the door, her bag rattling with Frankel silver. The girl in the red dress disappeared too. Overnight, she was overcome by thick crimson daubs, all trace of her obliterated. Papa sat back in his chair to observe his work. Elsa went to the piano. She played Scarlatti with the shutters closed.

At dinner, Papa took out his medal and propped it up on the table in front of him, leaning it against the pepper pot. Iron Cross, First Class. Won for gallantry in the war against France and England. He peered at the medal as he ate, barely pausing to draw breath between one mouthful and the next. When he had finished, he picked it up and tossed it up and down in his palm. Later that night, Papa was in the garden. When everyone had gone to bed she heard him digging, and the medal was never seen again.

Not long after the loss of Papa's job came the news that the money in his *Sperrkonto* had been confiscated. Even though Mama begged him not to, he wrote a letter of protest to the Gestapo, headed it 'Polite Request'. There was no reply. Money began to run short, then very short. He was desperate to see what the post brought each day and took to standing outside embassies in the hope that someone from somewhere would give them a visa. Eventually, it was Mama who made the decision to leave. 'It's not that we have anything left here. If we go to Hanne and Rudi in Amsterdam, at least we're with family. We can look out for one other.'

By the time Holland became a real possibility, it seemed almost local after Argentina, America and all those other places Papa had talked of. The relations there were Mama's. For all that, Elsa worried more about Mama than Papa when it came to living in Holland. Mama had always said there didn't seem to be a lot of point to Holland. In fact, none at all that she could think of other than tulips and she could manage to grow those well enough herself, thank you very much.

After Beate left, there was a change in Mama. Her convictions about even the most minor things had become stronger but they were always short-lived. She moved the furniture around incessantly and changed the curtains from winter to summer and back again every other week. She engaged in frenzied activity about the house; dusting, sweeping, emptying cupboards. She bristled when Elsa suggested they visit the shop for some food for the long journey to Holland.

'Shop? What shop? Hirsch, with his face crushed like a tomato? Or Goldmann? No more Hirsch. No more Goldmann, either, to let us live on credit.'

On the last morning in Zweibrückenstrasse, Mama and Elsa walked through the house to see if there were any last items they might try to fit in. Mama took a silver locket with a hollow centre from a drawer in the writing desk. She turned it over and over in her palm. 'If you put something you treasure in it, you'll keep it safe.' She smiled a little uncertainly as she handed it to Elsa.

Elsa went to her bedroom, to the old cigar humidor in which she'd kept her treasures ever since childhood. Most were things she didn't value any more and she could hardly remember why she'd ever kept them: Salzburg sweet wrappers, a wooden peg doll, an autograph book with the names of people long forgotten. From a small fold of tissue paper, she took the lock of Oskar's hair, fairer then than now, and placed a strand inside the locket.

Downstairs, Mama was selecting some volumes of Schiller from the bookcase for Papa. Elsa stood in front of the mantelpiece, as if trying to decide which photograph she couldn't bear to leave behind. Finally, she chose a photograph of her great-grandparents, surrounded by all seven of their sons, and left it on the hall table. Great Grandpapa was sitting open mouthed, a black slick of hair across his forehead. Great Grandmama looked like a stuffed doll, with fierce little eyes and a large hat.

It wasn't until they were on the train that Elsa realised she'd forgotten to pack the photograph. She had pinned the amulet to her underclothes but her great grandparents had been left all alone on the hall table. She felt ashamed to have remembered Oskar when her own people had been left behind.

Guest

From the moment they arrived in Amsterdam, the Frankels took up too much space. Mama seemed too wide for the narrow hallway and Elsa's limbs too unruly with so much china about. Aunt Hanne lost no time in getting everyone organised. She had lots of very neat friends with scrubbed faces and weak smiles: friends who knew things. In no time at all, one of these brought news of the Kindertransports. It seemed Elsa was still young enough to qualify as a *Kind* even though she was almost eighteen and had been wearing foundation garments for three years at least. Elsa would go to Belfast.

One evening, they all sat around the atlas. They looked for Belfast on the map of England. Elsa had never heard of Belfast before: no composer, no performer, not even a conservatoire. Mama drew a spiral around London with her finger then ran it up the coast to Scotland. It was a while before they realised that Belfast was not in England at all.

'So, Ireland then.' Elsa must have looked blank.

'Come on Elsa, it's just the next island along. The last one before America.'

Aunt Hanne's friend explained that, though it was Ireland, it was a part that England still owned. Elsa was lucky, she said. There was lots of open space in Ireland to grow good wholesome food. As for music, many people had a piano in the house. It should not be impossible for Elsa to keep up her music.

The day of the journey was one of scuffed goodbyes. Aunt Hanne said she wouldn't be coming along to the port. 'You mustn't take offence,' she told Elsa. 'It's just there've been so many, that's all.' Papa was unwell again. There was dread in his eyes but he seemed unable to express it. He got out of bed but

Mama decided it would all be too much for him and sent him right back again. He clutched Elsa's hand a moment, then slowly shook his head and walked away. As for Mama, she talked all the way to Rotterdam. Aunt Hanne had told her about the wedding of a distant cousin whom neither of them had ever met. Now, Mama discussed it as though she had seen it all with her own eyes: the Bruges lace in the girl's dress, her shell-pink roses. Uncle Rudi said not a word, his eyes fixed firmly on the road.

Later, Elsa sat next to the porthole. She rubbed at the glass with her sleeve to see out better but the haze and grime seemed to be on the outside. She imagined them on the quayside, their eyes straining in the morning glare then settling on someone in the same shade of blue. Nearby sat a girl of ten or so in a crinkly dress. She was sobbing, crunched up like a bonbon in its wrapper. For fear of being infected with such hopelessness, Elsa turned her back. When she could stand it no more she went up on deck but the girl's misery followed her like a fog. She knew she should have offered some comfort but somehow she was unable.

As she watched the flat coast slip under the horizon she began to cry herself and once she started, the tears tripped over one another. She tried to be quiet, to avoid setting anyone else off. She kept her shoulders set firm as a rack but soon she was howling into the North Sea. She leaned over the rails and shook her face back and forward into the sharp sea wind, tears smarting on her cheeks. When she had cried herself out, she walked along the deck, and there she noticed others, wailing just as she had done. Some were no more than babies. One tiny boy sat with his face pressed into the barrier, his thin arm reaching for the retreating coast. 'Mama,' he kept shouting. 'Mama.' Elsa tried to touch his shoulder but he pushed himself further into the rails and so she let him be.

In her head were girls who hadn't crossed her mind since the day she left school in Berlin. She could see her old classroom, that haze of heads in the rows in front of her, blonde and off-blonde. Gerda must be an accompanist all the time now. She'd be pleased with that. Even Marti can't have been too sad. Marti, with her loose blonde curls and her way of laughing with her teeth joined perfectly together.

'After all,' Mama said once, 'her father's made a fortune out of the boycott. They're doing well now. You can't expect Marti to be sorry things are as they are.'

The arrival at England took her by surprise. When she awoke, children were crowding around each porthole, the little ones hopping up on tippy toes to see better. When they docked at Harwich, there were lots of people, bright flashes. They seemed welcome.

'Here, Miss. A little smile for England. And again. Come on, little lad. Lift teddy up. Show him the camera.'

Elsa caught sight of the little boy she'd noticed on deck the night before. He came and sat next to her. Silently, he slid his hand into hers. When the women with papers came to divide the children into groups, they seemed confused by Elsa and the little boy. They conferred in whispers. Eventually, someone gently prised the little boy's hand out of Elsa's. He went off with a woman whose hat had cherries on the brim. He didn't cry but his eyes stayed on Elsa until he was out of sight.

A train ride the width of the country. All the way to Liverpool with just sugar-pink Lili for company. The mail boat to Belfast smelt of vomit and tobacco and there were so few other women or girls that Lili and Elsa curled up together on deck, shivering in the rain and spray. By the time the boat docked, they were exhausted. The woman who met them on the quayside drew her hands over her mouth in a pleased little peak and called them darlings. She placed a hand on Lili's wavy hair, picked lint off Elsa's coat. Her dress was old fashioned, Elsa noticed, and she spoke with great articulation. Each movement of her mouth was exaggerated, allowing a thorough display of her large teeth. The woman explained that, normally, they'd both be going out to the Farm. Lili, she said, would still be going there.

'I'm sure, Lili, you'll love farm life. We'll have you milking in no time.'

Lili looked horrified.

'Elsa, you, being just a wee bit older, are going Elsewhere.'

There were some, the woman murmured, half to herself, said so what if she's a bit older ... she'd be better off at the Farm ... fresh air ... exercise ... a tonic for lungs half starved in city air. The Farm sounded trying, Elsa decided, and she was glad to be going Elsewhere. Elsa was to be placed with a spinster in the east of the city, a Miss Jacob.

'No,' the woman said. 'Not as far as I know. No piano.'

It was a short drive from the port to the stolid reddish house that stood back from a long tree-lined avenue. Elsa gathered that, having the means and the space and being Jewish herself, Miss Jacob had been prevailed upon to take her in. A woman whose face seemed to sink into her chin, Miss Jacob showed little interest in what life had been like for Elsa. 'A bad business,' was all she said.

Every day, a lady came to polish and shine, jiggling like a jelly as she worked. At first, Elsa thought the woman might have a persistent cold, she seemed to sniff so much. Then, she came to imagine disapproval in those sniffs. One day, Elsa stood at the cupboard full of cleaning substances and tried to work out what each was for. She tried to remember what Beate used to do back home in Berlin before deciding she need no longer take orders from Mama.

Elsa adopted the cleaning of the brass on the front door and the broad plate that splayed over the threshold. Each morning she would stand there, clutching at the doorknob with a soft cloth, rubbing a little, watching the distortion of her own reflected face. This position, half in and half out of Miss Jacob's house, seemed to suit her. She was always first to see the postman, a little man with two stripes of hair plastered over his pate.

Mama's letters from Amsterdam were written in tiny handwriting on fragile paper. She talked of the weather, the flowers in Aunt Hanne's window boxes, Papa's bronchitis. Uncle Rudi played chess with Papa, she said. Elsa wondered if he let Uncle Rudi win.

'Papa is very hopeful that soon we will follow you to Ireland,' she wrote. 'Our application should be considered presently.'

Later, she stopped mentioning the visa application. Instead, she wrote about the canals, the pretty houses and Aunt Hanne's talent for homemaking. She mentioned no feelings of her own. There was never a word of Berlin.

When she wrote back, Elsa invented a beautiful Bechstein. In her letters, Miss Jacob was only a few years older than Elsa, a musician as well. She had glamorous friends who danced and told wonderful stories. Together they went to the theatre. The weather was not good; that much she admitted. No skating, of course. But the music, the piano. The opportunities she had to practise, to accompany Miss Jacob on the violin. She was building herself up, getting stronger. Soon she would be able to try more muscular music. Maybe, one day soon, her first concerto.

Meanwhile, life went on without music. On Thursdays, Miss Jacob and Elsa were driven into the centre of Belfast to a room of gilt and mirrors where elderly women in hats took afternoon tea, their chicken necks choked with pearls. The ladies would make polite enquiries as to the state of knees and hips before a hush fell on the room in readiness for the entry of the mannequins. On Elsa's first visit, the ladies ignored her, save for an occasional nod. She overheard one of them ask Miss Jacob who her wee guest was.

'That's my refugee,' Miss Jacob corrected her, and then a mannequin swept past the table and no more was said. Elsa felt their eyes on her and after that she was never quite sure how a refugee was supposed to behave.

A month without a piano and Elsa's head was so full of notes she felt it might burst. Her fingers ached for the cool precision of the piano keys. The only music in Miss Jacob's house was the ticking of the many clocks. They made time stretch through being so marked. Elsa took to sitting at the polished table in the empty dining room. She would sit there for hours with her eyes closed, playing things like the *Kinderstücke*, little pieces that required no concentration she knew them so well.

Her fingers flew across the table or sang out a melody or plunged deep chords into its surface until it seemed as though the wood itself began to yield, as though there was some faint reply from the living tree it had once been. Before long, she could tell immediately that she'd played a wrong note, hear that a thumb was thudding in among the runs of notes.

For all that, she found that she couldn't play her favourite things. A single phrase of Chopin tore into her heart like a ripcord. It made the walls of the little room dissolve and the music slide away from her. It made her see the world from high above her own head. Beneath her was this windy island, the grey corner into which she'd been tucked. Far over to her right was Berlin, where Marti and Gerda would be at the lake or having dancing classes with Herr Schreiber, whose hair gleamed like black satin. Somewhere in between was Amsterdam, flat on its back against the sea. This view of far-distant things brought too much pain and so she avoided Chopin. Her practice finished, she would take a soft cloth from the kitchen and wipe away the music from the surface of the table.

One Thursday, as Elsa was returning from the Ladies' Powder Room, just before the mannequin parade, she overheard Miss Jacob mention her name.

'You see, she's been spoilt rotten. Doesn't lift a hand. You do something out of the kindness of your heart and you get nothing back. Hours she spends, sitting in the dining room. I know, now, she's had it hard but you'd think the girl could show some gratitude. If you ask me, a guest should behave like one.'

A few days later, war broke out. Everywhere, the news-paper boys were yodelling about it. Miss Jacob and the ladies at the mannequin parade seemed amazed by the depth of Elsa's shock. While they were kind enough and kept refilling her cup with the dark orange tea they all drank, she saw them exchange glances when she muttered that she'd never really believed that this would happen. Miss Trimble placed her hand on Elsa's and told her not to worry. 'There's no war in Amsterdam, love,' she said. 'They'll be right as rain over there.'

One of the other women said it might do no harm to blend in a bit. Become Elsie, maybe, rather than Elsa.

The next morning it was raining when Elsa left the house to collect Miss Jacob's pineapple creams from the baker's shop at the end of the road. Each day since war broke out, she'd written a letter to Mama without knowing if it would ever arrive, though the little postman assured her that, 'So far, now, neutral places is fine.' She was clutching the latest in her hand, had barely strayed beyond the garden gate, when she heard the ping of something hard against the railings beside her. A sharp stone hit her in the calf and she gasped and jumped to one side. There were just two of them; little boys, no more than seven or eight, tongues out, thumbs waggling from their ears, shouting nonsense as incomprehensible as the newspaper boys on every corner. Then they started goose-stepping towards her, their fingers laid under their noses, their right hands jut-ting up in front of them.

At first, she couldn't believe that this was meant for her but soon realisation streamed across her mind like ink. The chil-dren were right up beside her now, their faces scrunched up into ugly little balls. She opened her mouth to scream at them but no sound would come. Sensing her defeat, they stepped up their insults. They walked round and round her but she'd plugged her ears against them. They came closer still, circling around her, dancing their war dance. One of them took a sharp pebble from his pocket and skimmed it towards her but this time it just glanced off the toe of her shoe. They seemed to lose interest then. Without another word, they ran off in the direction of the shop. When they were gone, she found she was crying and that seemed more shameful than anything else. In her head, she saw Papa with his head bowed and spit down the back of his coat. When she went back to the house, Miss Jacob was waiting at the door. 'Come in out of that, child.' She must have seen the tears but she said nothing.

That was when Elsa realised that Miss Jacob knew only as much as she wished to know. She longed to have someone to talk to. Even Lili, out on the Farm, would be better than no one at all. Her longing for a piano was stronger still.

That night, Elsa read all Mama's letters. For the first time, she noticed that they always began the same way.

'*My dear Elsa, I am so glad to hear that you thrive. We are fine here.*' The first few letters were practically identical, in fact. Elsa began to read them more carefully, to see if she could find something true amongst the flowers and canals. The real Uncle Rudi, perhaps: the Uncle Rudi who had begrudged Elsa the daybed in the living room.

'*I'd like to bake more, of course,*' Mama had written, '*but I must remember that we are guests here. A guest, Elsa, must never be an inconvenience. She must echo the needs of her host and place her own desires second.*'

That night, Elsa resolved that she would not become Elsie. She would let them all know that she was Elsa, who belonged in Berlin with her own piano. Elsa, who liked to skate in winter and picnic in the Tiergarten when summer came. Elsa, who once had friends. One of the Thursday ladies must have a piano. She would find a piano. When she did, she would play it so that they would, all of them, understand what it is to be a guest.

As the weeks went by, Elsa began to retreat into the past. Sometimes she thought of people who didn't matter at all: Gerda and the other girls she used to meet for ice cream when that was still possible; her first teacher; even the composer Richard Strauss, a man she'd once seen descend on the Conservatoire like a great emperor on a State visit. What did the old man make of it all? She had met him on that visit to the Conservatoire. Professor Schwartzkopf had insisted that Elsa be the one to play for him, no matter what anybody said. Elsa took to picturing Strauss at home in Bavaria. She imagined a house with blown roses on the side wall. Did he ever wonder where people like Elsa had gone? Had he simply decided to ignore it all? Did he, perhaps, approve?

Mostly, she thought of Oskar. She wrote to him, picking her words carefully, trying not to sound disappointed in him. She didn't rant, though she wanted to, though she wanted to scream it out, all down the page, *why don't you care?* She didn't send him love, either, because it was clear that was something he didn't want. After all, she had received no reply to the letters she'd sent from Amsterdam.

In case you'd like to know, I have been sent to Ireland until things blow over. It's something called the Kindertransport (don't laugh), apparently you're still a Kind at seventeen. Mama and Papa stayed behind in Amsterdam. Papa says they may get a visa to come to Ireland. Poor Papa, he is hopeful again but they have tried so many places. I suppose you have joined the others now. You'll understand if I don't wish you luck with it.

Your friend, Elsa

In time, Elsa came to feel that Miss Jacob had tired of having her around the house. It seemed so easy to irritate her that Elsa began to stay out of her way. She stopped taking Elsa to the Thursday mannequin parades. 'It's not your place to be bothering people about the likes of pianos,' she said. 'There's enough to be getting along with in this house without the playing of pianos.'

Not long afterwards, the woman who'd met Elsa from the boat visited the house. She talked in the same deliberate manner, as though speaking to a very young child or someone with only the most basic English.

'It's all right,' Elsa told her, 'I understand everything now.'

The woman looked a little puzzled at first, then hurt. Elsa wondered if it was just that she spoke to everyone like that.

'There's a bit more of a community in the Free State,' the woman said. 'Miss Jacob's the best in the world but she's getting on now. I've a family's willing to take you in. You'd be better off with a family.'

And so Elsa moved on again, to Dublin.

Beautiful Harbour

Bethel Abrahamson was a tailor with his own business. His wife Hilde was from Manchester, which was where the couple had met, at the home of one of Bethel's relatives. That was one of the first things Bethel told Elsa when he met her at Amiens Street. 'I couldn't believe my luck, Elsa. And in Manchester, into the bargain. There's no telling where the finest flower may grow. Just remember that. It mightn't look much to you, but who knows, Dublin might be the making of you.'

The family lived in a tight network of streets where everyone knew their neighbours; most families had come from a place called Lithuania half a century ago. The area was Portobello, which Bethel said meant Beautiful Harbour in Italian. It wasn't so beautiful, really, but it did feel like somewhere she might tie up awhile. The Dublin people called it Little Jerusalem, Hilde said. Elsa wondered why it couldn't just have its own name, instead of pretending to be somewhere else. There were bakeries where they sold things she'd not eaten since leaving Aunt Hanne. They even sold *hamantaschen*, with all kinds of fillings she'd not seen before. The canal that ran past the end of the street was like no Amsterdam canal, however. Its banks were a wild green jumble of nettles and long grass. It was a graveyard for old prams, and now and then a rat would plunge with a fat plop into the still water.

By the time she got to Dublin, Elsa had not played a piano for almost six months. While she'd continued to practise every day on the polished surface of Miss Jacob's dining room table, the sound of the music in her head had grown fainter. It was becoming more difficult to hear the wrong notes, just as the faces of Mama, Papa, Oskar even, were becoming shadowier too. It was in the comparisons between this new world and the old one that she sometimes remembered things she'd otherwise have forgotten.

In Berlin, the Frankels' *Havdalah* candlestick had been an exuberance of gold filigree with tiny jewels set into the knob on its spice drawer. The Abrahamsons had a small silver tower, simple and unadorned. The room they called the front parlour was overcrowded, every inch filled with furniture, china, bolts of cloth. In Zweibrückenstrasse, even the piano room was full of light, the floor a sea of gleaming oak, but that was before they closed the shutters.

The night she arrived, Hilde showed her into the back parlour where, it turned out, she spent most evenings embroidering the cloths that covered every surface in the front parlour where visitors were received. She'd hardly dared hope, let alone ask, but there was a piano. It was an upright, of course (there was no room for anything else), with two brass candle sconces that splayed out on either side. It was heavy, too, carved deep with flowers. She sat down without even remembering to ask first. She closed her eyes and breathed in deeply, and then she played. It didn't matter that the piano was out of tune. She played Chopin, even though she didn't mean to: a nocturne.

The next night, the back parlour was filled to the brim with neighbours, come to hear the German girl play. The night after that, they filled the front parlour too. By the end of the week, Mr Kernoff from down the road had organised a collection for her. 'That's a talent can't be wasted on the desert air,' he said, and others agreed. They'd send her to the College of Music, get her lessons, give her a gift after all her troubles.

The Abrahamson girls, Lottie and Minnie, were ten and twelve. Shy at first, they sat with their arms round one another when Elsa was there, whispering and giggling. One day she walked into her room to find the younger one, Lottie, feeling the material in her blue silk dress where it hung in the closet, wiping it slowly against her cheek. The girl jumped, blushed, then darted away. After that, she started to teach them some tunes on the piano and the ice was broken.

For a while, Elsa barely thought of Berlin. The little victories of Gerda and Marti no longer seemed to matter. When she wrote to Mama to tell her how happy she was, she didn't have to resort to invention any more. However, Mama's letters back did not change. She barely made reference to anything Elsa said. It was as though Mama's letters had all been written at the same time and posted one by one.

Elsa never read newspapers, not even back home in Berlin. Although her English was almost fluent now, she didn't start to read them when she came to Dublin either. The news on the wireless said little about the war on the continent, so she merely lived between the span of one day and the next, with her head full of notes. While the girls were at school, she helped Hilde with the housework, anxious not to make the same mistake as in Miss Jacob's house. She became more adept even than Beate when it came to laundering, and the brass on the front door gleamed. When the work was done, she played Hilde's piano – all afternoon sometimes – until it was time to prepare the vegetables for dinner. She didn't go out much, except to lessons at the college. The Abrahamsons protected Elsa so effectively, that when Holland fell to the Germans it came as a complete shock.

Walking home from college, she saw the headline on a newsstand. At first, they tried to pretend that it wasn't that bad. 'Sure, this could be a grand time for them to make the move across,' said Bethel.

But Hilde's eyes had darkened and she avoided any mention of the war while Elsa was around. Often, when Bethel was out, they would sit in front of the fire together, each brushing the hair of one of the children, and Hilde would share some tittle-tattle she'd heard at the market on Camden Street.

When Elsa asked Bethel how she could find out more about what was happening at home, he said that the papers never said anything out straight. The best you could do was read between the lines. 'Don't fret now, if you hear nothing for a while. Try to live your life.'

That night, Elsa cried like she had not done since the ship left Holland. Hilde must have heard, because she came in and took Elsa in her arms and held her like a baby. She no longer played Chopin after that. Instead, she drilled herself with Bach Inventions, playing so fast she'd no time to feel anything but the keys. Sometimes she played for so long her back hurt.

She would never understand what had happened to Oskar. She hadn't expected him to be so afraid, if that's what it was, to be too cowardly to come to the house. Where was he now, she wondered? He must be in the war. Everyone was. She couldn't imagine Oskar killing anything. He was always so very careful with spiders. It used to make her laugh, his elaborate efforts to trap them in one of the picnic cups, then fling them into the long grass. But even Oskar must be killing now. So many turnarounds, so many people who disappointed when it came to the bit.

She still wore the locket Mama had given her, pinned to the strap of her brassiere, smooth and cool as a pebble. One day, as she sat alone on a canal bench, she considered all the things that she had lost, even though she knew it wasn't good to dwell on it. Her parents, her friends, the café by the lake, the shops on Ritterplatz, her beautiful baby Blüthner, the cat that used to sleep on the summerhouse roof. She wondered if she would ever see any of them again. And then there was Oskar. She remembered the last day she'd caught sight of him. He was wearing a new uniform and he passed, whistling, in front of the house without even turning his head. She unpinned the little silver locket and rolled it on the palm of her hand. Then, she opened it and let the wind take the strand of his hair.

Now that she could play the piano whenever she wanted, she was improving fast. Miss Joyce, her teacher at the college, displayed all her certificates on the wall above the piano as though they alone were proof that she knew best. For all her qualifications, Miss Joyce let Elsa sail through bars where Professor Schwarzkopf would have stopped her with a rap of a pencil or a sharp pinch on the shoulder. So Elsa became her own critic, stopping, recapitulating, while the new teacher sighed at such perfectionism.

As for the war, she learned that people preferred not to speak of it. Hilde looked uncomfortable when Elsa asked how long she thought it would last. People talked about the Emergency but they didn't seem to approach it with any urgency that she could see. When one of Bethel's sewing machines broke down, he sighed about the difficulty of getting hold of spare parts but that was all. The war seemed very far away.

Then, one January day, a stray German bomber flew over Dublin. Perhaps it got lost, perhaps not. It dropped two bombs as it passed over. One of them hit the synagogue in Donore Avenue, and for weeks afterwards people were in a state of panic. Mr Kernoff said it showed what they could do if they wanted to. Pin-point accuracy, was what it showed, he said. Other than that, the war might as well have been on another planet.

Miss Joyce suggested Elsa enter for a music festival whose name she could not decipher, other than that it began with an 'F'. It would provide a focus, she said. She might polish up some of the old Berlin repertoire for it. If she wanted, she could try some more muscular music, a movement of a concerto even. Lottie sat for hours with her, page-turning and offering encouragement as she made her way through the work.

When the Feis arrived, she was amazed to see that people came to listen to the competitions as though they were a real concert. The hall was full when she arrived, even though it was the middle of the afternoon. All sorts of people were there;

elderly ladies with knitting, men leaning against the wall at the back as though they were just passing through and would soon be off again. A singing class preceded her own. Tenors. There was a minister of religion who sang with his hands clasped girlishly, a florid-faced man who looked as old as Bethel, a young man with a face like a ripe peach.

She hadn't played on a stage in so long she wasn't sure how it would feel, but when her turn came she recognised the sensation of losing her hearing, of somehow drifting to the stage, of producing music she could not remember having learned.

'Once you have thoroughly mastered a piece,' Professor Schwartzkopf had told her, 'you must lose all self-consciousness and let the music play for you.'

When she had finished playing, she sat there for a moment, dazed, as though she'd swum too deeply underwater and had almost forgotten that there was a surface to it at all.

'You're freezing, Elsa,' Lottie said when she got back to her seat. 'Look, you're shaking like a leaf.' She shoved the hot water bottle onto Elsa's lap. Gradually, she was able to make sense of the random sounds in the hall, a dry cough, the rustle of a sweet paper, a child's whine. She was aware, too, that people were looking at her. A man who was leaning against the wall smiled at her. One woman pointed her out to her friend. The next competitor seemed agitated, standing at the side of the stage while she mouthed something at a woman in the audience who appeared to be telling her to hurry along.

'Poor thing, having to play after you,' Lottie said, pinching Elsa playfully on the arm.

Winning made her happy, until she reminded herself that she was Elsa Frankel from Berlin who had no right to be happy. Lottie was happy, though, and she raised Elsa's arm like a prizefighter's, until she was able to shuffle it back down again.

Charlie

Anatomy of the Heart

The rain was tumbling from the gutters, rushing through the drainpipes outside the lecture room windows. It was hard to believe it was still raining, thought Charlie. It seemed to have rained all month long. Professor O'Malley stood before a large anatomical chart, cane in hand, his tweed waistcoat buttoned tight across his belly. He traced the route of the phrenic nerve on his endless journey through the byways of the human heart. The cluster of ducts and paths and lines was like a little life, pulsing with alternatives.

Charlie ached to be done with his studies, to leap out into the real world and find his own way. He knew that sometimes the way opened up for a man without his giving it a moment's thought. Forging one's own path was a finer thing, he believed. He admired the lad who would prospect in a river, join a wagon trail, travel far in search of new things.

At home in Foynes, he often marvelled at the flying boats coming in to land. Once, he stood and watched the people disembark. There was a sheen to those people; they seemed warmed by a different sun. It seemed a miraculous thing, to take to the sky in such a machine and then to step onto land again in another place entirely.

He glanced around at his fellow students. Many were doctor's sons, just like he was himself. There was Ringrose, Des Hennessy, and two or three more in the immediate vicinity. It wasn't that they'd been conscripted into medicine: not exactly, not like those blighters in the North who might be conscripted soon enough into the fight. Most were there willingly. All the same, he wondered how widely his fellow students had looked around for an alternative.

When the lecture was over, students clustered at the front door. Bobby Coyle and Des Hennessy were lighting up, their backs bent against the driving rain.

'I reckon the golf's off,' said Bobby. 'It'll be a bog out in Portmarnock.'

The three of them headed off towards O'Neill's, where, on race days, Bobby used one of the snugs as his office, fielding queries and dispensing tips. Charlie whistled through his teeth as they barrelled along Grafton Street, heads down against the rain. 'There's no bloody end to this weather. I tell you, when this is over, I'm off to the Transvaal like a shot.'

'You'll be taking up the German, so,' said Bobby. 'The way your man Rommel is headed, it's German they'll be speaking there by the time the war's over.'

'All I know is I've seen enough rain to last me a lifetime.'

'It's a whole new kettle of fish out there,' said Des. 'Dengue fever and dysentery and God knows what. There'll be a deal more book-learning before you're any use out in Africa.'

'How's the volunteering, Bobby?'

'Not a bother.'

'Not a rifle, more like.'

'Well, we've a new lot of Springfields arrived last week. We'd give them a run for their money anyhow. Mind you, it's patchy.' Bobby dragged the base of his glass back and forward over the beer mat. 'In some places, it's just a farce.' He took a swig from the pint.

'I heard about one unit up in Dundalk. All they had was a couple of powder-and-ball efforts. Last seen action in 1798.'

'Sure that's nothing,' said Charlie. 'I knew a lad was given a blunderbuss. Fellow says he felt like Captain Hook. Just shows you, whatever MacNeill might think with his Division up there facing North, the British could walk over the border tomorrow if they wanted to. Knife through butter.'

Charlie wondered if Bobby really believed that anyone could defend Ireland if it came to the bit. But Bobby had moved off the subject. By now, he was preoccupied with the arcane ailments that seemed constantly to plague his horses. Des was telling him he'd be better off in the veterinary field, and it was clear that even Bobby could see he had a point.

Now that the golf was off, Charlie was at a loose end. He had little time for the horses himself, and his eye lit on a Feis Ceoil poster pinned to the snug door. He could hardly believe it was that time of year already; the spring weather had been so bad. He'd always enjoyed a bit of music, even though he'd refused point blank to learn the piano with his sisters. Singing, that was more his style. He had a light tenor voice and lately he'd been going along to the Rathmines and Rathgar. Billy Fitz had told him they were always short of tenors and that there was a great social life to be had, with so many girls in the chorus. There seemed to be three classes on this afternoon, one of them for *Lieder*. He had a soft spot for a bit of *Lieder* and he remembered then that a chap from the Society, Ulick perhaps, had entered one of the singing classes at the Feis. More than likely, there'd be a crowd there to cheer him on. Charlie made his mind up there and then, and the thought that he'd escaped an afternoon exploring the left ventricle cheered him up no end.

He left the others poring over the afternoon's runners at the Phoenix Park and crossed the river to the hall in Abbey Street where the Feis was being held. When he got there, the hall was already full and he had to stand in one of the side aisles. On the stage, a trestle table was laid with a thick velvet cloth. There was a row of highly polished trophies and an extravagant arrangment of lilies. On one side, an accompanist was sorting through sheet music in preparation for the next competitor. On the other, two ladies in kilts took turns to change the competitor numbers displayed on a wooden easel. The adjudicator was an elderly man with a face like a weasel. Seated on a raised platform in the centre of the hall, he presided like an ugly little god. On his desk was a flat round bell, which he slapped now and then with the palm of his hand.

The first singer had a pinched face and wore a tight-knotted tartan tie. The adjudicator tapped the bell after a few bars, which struck Charlie as unnecessarily brusque, even for a reprise. It was only when Ulick sauntered out onto the stage, and a great whoop went up, that Charlie realised that half the Society seemed to be up there in the front few rows. Ulick gave someone the thumbs up, then settled his gaze on the middle distance as he prepared to sing. The adjudicator gave Ulick no more than a raised eyebrow for his trouble; another R&R man got no discernible reaction at all. In the case of one plump little man with prominent teeth, the adjudicator rubbed irritably at the end of his thin nose, as though he was allergic to the sound the man was producing.

Charlie's concentration wandered to a trio of girls on the other side of the aisle. He wondered if they were pianists; they were sitting with their hands on hot water bottles wrapped in large ragged towels. The younger two might have been twins, with their long thin faces. The third girl, though, was older. Eighteen, maybe even twenty like he was himself. The two younger girls began to giggle as the little adjudicator mounted the stage and cleared his throat with elaborate emphasis. But it was the girl nearest the end of the row that Charlie wanted to see. He craned his neck to get a better look. Her thick hair fell around her in heavy waves. On each side, a lock was drawn back, and they were tied at the crown of her head in a long blue ribbon. She looked delicate, too pale to be healthy. A little anaemic, perhaps. Her eyebrows, which formed a single heavy line over the bridge of her nose, gave her an appearance of intense concentration.

The adjudicator waxed lyrical for such a weaselly looking man. He said the standard of performance easily surpassed anything he'd experienced at festivals across the water. There was a collective murmur at this; the little god had hit the right note. Charlie was more interested in the girl. He imagined her consulting him at the surgery, coughing delicately but fatally. She caught him gaping at her, and it was a moment before he realised that the man being presented with the prize was none other than Ulick himself. Acknowledging his supporters, he spotted Charlie and saluted. The girl decided Charlie was worth a second look. She smiled this time, now that he was a winner's friend.

'Would all competitors for the Esposito competition for pianoforte please form a queue with their entry cards to the side of the stage.'

He didn't know a great deal about the piano and after a couple of performances he wondered why he was sacrificing his drink with Ulick and the others. But then the girl with the blue ribbon left her seat. She looked like she was used to this game; she bowed as she reached centre stage, then took as long as she needed to settle herself at the piano. She fiddled with the knobs on either side of the stool to adjust the height, then flexed her fingers over the keys. Charlie felt for those fingers. He wondered were they still warm enough or had she been sitting in the wings so long that the benefit of the hot water bottle had worn off. He held his breath as her hands seemed to hover over the keys a moment before plunging down into melody.

By the time she had finished playing, even the little ladies in the kilts who marked off the competitors were gawking up at the stage. A woman in a brown pillbox hat who'd been knitting furiously throughout the singing class had laid the knitting to one side. When she stopped playing, the girl herself seemed dazed. As she rose from the stool, she gripped onto the side of the piano to steady herself. Her two young companions – sisters maybe – clapped energetically and the hall was alive with gasps and excited chatter.

He overheard the usher remark to the woman with the knitting, 'They're quare piano players. There's no bating them at that caper.'

Charlie didn't take in either of the performances that followed hers. The result was a foregone conclusion anyway. When the adjudicator presented the girl with a large silver urn, he lost sight of her face a moment and found himself straining to catch her again. He searched for her name in the programme and by the time he looked up, Elsa Frankel had left the stage and the adjudicator was presenting second and third place medals. The aisles were clogged with competitors arriving for the next class. There was no way of getting through and he watched the three girls disappear through the back door. He was mad at himself for not having gone over there when he'd had the chance. He could have paid her a compliment, instead of just staring at her like she was something in a specimen jar.

That evening, back in his digs, Charlie was restless. There wasn't much room to pace but he couldn't sit still. While he recited to himself the anatomy of the heart, he marched back and forwards across the space between his narrow bed and the desk he'd moved to face the window. Once he had it off pat, he threw himself onto the bed and all the springs twanged. All he could think of was Elsa Frankel: who she was and where he could find her again. He ran a bath without getting Mrs Curran's permission and scrubbed vigorously at his back to get the circulation going. Even after he'd soaked in the bath for so long that Mrs Curran came banging on the bathroom door, he still felt agitated. Despite the banging, he lay on in the water and contemplated his wrinkled fingertips. He wished he knew the name of the piece she played. It was beautiful, but it was also the saddest thing he'd ever heard. Like a great snowy plain that stretched away as far as the eye could see.

The Bohemian Girl

Next morning, Charlie ate the breakfast that Mrs Curran made him every day, winter or summer: fried eggs with crispy edges, sausages, rashers, white pudding, black pudding. The only other lodger, another Surgeons man, had left at the end of the Michaelmas term but Mrs Curran still served up the same quantity of food. He'd no idea where she managed to get all the eggs and pork, unless she had people down the country with a farm. When he asked her once, she just tapped the side of her nose and bustled off again. He didn't really want it but he hadn't the heart to tell her that. Once he'd hinted that she really didn't need to cook every morning but she wouldn't have it. 'It's all included in the price, Mr Byrne. Room *and* board.'

So, each morning, he ate what he could. He drank the strong tea awkwardly because his fingers were too large to fit into the delicate handles on Mrs Curran's pink and gilt cups. She never sat down for breakfast herself, but shuttled between kitchen and breakfast room, munching on morsels from the sideboard, relaying the latest news from the wireless she kept on the kitchen shelf.

'More bombs, Mr Byrne.' She'd just offered him more toast, so it took a moment for the word to register with him. He looked up to see her neat barrel of a body disappear through the kitchen door. Her head protruded through the hatch in the wall. 'Belfast, Mr Byrne. Bombed again.'

Mrs Curran was a woman of few words. Charlie thought she might be from the North herself. 'You don't have people up there, do you Mrs Curran?'

'Indeed I do not,' she said and bustled off.

They said no more about bombs and Charlie headed off towards the college. The news of Belfast left him feeling melancholy as he walked towards St Stephen's Green. The day was fine; a season away from the day before. His first lecture was not for an hour, so he stopped and bought a copy of *The Irish Times* in the hope of finding a report on the previous day's competitons at the Feis. He went into the Green and sat for a while on a bench by the duck pond, skimming through the pages.

News of the night's bombing raid had not yet made it to the paper, which was full of the innocence of the day before. There was a picture of some golf club members down in Waterford, bent double in their plus fours, planting potatoes on the section of the course they'd dug up for the purpose. He hoped it would not come to that at Portmarnock. He looked for Bobby's horse in the results of the Laidlaw Plate but it wasn't placed. In amongst the advertisements for Guiney's anniversary sale and the Bracer that Builds you up, he found Elsa Frankel.

> *The large audience … two important piano competitons … Dublin's interest in piano work continues unabated. Competitors should eschew the modern craze for speed in favour of a concentration on clean detail and a proper singing piano tone … highest praise for the winner of the Esposito Cup, Miss Elsa Frankel … Extraordinary maturity … emotional depth …*

The report gave her address as Stamer Street but it didn't say which number. He knew Stamer Street; the houses were tall, narrow, red brick. He might have to go knocking on doors until he found her. But what would he do then? He didn't think she was the type of girl you would ask to a dance. The cinema, maybe? He'd noticed that the new picture with Nelson Eddy and Jeanette MacDonald was on at the Metropole. It had a romantic sort of a name, something to do with the moon. Maybe she would like that. He didn't know if there was opera on at the Gaiety or if there was, how much it cost to buy a ticket. He wasn't sure the opera was up to much, anyway. He'd heard they had some awful fellows singing the leads now that there were no Italians coming over to fill them. It might be safer to stick with the pictures. The idea of finding Elsa Frankel was such an appealing one and the day so fine that Charlie decided the pericardium could wait another day.

The unexpected sunshine had him full of the joys. When he reached Stamer Street he marched straight up to number 1 and gave it sharp little rap. The man who answered the door had his shirt open to the top of his vest and a drip of lather on the end of his chin. Charlie came straight to the point. 'I'm looking for a girl called Elsa Frankel,' he said.

'So why'd you come here then?' the man replied and closed the door in his face.

He worked methodically through the numbers. He'd got to number 9 when a man emerged from one of the houses he'd already tried. 'I hear you're looking for the German girl, the one who's living with Bethel and Hilde,' he said and pointed Charlie in the direction of number 17.

As Charlie approached the house, the sound of a gramophone wafted across from the other side of the street. *I dreamt I dwelt in marble halls.* The sound was faint and cracked but the voice was unmistakeable. It was Margaret Burke Sheridan, the opera singer his father worshipped, the one they all referred to at home as Maggie from Mayo. *But I also dreamt, which pleased me most, that you lov'd me still the same. The Bohemian Girl.* Charlie took this as an auspicious omen, and it fortified him as he made his way towards Elsa's house.

When he got closer, he passed two women who were standing in the street with their shopping baskets, speaking a strange guttural language he couldn't place. He could tell they'd noticed him but they pretended they hadn't. Just then, the girls who had been with Elsa the other day at the Feis came bounding through the door of number 17. If he hadn't stood aside they'd have crashed right into him as they raced down the steps and went skipping off down the road.

He'd already had his foot on the bottom step but now he changed his mind. The moment had passed and his courage failed him. He imagined her in the hallway, putting on her coat and getting ready to leave the house herself. It was probably an awkward time. And anyway, he'd come on a whim without announcing himself or even thinking out what he would say. He walked away in the direction of town. Instead of trying to catch the end of his lecture he went back to his digs. He wanted to do this properly and he decided a letter to her parents would be the proper way.

Dear Mr and Mrs Frankel,

I am taking the liberty of writing to you in English in the hope that you have the language. I am aware that you are a German family. I do not have a knowledge of that particular tongue but I'm sure you will agree that the love of music transcends such barriers.

As a music lover myself, and a medical student at the College of Surgeons, I am writing to say that I was privileged to witness the piano playing of your daughter Elsa at the Feis Ceoil the other afternoon. I am not one of the cognoscenti but I take an interest in light music myself, being a tenor with the Rathmines and Rathgar.

I wonder if I might be so bold as to ask whether I could come and meet Miss Frankel. I thought it would be more appropriate for me to approach you in the first instance so that you could discuss it with her. It would be a great honour to be introduced to Miss Frankel and perhaps even to hear her play again.

Yours sincerely,
Charles Carolan Byrne

Mrs Curran left a letter on his side plate at breakfast a few days later. She busied herself at the sideboard, waiting for him to open it, but he took it off to his room and sat down on the edge of the bed to read it.

Dear Mr Byrne,

I am in receipt of yours of the 4th inst. You are welcome to call for tea on the afternoon of Thursday coming, if that would be convenient for you. Elsa is staying with us for the time being and she has a brave bit of English now. I hope you are a lover of Chopin as that is the usual bill of fare.

I look forward to making your acquaintance.
Yours, etc.,
Bethel Abrahamson

The next Thursday, the two men sat together in the front parlour of the house in Stamer Street. The tall, narrow room was dominated by a large lithograph depicting bearded men in flowing gowns, so ancient and knowledgeable they might be prophets. There was that much in the picture, what with garlands of leaves, inscriptions and a whole menagerie of beasts, that Charlie found it hard to tear himself away from it. In fact, the whole room, lined with heavy carved furniture so dark it was almost black, was as crowded and richly decorated as the print. Every surface was laid with fine embroidered cloths and there were huge bolts of cloth piled up beneath the sideboard.

'Right then, Byrne,' said Abrahamson, rubbing his hands together heartily. 'You'd like to visit Elsa.'

'I would, Sir.' He slid the posy he'd brought with him onto the floor, not quite sure what to do with it.

Bethel cracked the knuckles of one hand, then the other. He looked at Charlie, sizing him up. 'She's an only child, Byrne, from Berlin originally. The father was a professor of some kind, back in the day. Of course, that's all changed now.' He seemed distracted a moment. 'Things got very hot for them in Berlin, so they had to get out of there, went to family in Amsterdam. Elsa was the lucky one. And now, with Holland occupied ...'

'But couldn't they just come over here?'

Abrahamson looked straight at him. 'It's not for want of trying. We've had people onto it ever since she arrived. In fact, it looked like we might be getting somewhere until this time last year, and the Germans blasted their way into Holland. I'd say that's put the kibosh on it, for the time being anyway. No, Byrne, right now my main priority is Elsa herself. It was tougher for them over there than either of us can appreciate. It's up to me to make sure she doesn't suffer like that again.' He looked levelly at Charlie. 'You might be aware that, even in Dublin, there's people only too happy to make problems for a Jew.'

Charlie had never met a Jew before, much less made problems for one. He didn't know what he was expected to say.

'If our friend Esther had her way we'd have Elsa up at Dublin Castle filling in forms. Becoming Official, whatever that means. Sure you wouldn't want to be taking any risks with officialdom. She's grand where she is.' He leaned over and gave Charlie a brisk pat on the leg. 'I'm just telling you all this, Byrne, so you've the bit of background. So you know the score.'

Charlie nodded, swallowed.

'As for how much you should talk about the war and all that, it can be hard to know how to handle it, sometimes. There's been no word from the parents this last while, you see. Not a dicky. Elsa is like you or me on the surface of it but life's not easy for her.'

There was a break in the conversation and for the first time Charlie could hear the sound of a piano in the next room. Bethel seemed unaware of it, his eyes on the carpet. Charlie looked down to try and see what was engrossing him. He seemed to be following the intricate path of one of the boughs on its tree of life pattern. Charlie began to rack his brain for something to say. 'It's hard lines, being far from home,' he said at last. The longer the statement hung there, the more foolish he felt.

Bethel looked up and gave him a half smile. 'It is,' he said, nodding slowly, 'but it's hard to get your head round, isn't it? People scattered, like that. Not able to live with their own people in the place they were born.'

Charlie felt inadequate, suddenly, in the face of so much turmoil. His own upbringing seemed impossibly dull and self-satisfied by comparison.

'That's a miserable state of affairs, Byrne. Living somewhere you've no real love for because it's not safe for you to be any-where else.'

'So I'd imagine,' Charlie said quickly. 'You don't feel that yourself, Sir, I hope?'

Bethel looked taken aback and Charlie hoped that the ques-tion didn't seem too personal.

'Sure I'm Dublin born and bred.'

Charlie felt clumsy, embarrassed. He felt his face redden.

'But you're right, of course, for all we're born and bred, we're always set apart a little bit. In these times, now, we have our worries, sure we do. Between you and me, Byrne, I'd say we're on some list already, somewhere in Berlin. If it came to it and there was a German invasion, we'd be in the soup.' Bethel seemed to be thinking aloud now. 'Don't know where we'd go if that happened. Not many places left when you boil it down. My own father, now, he left Kovno fifty years ago. From there, he went to Konigsberg, then onto Halle. Leipzig, Magdeburg, Hanover.' He reeled off the placenames like a well-worn litany. 'They stayed there a month or so with some relatives, then off on the road again. On again, to Amsterdam this time. He used to say sometimes that maybe he should have stayed in

Amsterdam. He liked the size of the place and the canals. But he travelled further. Antwerp, though I don't know why, and then back to Rotterdam, where he got the boat to England. A place called Hull, a port over there on the east coast. Then Leeds, then Manchester. They stayed in Manchester a long time. Some of the family still live there but our side came over to Dublin and we've been here ever since.'

Charlie nodded, eager to show interest, but he could see the posy on the floor out of the corner of his eye and he was worried the flowers would have wilted by the time he got to see Elsa, whenever that might be. Bethel seemed to detect Charlie's impatience. 'But none of this is why you came visiting,' he said briskly. 'So, Byrne, you're a medical student, then. You liking that?'

Charlie wondered whether he should bother pretending but Bethel didn't wait for an answer anyway. 'In this house now, it's music, music, music.' That seemed to cheer him up. 'And not just Elsa, either. She has my own two at it as well now.' Charlie laughed along with him, wondering whether he would get to see Elsa today at all.

Hilde nudged open the door with her shoulder. She laid a tray of tea on one of the heavy sideboards, gave Charlie a brief smile and nodded over at her husband.

'Elsa's ready for us, now,' Bethel said. He began pouring the tea, and placed a cup and saucer on the arm of Charlie's chair. It was all very like how his grandmother had described courting in the old days. He uttered some inanity or other and slid himself forward onto the edge of the chair in preparation. When he ran his hand around his chin, he remembered the little nick he'd made that morning, trying to shave without a mirror.

Elsa was even smaller than he remembered. A smile flickered across her face and was gone almost before he could catch it. Charlie gripped the arms of the chair to lever himself out of it and almost knocked over the teacup in his haste. Avoiding that disaster, he managed to trample on the posy. He could tell that Elsa had taken all this in but she didn't say anything. No one said anything for a moment.

'Elsa, this is the Charles Byrne fellow I told you about. The boy who tracked you down from the Feis Ceoil.'

He didn't like 'boy'. He didn't much like 'tracked down' either. It began to dawn on Charlie that he really had no pretext for being there, and his cheeks flared.

'Do you remember I told you Mr Byrne here has a bit of an interest in music himself?' Bethel said.

Put kindly enough, thought Charlie. 'I'm in the Rathmines and Rathgar,' he said. 'We could do with an accompanist.' It must have been the need to explain his presence; some urge to justify himself. Anyway, it was out before he could stop himself.

'It's light music, Elsa,' Bethel put in. 'An operatic society. Amateurs. Sociable fellows.'

Charlie nodded, wondering how he was going to get out of this.

'They probably need someone to help out at rehearsals. Would that be it?' Bethel asked, clearly trying to help him along.

'It would.'

Bethel poured the tea and for a moment the room was quiet but for the clink of teaspoons.

'That piece you played at the Feis,' Charlie said. 'Is there any chance you could give us that again? When you've had your tea, would you play it, maybe?'

She gave him a quick smile, and after that he could barely keep track of what Bethel was saying about the spring this year being the worst he'd ever known it. When the tea was done the three of them trooped next door to the piano.

As she'd done at the Feis, Elsa twisted the knobs on either side of the stool to trundle it up to the right level for her. When she turned back to the piano, her body slackened. She took a long breath and began to play. She seemed unaware of anything but the music. He didn't recognise the piece she played but the melody sang out like the song of a bird. He found himself trying to interpret the expression in her shoulders, just as he'd tried to read that elusive look on her face the first time he saw her. When Hilde put her head round the door, Bethel got up and left the room while Elsa was still playing.

Elsa played on for a little while and then she stopped. She sat silently, with her back to him. Charlie's eyes leapt around the room looking for a conversation piece. When finally she turned around to face him, his cheeks were hot with the effort of appearing in control. They both started to speak at the same time.

'Isn't that a girl's name?' She looked at him from under her lashes, her head to one side.

For a moment, he didn't know what she was talking about

'Caroline. That's how you signed your letter: Charles Caroline Byrne.' She rolled the syllables so that they sounded incapable of being applied to anything male.

'No,' he said, flustered. 'It's Carolan. After Turlough O'Carolan, the blind harper. It's a man's name.'

'Harper?'

'Fellow who plays the harp, musician.'

She looked amused. His face was burning.

'Did your mother want a musician for a son?' she asked.

The idea had never occurred to him before.

'Something different,' he said. 'I suppose they wanted something different.'

'And are you?'

'I don't know.'

She sat in the chair opposite him and placed her hands in her lap. 'I don't want to be an accompanist,' she said.

He felt such a great surge of relief that he must have smiled. 'Oh that's all right,' he said. 'I don't know if it would be up your alley anyway. It's Gilbert and Sullivan, mainly.'

She wrinkled her forehead, then dismissed the whole thing with a wave of her hand.

'Would you come out with me, Elsa Frankel?' he asked quickly, in the half hope that it would slip out without her noticing. 'We could go to a concert, if you'd like?' He had the spring concert in mind. In the Damer Hall.

'Yes,' she said, and he felt like he was stepping off an old, half-dead planet onto one that was fizzing with life.

Reeling

It was Friday night, and Mrs Curran stopped in her tracks as Charlie came down the stairs. 'Begod, you're the cat's whiskers,' she said. 'Is there a dance on?' Her behind swayed off through the living room door in its business-like way. He'd had Clark Gable in mind when it came to the hair and he hoped he hadn't overdone the Brylcreem. He glanced at himself in the mirror and decided he'd do, then he took his bicycle clips out of the drawer in the hall stand and walked out the door.

When he arrived at Elsa's house, he thought he could hear the sound of girls laughing. Twittering would be a better word, he thought, like little birds. Mrs Abrahamson showed him into the front room and gave a little nod of approval as her eyes travelled from the polished toes of his shoes to the Clark Gable hair. She closed the door behind her with a little click. Moments later, there were shuffles and whispers ouside, and more of the twittering. He eased himself towards the door. When the moment was right, he dropped down suddenly so that his eye looked straight through the keyhole. The eye on the other side blinked. There was a sharp intake of breath and then the sound of muffled shrieks, feet pounding up the stairs.

Seconds later, Elsa was in the doorway like a kind of a vision. Her hair gleamed and the ribbon was yellow tonight.

He felt it would be rude just to leave without a word to the Abrahamsons but there was no sign of either of them. Then, just as they were moving out into the hallway, Bethel came out of the back room. 'Take good care of her now,' he said. He patted Elsa on the back and his hand looked like the paw of a bear against the narrow span of her shoulders.

Charlie decided he didn't know her well enough yet to invite her onto his crossbar, so he left his bicycle propped up against the railings. He didn't know whether he should offer her his arm, so he didn't. She was only as high as his shoulder but every sinew of her seemed more fully alive than most other people.

'So, harp man, we're going to hear some music?'

'Oh, it's just a variety concert. It won't be top notch, just a bit of everything.'

He'd hoped that by understating his expectations the concert might be a pleasant surprise but the first couple of items were dreadful. First, a lady whose feet spilled out over the top of her shoes took to the stage to warble mournfully about the spring. Then, it was a trio of pale girls who sang 'Three little maids from school are we' and fluttered their paper fans and batted their eyelashes so ferociously it was exhausting just to watch. One girl let go in mid-flutter and her fan went flying off over the heads of the audience and landed with a clatter at the back of the hall. Maybe Nelson Eddy would have been a better bet.

Charlie had tried to position himself so he could to see her face without gawking straight at her. As the performances went from bad to worse, he contented himself with looking at her hands. By the time they'd heard a hooting contralto, a recorder ensemble and a histrionic recitation of 'The boy stood on the burning deck', Charlie had plucked up the courage to lay his hand gently on top of Elsa's. When she didn't move it, he mustered up the courage to look at her only to find her doubled up and shaking. He was alarmed for a moment, tried to remember if they'd covered fits and convulsions yet, until he realised that she was laughing fit to burst.

He longed for the interval. When at last it came, they stood by the wall in the foyer and drank bright-coloured minerals, and Charlie tried to find something appropriate to say.

'I'm sorry it's not better,' he said at last. 'We don't have to stay, you know.'

Elsa looked horrified. 'But of course we must stay. I would hate to leave. That spring lady, she might even have another song for us.'

He must have looked confused because she dug him in the ribs and threw back her head and laughed and laughed. He was glad she was enjoying herself, even if he was not sure it was right to laugh at people who were only trying their best.

Sure enough, the spring lady led the second half of the programme. She sang in Italian this time; something tragic for which she wore a feather headdress. Elsa ruffled his sleeve with delight. Next, a group of Irish dancers filed onto the stage. They stood there stiffly; black-stockinged knees raised and cross-laced feet pointed. There was a wheeze from the accordion at the side of the stage. The girls lifted their arms to form a chain and they were off. The fiddle sawed out the melody and the girls wavered across the stage. One-two-three-four-five-six-seven. One-two-three, one-two-three. Then curled into two circles. One-two-three-four-five-six-seven. Then in pairs. One-two-three, one-two-three. Elsa sat forward in her seat. She moved her head in time to the music and soon she was tapping out the rhythm on the edge of her chair. It wasn't the kind of thing you do for Irish dancing, but no matter. He noticed a few people looking at her with curiosity and he felt proud that he was the one she was with.

When it was all over, they walked back up towards Portobello.

'What was that last one they were doing, those four girls?' she asked.

'Oh, that would be an eight-hand reel,' he said.

For some reason she found that hilarious. When she laughed, her laugh seemed almost too big for her, as though she would snap in two with the force of it.

The rain came down and before they knew it they were in the middle of a downpour. They sheltered in a doorway not far from Kelly's Corner. Charlie knew they were so near Stamer Street they could almost make a run for it but he didn't want to leave the stillness of the doorway. He couldn't bear the thought of saying good night. She'd only a light cardigan on, so he took off his jacket to drape it over her shoulders. Her hair was drenched now, hanging in rats' tails down her back, but she still looked beautiful, even though she was paler than any girl he'd ever seen. He wondered would she be offended if he asked about her iron intake. He realised that this was not the moment to mention it, but made a mental note to remember to talk to her about her diet.

'Let's dance in the rain,' she said suddenly.

He wished she wouldn't do that to his jacket, but before he knew it she was whirling him around. Round and round in the pouring rain. One-two-three-four-five-six-seven. One-two-three, one-two-three. She was light as a feather and threw her head back and laughed at his clumsy, scooping clodhopper of a waltz. He was a little offended, until he realised that she was enjoying herself hugely with him. The laughing was nothing to take offence at.

Maybe next time a dance would be the thing, and maybe by then he'd feel he knew her well enough for the crossbar. The rain had eased off by the time they got to the bridge. They were just turning the corner to walk home along the canal when he heard the hollering, like an Indian war cry: the type of sound you make when you're a little boy climbing a tree and you fan your hand back and forward over your mouth.

'Charlie Byrne.'

There were two figures in the road in front of them. He noticed that Elsa had slipped a little behind him.

'Charlie Byrne. You're a dark horse, boy.'

As they got closer, Charlie realised it was Bobby Coyle, drunk. The other fellow was an old schoolfriend of Bobby's he'd met once or twice in O'Neill's, a civil servant of some sort. They were both in their LDF uniforms.

'Come here to me, Byrne, and show me your young lady. Don't be shy, now, she's a fine-looking girl. Isn't that a fine-looking girl, Sullivan?'

Charlie sensed Elsa move closer to him. He reached out and took her hand. When he caught her eye, he realised that she was trying to interpret the situation from his own reactions, so he did his best to smile at Bobby. 'This is Miss Elsa Frankel,' he said.

Bobby looked over at Sullivan and made a face. Sullivan tittered like a girl. 'Was that a reel you were attempting, Elsie?'

Elsa turned into Charlie's shoulder and he put his arm round her in response. 'Leave her be, Bobby, she doesn't understand a word you say.'

'So, you're not a Corkwoman then, Elsie?' said Bobby. He and Sullivan collapsed in laughter. Sullivan was wrapped round the lamppost at his friend's wit, clapping his hand on his thigh. 'You're some fella, Bobby. No bout adoubt it.'

But Bobby wasn't listening. 'What name, did you say? Rankin? Franklin?'

Elsa said nothing but her grip was tightening on Charlie's arm. He put his hand on hers, rubbing it in what he hoped was a reassuring kind of way, but she gripped tighter still.

By now, Sullivan was recovering from his laughing fit. 'You're a right dark horse, Byrne. Where've you been hiding this one? A bit backward in coming forward isn't she, Byrne? A dark horse like your man, are you Elsie?'

Charlie's arm was beginning to hurt. He'd be amazed if there wasn't a bruise in the morning.

'Jesus, I love you,' said Bobby. 'I hope she's a bit friendlier with you, Charlie. I hope you get a bit more out of her than that. Sure we haven't heard a peep yet. Have a go there Sullivan, see what you can get out of the lovely Elsie Rankin.'

Sullivan took one step towards Elsa and she was off. 'Thanks for nothing,' Charlie shouted back at the two men as he set off after her.

He caught up with her in no time, just a street away. She was panicky, huddled against a wall, her face shiny with tears. He was puzzled. It seemed to be such an overreaction. Bobby Coyle was an awful eejit, but he wasn't a thug. As for Sullivan, he was just a muck savage. It was an unpleasant end to the night but if she'd stood her ground they'd just have gone away. He couldn't understand what had frightened her so much. Because he was sure now that fear was what he'd seen in her eyes. Not annoyance or irritation but fear.

At first, she shrugged him off. He drew away a long strand of hair from in front of her face. She breathed in sharply and turned to look at him. It was as though she'd emerged from a tunnel. She let him put his arms around her and buried her face in his shoulder. As he held her, he could feel her sobs come in a little bundle, then subside again until eventually her breathing evened out.

'If you knew Bobby Coyle, you'd laugh that he could be given a uniform by anyone.'

He expected her to laugh but she didn't. She looked up at him. 'Where I come from even the worst of men have a uniform.'

He realised that she was soaking wet, what with having no Mackintosh and her shoes just light patent leather things. He felt terrible sending her home to the Abrahamsons in this state. The first time he'd taken her out and here she was, sodden with tears and Dublin rain. They walked up to the next bridge then back down the other side of the canal. Along by the backs of the houses, he asked her what she meant about the uniforms.

'They don't need to wear uniforms to be cruel. Sometimes it's enough to be called Professor, Doctor, whatever. But the ones who wear uniforms are even worse because cruelty is what's expected of them.'

'All this and yet it's your home.'

'Home is gone. We don't have any home.'

'But your parents, your school friends, all your memories must be there.'

She screwed up her face and shook her head so fast it was blurred. He started to ask her more but she held up her hand to stop him.

'Are there letters?' he asked. 'Can you write to them?'

As soon as he said it, he remembered what Bethel had told him and he wished he could bite back the question.

She shook her head, just once this time. 'Not any more. How do you write to people who are trying not to exist?'

They sat on a bench, half hidden by the reeds that arched up behind them.

'I'm not even meant to be here,' she said. 'They didn't know what to do with me in Belfast. There wasn't anywhere else to go, except for the Farm. What would I do on a farm? It was so long, that time in Belfast with no piano, no one to talk to. I just want to stay where I am.' She gripped his arm, and that alarmed him all over again because he wasn't sure he knew enough about the world to be able to keep her safe in it, and he knew that he wanted, more than anything, to be the one who could do just that. 'I didn't know they put your name in the newspaper, your address even, just for winning a little competition.' She began to cry again, swiping away the tears with her knuckles. 'Bethel says don't worry. He says they'd never send me away. Not now. He says that's not the way they do things in Ireland. Someone would just turn a blind eye and that would be fine. It is just another thing I am not to worry about, now that I am in Ireland, where there is no war. I am not to worry about Mama or Papa. Certainly not Aunt Hanne or Uncle Rudi. As for old Frau Hirsch who lives on her own

… Don't worry. Don't worry.' Her hands were clutching at the hem of her skirt, stretching it taut, then pulling and pulling, as if she might rip the cloth in two.

Charlie placed his hand on top of hers as gently as he could. After a moment or two, she seemed to relax a little, and then she spoke. 'Every night I worry about them all. I worry about myself too. I worry that someone will come to the door. Someone in uniform to tell me I'm not wanted. Bethel and Hilde say that things aren't like that here. Make some friends, they say. Try to live a normal life. Try to forget. You'll see them all again when things calm down. But even I can tell they don't really believe it's possible just to forget.'

Charlie wished he was better at finding the right things to say. He put his arm around her shoulders and they sat there for a long time, just listening to the sound of each other's breath. When it was time to go, he turned to look at her. Her eyes were wide open, unblinking, as she gazed ahead into the dark water of the canal.

Dublin

Hedy Lamarr and the Parachute Man

Kitty had been out with a fair few fellows up in Dublin. Without exception, they were a shower of octopuses. There'd not been a hint of that with the German. Maybe he was just brought up to be gentlemanly (not that it made a blind bit of difference to the octopuses, and them indoctrinated against the sins of the flesh since they were in short pants).

It would give you the pip: fellows lining up to take her out that summer up in Dublin before Father became ill but not a flicker of interest from the one who'd fallen out of the sky. She imagined dandering down Grafton Street with Oskar on her arm, taking tea and little cakes in Bewley's. It would be dreamy to be away from Dunkerin with somebody as glamorous as him. Rita was driving her mad with her letters: this dance and that one. To hear her, you'd think Kitty was out at dinners in Jammet's every other night of the week. Oh, to be back in the land of the living with Oskar to show off around town. There's no way Rita could beat that: a man who'd floated down to earth like a dandelion clock. Sure she wouldn't have to say he was a German at all. She could pass him off as some other class of a foreigner; do the talking for him, if she had to.

As for a place to stay, Aunt Effie would put them up. She wouldn't bat an eyelid. Effie didn't give a fiddler's what anybody thought. Didn't they say she had a fancy man herself, some fellow with a funny name who dressed up in Indian clothes and pretended to be the doorman? That's what Father used to say, anyway. Mother was horrified. 'Whisht now, Frank,' she'd scold. 'That's an awful thing to say. Sure he's just one of those poor divils who come to Effie looking for the Light.'

'So that's what they're calling it these days.'

She couldn't make head nor tail of Oskar. Whatever about the lack of movement on the romantic front, there was no sign of him making any move for Wicklow either. If he was a spy, which she very much doubted, then he didn't have a lot of get-up-and-go about him. She'd reached the conclusion that he was a bit of a dreamer, really. She wasn't surprised he'd left the war. She reckoned the war would do just fine without him. She couldn't for the life of her imagine him being any good at all when it came to dropping bombs. All Oskar seemed to do was sit and dream and fiddle around with his knife on scrag ends of wood. One morning, when she arrived at the shed, she jumped with fright when she saw the knife, until she realised he was just whittling away at something. He had a little leather book that he wrote in, too: pages and pages of spiky script.

The thing that puzzled her the most was that she still couldn't see how he'd reached Dunkerin in the first place. If his plane had crashed, wouldn't they have found it by now? If he'd been dropped deliberately, then he was a spy, and she didn't believe they couldn't find someone a bit more like Humphrey Bogart for a job like that. If he'd really done what he said he'd done and just jumped out of the war, then he was a deserter. It must have been a pretty desperate state of affairs to drive somebody to jump out of the war, out of everything he'd ever known, too. She couldn't imagine what would drive a man to that. Besides, once you deserted there was no way back. People hated you for it. Up in Dublin, she'd seen a picture once where the French Foreign Legion did awful things to deserters out there in the middle of the desert. From what she'd heard of the Germans, they weren't likely to take too kindly to deserters either. As for all that about not wanting to harm anyone, that was a bit rich, what with Belfast blown to bits.

Kitty considered Hedy Lamarr, and what she would do when it came to a parachute in the lime tree. Hedy Lamarr would likely bide her time and the fellow would come running to her anyway. That was all very well, thought Kitty, when you were Hedy Lamarr, but what's floated down can just as easy float off again. So instead she was bold as brass. The night Mother was due to stay over with the Kennys after the musical evening for the Red Cross, she told Oskar there was a bed for him in the house. When he arrived, he stood at the bottom of the stairs until she told him to come on up. He came up all right but he hardly said a word to her. He plonked himself down on the bed in the old nursery and was asleep as soon as his head hit the pillow. She couldn't help thinking there was an insult in that, and for the first time she thought how easy it would be to have him locked up.

Journal of Oskar Müller

Day 3, 20 April 1941
The days are very long. It's frustrating still to be here, but my knee has swollen to the size of a grapefruit, not that there are any grapefruits around here. I don't know if I can trust Kitty but I feel sure she will not have me arrested while I'm still a novelty. She is barely more than a kid and she seems to know little of the world outside her village. She is the only person I've had contact with, so it's not easy to get an idea of these people. There is a mother, though I haven't heard her speak. I have heard men's voices: an old man who works around the place and, last night, two younger men who found sport in hunting me down. The place itself is rather down-at-heel: a small farm, perhaps, that the family can no longer manage. The house is a reasonable size, surrounded by trees, mainly chestnuts and limes. Beyond it, there is only wilderness.

Day 4, 21 April 1941
Kitty does not seem interested in the war. I suppose that's in my favour. She asks question after question about Berlin: the shops, the cafés, what hats the ladies wear. She prattles on about Dublin, the only city, I suppose, she has ever seen. How she lived there once. How she wishes she had never left. She talks of an aunt who lives there still. The aunt was the first vegetarian in Ireland, she tells me, as if such a thing is possible. Even though she was christened Eileen everyone calls her F.V. After a while, I stop listening to Kitty's long stories about this splendid aunt of hers; FV or Effie or whatever.

Day 5, 22 April 1941
I am so far from Wicklow. How I shall get there in this state and without money, I don't know. I don't wish to steal from Kitty, though sooner or later I suppose I'll have to steal from someone. I have already broken one boundary, who knows how many more I'll have to break? I don't suppose any of my comrades see me as a person of honour any longer.

Day 6, 23 April 1941
I am impatient to start my journey, and yet there is a kind of paralysis about me. I am almost afraid to leave this place. I am like the first man on a new planet. I have no way of getting back and yet I do not know if what I have done is a calamity.

Day 7, 24 April 1941
Last night, Kitty brought me inside the house and I slept like a baby in a room with rosebuds on the walls. She is pretty, lively and there is a sharpness about her that amuses me, but I have no inclination to complicate matters by playing the handsome stranger. This morning she barely spoke to me and there was no breakfast. It will soon be time to leave.

Day 8, 25 April 1941
I left the shed early, before first light. I took from the kitchen
what food I could find, and filled my watercan. I had almost
reached the gate when I heard Kitty running after me. She says
this aunt does not believe in wars. Her evidence is the aunt's
vegetarianism. I almost laughed. Our own vegetarians are much
more warlike than any meat eater in this damp little place. But
it seems Kitty has everything planned. Not much of a planner
myself, I find this astounding. She has even kitted me out in
clothes belonging to her brother, dressing me like a new doll.
How the boys in Vannes would laugh to see me now! I am a
country gentleman with a waistcoat. My flying suit, uniform –
everything but my boots – she burnt with some garden rubbish,
dashing precious paraffin over it like a mad thing.

Am I wise to rely so much on this girl? She can't be entirely
stable. But it's true that I will be less conspicuous with her than
on my own. Once I reach Dublin, it will be a simple matter to
find Wicklow, a mere day or two by foot, and then to disappear.

Sean Galligan took Kitty to the station in the gig in time for
the early train to Dublin. The morning was overcast and she
sat wrapped in the travelling rug, her stomach raw from nerves
and lack of breakfast. Oskar had already left on her bicycle. She
didn't like letting him off on his own, in case he had to speak
to anyone, but he didn't look too worried as he headed off
down the driveway, whistling through his teeth.

At the station, there was a straggle of commercial travellers
waiting for the first train of the week. Most of them seemed
to know one another and they stood together in little clumps.
She bought two tickets and tried not to let it bother her when
the man behind the counter gave her a funny look. On board,
she moved like a crab along the narrow corridor. When she
found the right compartment, she placed her small suitcase on
the rack and waited for him to find her.

She didn't look up when the compartment door slid across but she spotted his boots, with Desmond's tweed trousers tucked inside them. She was still feeling a bit mad with him for heading off on his own without so much as a thank you, but now that he was here she was prepared to let bygones be. He was just sitting down next to her when she heard the sound of someone moving smartly down the corridor, then stopping just outside. Suddenly, Oskar was all over her. It was like one of those clinches in the pictures, with the violins going for it like mad. *Gone with the Wind* or something like that. When the door of the compartment opened, she tried to pull away from him for modesty's sake but he held on tight, his head buried in her shoulder. The man in the doorway glanced from Kitty to Oskar then back again. He looked like an official type, in his Mackintosh and hat. He cleared his throat. She was sure he was about to ask for their papers but he seemed to think better of it. Instead, he wished them a good day and was gone. No sooner had the man left than Oskar pulled back from her. 'Excuse me,' he said, as if he'd passed wind. She half expected him to try to wipe the kiss away from her lips with his handkerchief.

'No bother,' she said, but she was woozy from the kiss, and parts of her felt so pinprick sharp from it, too, that she wouldn't have minded if he'd been an octopus, not at all.

As they pulled out of the station, she imagined she was seeing everything for the first time, with his eyes. She wondered whether he thought the place beautiful, for all the lack of a bit of sun. She wondered what he thought of her. Just then, she noticed he'd taken Desmond's valise: the one with his initials on it. She couldn't remember having given him that and she thought to herself what a blasted cheek. She didn't say anything, though, because she liked the warmth of him next to her and she still hadn't got over the kiss.

The train was travelling slowly enough as it was but it began to decelerate to little more than walking pace, then shunted to a stop in the middle of open countryside. Kitty had fallen asleep on his shoulder, so Oskar wedged his rolled-up jacket between her head and the wall of the compartment and carefully extricated himself. There were no waiting passengers and he didn't think they'd stopped for a signal. During the ten minutes or so that it took for the train to get going again, he was sure the game was up. Then, a whistle and a hiss of steam and they were off. His heart jolted as the compartment door slid back again. This time, though, it was a young woman. 'Mind if I join you?' she said.

He shook his head and closed his eyes to avoid the need for conversation. The train seemed practically empty, so he wondered why the woman hadn't taken one of the other compartments. For her benefit, he drew Kitty's head back down onto his shoulder and began stroking her hair. The woman started rustling at something. Ravenous by now, he hoped she wasn't about to unpack a picnic. He felt it was important to keep an eye on her, so he allowed his head to fall back so he could watch her from under his eyelids. His view of her began at the blue toque on her head and ended at her waist. It worried him that he couldn't see her hands.

'You're not from around here, are you?' she said. She was eating sandwiches, ham he thought, and he had to stop himself from just reaching out to take one.

'Hel-lo-oh?' She leant forward; he could see the veins at her temple, smell mustard on her breath. 'Well?'

Eventually, he made a great show of rousing himself, stretching and yawning on an operatic scale.

'Honeymooners?'

Oskar took Kitty's left hand and kissed it. The woman's eyes darted to the empty ring finger. 'You divil,' she said and smirked at him. 'Do you not have a word?' She leant forward.

'Parlez-vous anglais? Speaky ze English? Pogue mahone?' She chuckled to herself. 'Doesn't look like it.'

Kitty sat up, still half asleep. The woman tapped her on the knee. 'Welcome back, sugarplum. Any more where he came from?'

Kitty was on the point of blurting out that they were to be married, when she remembered that was only in the dream she'd been having. She blushed in mortification at the thought.

The woman winked at Oskar and pointed to her own ring finger. 'You'd want to get a move on and buy the bit of tinsel.'

By now, it was clear that neither Oskar nor Kitty was likely to contribute much in the way of conversation, so the woman was reduced to delving in her bag for something else to amuse her. She pulled out a book of knitting patterns and flicked lightly through it, as if to demonstrate her disdain for such things. She left the compartment at the next stop, though Oskar was sure she hadn't actually got off the train at all.

The railway track began to follow the course of a canal and they passed a sailing barge loaded with crates and boxes. It was only when the barge overtook them that Oskar realised the train had come to a stop. He hoped this had nothing to do with him. Doors creaked open and slammed shut. Feet crunched on gravel. Some of the passengers were now outside the train and he shoved down the window to get a better look. They seemed to be collecting wood from beside the track and carrying it to the front of the train. One group was dismantling a wooden fence. He realised then that the passengers were foraging for fuel to allow the train to limp on to Dublin.

It was close to nightfall when the train pulled in at Broadstone Station. What remained of the light seeped through a dirty sky. Kitty felt a little jab of irritation at Oskar for marching on ahead of her. He was like a dog let off the leash and there was no sign of any bother with his knee. Once they were clear of the station, she noticed a man and woman heading up the hill together. It was only when they stopped at the kerb that she realised who they were. The fact that the Mackintosh man and the woman with the knitting book seemed to know one another made her very uneasy. She glanced over her shoulder to see if there was anyone else hanging about watching them but there were only a couple of porters dragging on fag ends, and an aul' fella muttering into his beard.

Oskar, meanwhile, was almost at the river. Even in Desmond's clothes, he stood out like a sore thumb. The short blond hair didn't help but it was more the set of his shoulders and the way he didn't feel the need to keep his head down that was the dead giveaway. At least he'd left off the yellow scarf. When he realised she wasn't with him, he turned and waved over at her to come on, not that he'd the slightest idea where he was going. For the love of Mike, she thought, has he no idea how to keep a low profile? He was standing at the river wall, gandering all round him as if he'd just found himself on Mars.

'You'd want to catch a grip,' she said. 'The place is crawling with people looking for the likes of you.' When she told him what she'd seen, he just shrugged. It made her mad that he seemed so relaxed about everything and she was the one up to high doh. 'And who's to say there isn't someone watching us right now? Who's to say your card isn't marked already?'

He looked at her as if she was away in the head. What was that medical word Desmond had used the other day?

Mister Germany

By the time Oskar and Kitty arrived at Pembroke Road, the night was like a bucket of pitch. Kitty had sent Aunt Effie a letter to warn of her arrival with a friend of the family but she hadn't said it was a man, much less a German come down out of the sky. Now that they'd actually arrived, she was apprehensive. Effie was unpredictable at the best of times.

The man in the white shift must have been watching out for them. No sooner had they reached the bottom of the steps than he was standing in the open doorway. Kitty wished him a good evening but he said nothing back, just stood to one side to let them pass. He had a face like a radish and watery eyes. In fact, he looked a bit like Sergeant McCreesh in fancy dress. Then, she realised from the shift that this must be the fellow with the Indian name: the one who lived with Effie because he was looking for the Light.

Aunt Effie was upstairs in the Receiving Room, lying on a chaise by the back window. An oil lamp on the table beside her cast a yellowish light around itself but otherwise the room was dark. Kitty left Oskar in the middle of the room with the bags.

'How are you, Auntie?'

Effie lifted an arm and waved it vaguely. 'I'm on my last legs, child. Ranjit doesn't have any truck with that kind of talk, but I know myself when I've run out of steam.' Kitty started to protest but Effie just shook her head and patted the chaise next to her. 'Sit down here, child.' She ran her thumbs down along each side of Kitty's jawline from the tips of her ears to the point of her chin. 'As I thought, that'll be a Daly chin by the time you hit thirty,' she said finally. 'Oh well, you can't cheat kismet. How's your Mother? Still as mad as a March hare?'

'She's bearing up, thanks Auntie.'

Effie's eyes lit on Oskar and she seemed to perk up. 'Who in the name of Isis is that? You've not done a flit with some mountainy man, have you?

'Can you put him up, Auntie?'

'Bring him over here so I can get a good look at him.'

Oskar walked slowly towards the chaise. He didn't quite bow but inclined his head curtly in Effie's direction.

'He's called Oskar,' Kitty said quickly, for fear he might click his heels.

'He's not from the mountains, anyhow. I can tell that by the cut of him.'

'He's an archaeologist,' said Kitty, remembering the Germans the boys had talked about who worked in the museum. 'He's fierce interested in dolmens,' she added, to add a bit of substance.

'Dolmens? In Dublin?'

'Oh no, he'll be off down to Wicklow soon to study the ones they have down there.' She jumped at a scream from the garden.

'Relax,' said Effie, 'it's just the peacocks. They've barely space to open up out there but sure they brighten the place up a bit. God knows everything's got so drib and drab these days.'

Kitty wanted to ask how you got hold of peacocks in Dublin, but Effie was concentrating on Oskar. She made a megaphone of her hands and took a deep, wavering breath. 'You Are Away From Your Home.' She dropped her hands into her lap with a little smack, breathless and swaying slightly.

Oskar took a few steps towards her and gave the same curt little nod. 'I am very grateful for your hospitality.'

'I haven't offered you any yet.' Effie's sharp little eyes narrowed as she examined him from the top of his head to the toes of his Luftwaffe-issue boots. 'Good Isis, child, is it a German? And I thought there was a war on.'

Effie made another megaphone and turned back to Oskar. 'I Thought There Was A War On.' She cocked her head, as though trying to catch an answer somewhere in the ether. Then she turned to Kitty. 'I suppose this is your Mother's doing, landing you up on top of me with a German. Well, Mr Germany? What have you to say for yourself?'

'I am not part of the war. Not anymore.'

'Oh we're all part of the war, whether we like it or not. Call it an Emergency, pretend nothing's happening but we're all part of the war.'

Oskar looked at her with that direct gaze of his. 'I do not want to fight for my country any more.'

'Well couldn't you fight agin them then? It strikes me a lump of a fellow like you should be doing something useful at a time like this, much as I like the dolmens myself.'

'I have a project,' Oskar announced.

'That sounds very grand altogether. What kind of a project, I wonder? Nothing nefarious, nothing wicked, nothing that might leave us all dead in our beds?'

'No,' said Oskar, 'not like that.'

Effie pushed a bell at her elbow and the man with the red face and the Indian name appeared again, dragging a copper tea urn in on a trolley.

'Drink, Mr Germany. Wet your whistle. You can talk later.'

They had their tea, which Oskar was disappointed to discover wasn't real tea at all but something that tasted like lettuce. Immediately afterwards, Effie, whom he decided was the strangest-looking woman he'd ever seen, instructed the man with the Indian name to 'Stick Mr Germany out in the Austin for the night.'

Oskar had no idea what that meant. Ranjit looked like he was beginning to enjoy himself. He no longer bothered to hold the door open but marched on ahead of Oskar towards the front door. It was only when he was outside that Oskar realised that 'the Austin' was in fact a motorcar. It was wedged in under a dead tree on the gravelled forecourt of the house. The left front corner was completely compressed, the windscreen covered in layers of sap and bird droppings and the dusty green detritus of whatever young tree was growing alongside the dead one. He wondered how someone could simply have abandoned what must have been a fine machine until he remembered that there was probably no petrol for it anyway.

Oskar soon felt uneasy inside the motorcar's metal shell. It reminded him too much of being back inside a Heinkel. Visibility was next to nothing through the windscreen, so he sat crouched to starboard peering through the cloud of blossom that trailed across the driver's window. He was glad to have retained his gunner's instincts, even if he had evidently taken leave of his senses by throwing his lot in with such outlandish people. After all, he was there for the taking. Suddenly, his assumption that they would simply help him in whatever it was he wanted to do seemed hopelessly naïve. Little by little, his doubt that they would help him swelled to a certainty that they would turn him in. He thought about sleeping outside the motorcar so that he would have a better chance of escape if someone was indeed on to him, but in the end he decided he was less conspicuous where he was. He resolved to stay alert and to keep the window rolled down so he could hear them approaching across the gravel when the time came.

He awoke to daylight and a hard rain clattering off the windscreen. He ducked below the level of the glass, covering his head with his hands. He was sure this was the capture he had foreseen the night before and cursed his decision not to take his chances somewhere else. He waited for them to surround the car, but he could hear no approaching footsteps. Suddenly, it struck him that perhaps they wouldn't bother arresting him. Perhaps they would just shoot him there and then. He gripped his temples to deaden what was to come. Then, from somewhere beyond panic, came a voice. He strained to hear it. 'Mis-ter Ger-ma-ny.'

He began to uncurl himself, peering out from under the crook of his elbow. There was a long whooping whistle. Then another. He took a look through the side window and saw that it was the man in the white dress, standing there with a fistful of gravel looking very pleased with thimself. He let the gravel slip through his fingers, then jerked his head in the direction of the house and left. Oskar kicked the door in annoyance. When a dignified period had elapsed, he clutched Desmond Hennessy's coat and made his way to the house. The door had been left open and the man who thought he was an Indian was standing with his back to him with one foot on the lowest stair.

The room on the first floor seemed a very long way from breakfast. There was no smell of food and no indication that any was on its way. The curtains were closed and it was almost as dark as it had been the night before. Oskar sat at the end of the table, and cast one leg over the other in as jaunty a fashion as he could manage after a night spent folded in half. Soon after, Effie arrived, trailing layers of wispy fabrics behind her. She stopped and squinted at him. 'I can see you've had a bad night, but you'll just have to put up with it. I'll not have you in the house, Mr Germany, till I know what you're up to. After that, we'll see.'

'I am grateful.'

'As well you might be.'

Kitty arrived at the door and peered into the half-light, 'Come on, Auntie, you're not a vampire. A little bit of light at breakfast wouldn't hurt.' She tugged at the heavy curtains but they only seemed to part a matter of inches.

When Ranjit arrived with porridge and dried fruit, he placed everything as far away as possible from Oskar. A shaft of sunlight sliced through the gap Kitty had made in the curtains, forming a slender triangle in the centre of the table, but Ranjit was quick to pinch the curtains back together again and snuff out the light.

'So, Mr Germany. You, and your dolmens ...'

'Today I will go to Wicklow.' He made it sound like a chest rub, and Kitty sniggered.

'What else would you be doing? And you in the middle of a war. I suppose you know where you're going?'

'The place is called Whitecrest.'

'Never heard of it. Kitty, ever hear tell of a Whitecrest?'

Kitty shook her head without looking up. Aunt Effie peered into a small bowl at her elbow and picked out a raisin. 'White*hall*, maybe? There's a Whitehall over on the Northside. I can't think of any other Whites mind you. Could it be a boarding house out in Bray, Kitty?'

Kitty shrugged.

'I need something more exact than this,' Oskar unfolded the page Kitty had torn out of Father's atlas. 'I need a map, not a picture of your country. This will be no good at all.'

Kitty had heard enough. 'I'll be in my room,' she said.

Effie dipped her hand back into the bowl beside her. She extracted a walnut and studied it, revolving it between her thumb and forefinger. She waited for Kitty to shut the door behind her before dropping the nut back into the bowl. 'You needn't bother with any more guff about dolmens.'

Oskar nodded, drawing his chair into the table.

'You'll have to come up with something better than that if you want this roof over your head. You can't really expect me to believe this is a social call in the middle of a war?'

Oskar found that he was watching the dark red bow of her lips purse and stretch instead of following what she was saying. He made himself concentrate.

'Maybe you found war wasn't to your liking?'

Oskar realised that he didn't know what to call her. Effie sounded too familiar, Aunt Effie ridiculous. 'I tried to explain last night, Miss Effie,' he said. 'I am no longer a member of the German forces.'

She seemed to like being called Miss Effie. At any rate, she was mildly amused by something or other. She offered him a little dry bun. He bit into it but it tasted like sawdust.

'After we put you out in the Austin last night, Kitty told me something about a parachute. But was there not a plane stuffed with fellows trying to hold you down?'

He recalled the scamble there'd been once Willy had realised what he was about to do but he didn't care to go into all of that, so he shook his head.

'What are you doing here?'

'I am looking for someone.' He'd never actually said it out loud before and now it sounded mad, even to him.

'Someone?'

'A girl.'

'Now we're getting somewhere. You have the look of the young swain about you, right enough. Has she a name?'

He stood up and walked the length of the room, pretending to examine the murky prints that lined the walls.

'Ah, what's the use,' she said eventually. 'You could just as easy make up a name as tell me the truth. She's a sweetheart, this girl?'

He felt himself nod, though he wondered what Elsa would make of the description. When he was sure he was in control of himself, he blurted it out, 'Her name is Elsa Frankel.' Now that it was out in the open, it seemed possible – likely even – that he would find Elsa. Gradually, a weight was lifting from him.

Meanwhile, Miss Effie had moved on.

'The first thing you'll see of Wicklow is two hills: pyramids, both of them, a large and a small. What comes after them, I couldn't say. We've no call for maps of the here and now in this house. You'd want to go into town for the kind of thing that gives you names and distances and that sort of palaver. O'Connell Street, I suppose: our own bit of Paris. Turn left when you get to the gate, pass the Green, cross the river and look for an Englishman stuck up on a pillar with his nose in the air.'

She described bridges and stations and streets, and he became enormously confused, losing track of which was which. He got particularly lost when she started talking about a swastika and a laundry. Whatever it was seemed to perturb her greatly but he could think of no possible connection between the two.

All this was enough to secure him a room at the top of the house. Ranjit was no longer hostile but neither was he interested in conversation and they tramped in silence together up the stairs. Oskar laid out his little pile of possessions on the bed and jotted down in his journal some of the instructions Miss Effie had given him. He'd no idea how much maps cost, but deep in an inside pocket of Desmond Hennessy's coat he found some copper coins and a couple of larger, silvery ones. He wasn't sure what they would buy, if they still bought anything at all, but it seemed another small stroke of luck. Later that morning, he strode out into a world where Elsa could only be a day or two away.

Blue

Oskar turned left out of the gate, and followed the street across a hump-backed bridge until it widened out into a garden square bustling with bicycles and trolley buses and the odd spluttering motorcar. A bus trundled past. Gold Flake, it said. There was a grand hotel whose entrance was guarded by two torch-bearing statues and, on the other side, a park. He thought of the Tiergarten, where the trees had been replaced by burlap strung over metal poles. It seemed astonishing that there could still be a park. The flowerbeds were as neat as Mutti's samplers, embroidered onto close-cut lawns. Once he was through the park gates, he came up against a stream of schoolgirls in navy blue gymslips. One of them turned and gave him a wave, like she was rubbing a small mark from a window. The little nun accompanying them clapped her hands and the girl fell back in line. When they reached a bandstand, the nun began to arrange the girls in height order, and it dawned on him that they were a choir. He didn't like choirs, so he walked on. It was when Emmi joined the choir that the trouble started.

She'd joined the BDM along with all her friends, and for a couple of years she remained unchanged, still laughing at the fervour the others showed for the Fatherland. When the choir trip came up, she wasn't even sure if she wanted to go but Mutti persuaded her to give it a try. When she returned to Berlin, they met her at the station. She was all gasps and exclamations, and they could get no sense out of her at all. She said she had a story to tell, insisted it get a proper airing, so they all sat down at the little table in the parlour while Mutti fed her coffee and cake, and Oskar whittled away at a stick.

When she was ready, she stood and clasped her hands together, just like Mutti did when she was about to burst into song. 'We went up to Berchtesgaden,' she said.

She whispered the name, as though it was some magic kingdom. He remembered Mutti tapping the palm of her hand up and down on the table in delight. They'd been taken there, Emmi said, in the hope that the Führer would come and greet the wellwishers outside after his lunch, as he did now and then.

'Oh Mutti,' she sighed, 'the weather was dismal. It was so disappointing. All the way up the mountain, the rain was so heavy we could hardly see anything at all. But when we reached the Berghof, the sun just burst out from behind the clouds. Everything shining, like glass.'

Mutti crossed herself quickly. 'Go on.'

'I was happy enough as it was, the rain having cleared. But then a door opened.'

It must have been around then that Oskar's knife slipped. He remembered Mutti drawing out a handkerchief from her pocket and waving it in his direction without once diverting her attention from Emmi. He'd wrapped the handkerchief tight around his thumb and folded it over several times but still the blood seeped through.

Emmi no longer seemed to be talking to them at all but describing some vision that was revealing itself to her as she spoke. 'It was the Führer, Mutti. But dressed, well, like Vati or someone. Just like an ordinary man. So humble; just a grey suit with a felt hat. We all cheered and he raised his hat at us. He seemed to be about to go back through the door when one of his attendants came over and asked where we were from. He must truly love Berlin, Mutti, because when he heard he insisted on speaking to us.'

Mutti was nodding vigorously. 'Of course he does, my darling. Berlin has a special place in the Führer's heart.'

Emmi barely seemed to hear what Mutti was saying. 'He brushed against a shrub, and the cloth on that shoulder was sprinkled with raindrops. And then, he stopped in front of us.'

Oskar remembered how curious it was that the story no longer seemed to be Emmi's story at all. It was as though the day had been memorised and sealed so that it had become part of some other, bigger story.

'When he saw me, standing there holding Papa's camera, he offered to pose for a photograph with the others. I was pleased, of course, but disappointed too because I would miss being in the picture. Can you believe it, Mutti? Not a moment's hesitation. Right away, he turned round to one of his staff members and asked him to take the photograph so that I could be in the picture too.'

Oskar recalled Mutti shaking her head in wonderment at the depth of the Führer's feelings for his people, at his unfailing intuition. 'Wonderful,' she kept saying over and over again. 'A man who can make the sun shine.'

After that, Emmi and Mutti always referred to a blue-sky day with bright sunshine as Führer weather. Eventually, everyone else did as well.

Oskar preferred not to think about Berlin and the sunshine that belonged to the Führer. Instead, he allowed himself to be distracted by a huddle of boys crouched at the edge of a pond that was busy with ducks. The thin sun caught the glint of metal in their hands as they cast off a row of empty sardine tins into the water. As the light breeze took them, the curled lids became sails and the tins scuttered along in among the ducks. He remembered summer afternoons at Teufelssee when he was nine or ten; he and Horst with their own little boats whittled from the bark of the sycamore tree. He was just thinking how lucky the boys were, and how little they realised it, when someone parked a black perambulator right in front of him, obstructing his view. Inside, a large red baby was holding his breath with fury. As it let loose a blood-curdling scream, a woman flopped down on the bench next to Oskar. She shook the handle of the pram but the baby yelled even louder.

'You're one of those lads from the Legation, aren't you? Pleased to meet you,' she stretched her hand out for him to shake it. 'I'm Cissy.' She reached into her pocket for a large pink dummy, and shoved it into the baby's mouth. He began sucking on it, in an exploratory kind of way; when he decided it would do, he shut up.

'You must have an awful time with that boss of yours. I hear he's a right so-and-so. Mrs Lacey had himself and the wife to tea one day, and she said he hadn't a word to fling at the cat.'

Oskar started to edge away from her but it didn't seem to matter whether he answered her or not.

'No offence, but Mrs Lacey says they're an awful shower. Dull as ditchwater. Present company excluded, of course. Mrs Lacey says they're even worse than the British, and God knows they're bad enough. Still and all, she says, you have to keep inviting both sides. It's like children, isn't it? You've got to keep an eye on them for fear of what they'd get up to once your back's turned.'

Oskar looked to see if she was being overheard but no one else seemed to have noticed him. The boys were still at their race, making waves in the pond with bits of stick, and a little cluster of older boys had begun to gather around them. The girl leaned over the pram to adjust the baby's blanket, and Oskar took the opportunity to move away from her. He had almost got to the end of the pond, when she caught up with him. He felt a sweat begin to break on his forehead.

'Between you and me, though, I'd rather the Germans than the other lot. They had their chance, God knows, and what they didn't do to us isn't worth talking about. A few Germans round the place might do us the power of good. You'd not have a road the state of the one out there if the Germans were in charge.'

Oskar looked back to see a group of women gathering around the abandoned baby who had now begun to scream louder than ever. The sound of the crying stopped the nursemaid in her tracks. As she turned, Oskar began to walk briskly away, moving as fast as he could without breaking into a run. It wasn't until he went to unfasten a side gate onto the street that he realised his hands were shaking. He was shocked that, tweed coat or not, he was so obviously a German.

The people who passed him on the streets were pasty-faced, their clothes poorly cut and colourless. The shops, too, were drab. A scattering of dead flies adorned a stack of faded biscuit tins in a café window. He stopped at a butcher's, where strings of sausages lay coiled next to slabs of meat grained with yellow fat under a curtain of swaying carcasses. As a display of plenty, it was impressive. Each product was pierced by a triangle of white card bearing a price. He jingled the change around in his pocket but it was clear that it would barely buy a few sausages. He fingered grandpapa's watch in his pocket and decided he'd pawn it if he had to.

He felt the whip of the wind as he crossed the river onto a wide boulevard dominated by a tall column with a statue on top. He'd never been to Paris but he'd seen photographs of the troops marching down the Champs-Élysées when the city fell. He didn't think this street was very much like Paris, but maybe Miss Effie had been making a joke. Here, the people seemed poorer still. There were hollow-eyed men on every corner and women in plaid shawls begged with their babies. He caught a glimpse of himself in a shop window and couldn't understand what had given him away. He loosened his collar, and shoved his hands in his coat pockets to look a little less military. There wasn't much he could do about his hair, which was too short and too blond. He made a mental note to look for a hat when he returned to Miss Effie's. He spotted a pawnbroker's sign in the distance. When he went to cross the road to reach it, a ragged woman pushing a battered pram swerved to avoid him. He glanced into the pram but there was nothing inside but a scattering of coal on a dirty pink blanket.

When Oskar reached the pawnbroker's, the window was coverd by a blind the colour of tallow. Through the glass door, he could see that the hallway was empty but for a pile of old boxes and an unstrung harp. It seemed the pawnbroker had moved on. He was just wondering what to do about a map when his attention was caught by a streak of blue. The girl was dark, light-footed, and she was moving in the direction of the river. He thought he remembered that dress, blue as lake water. He hardly dared breathe for fear she might vanish before his eyes. He lost her a moment but then he spotted her again, rounding the side of a large building that was black with soot. Then, almost before he knew what had happened, she stepped onto a tram and was gone. It all happened so fast that he told himself it wasn't Elsa. She could not have been and gone, just like that. He could not have been so close and then lose her. He had always had faith in happy endings but then so had Joachim, so certain that one day he would play that clarinet of his in Bourbon Street. Faith was no guarantee, but he was beginning to doubt, and he couldn't afford that.

Another tram arrived and he found himself jumping aboard it. He crouched at the window, scanning the street for a girl in blue. He handed the conductor Desmond Hennessy's coins one at at time until the man's fist closed over them. All the while, he was scouring the street outside, trying to cover both sides at once. The other tram was just up ahead and he was sure he would have seen her get off. But they reached the end of the line and there was still no sign of her. Dejected, and with only the two silvery coins remaining, Oskar got off the tram. That was when he saw the sea, unfolding grey in front of him. Gulls dipped and soared and wheeled across its surface. He filled his lungs with the smell of it and let the air wrap itself around his head. It was astonishing that this was all that divided him from the people he'd been bombing for months. He looked out to sea and tried to imagine what was on the other side of it. He'd heard that the English appreciated leisure above all else; that they would rather invent another ball game than fight another war. Vati used to say it was a pity it always seemed to be the English because they were just too damn easy to underestimate. They were that lazy idiot cousin who wasn't much good for anything, yet somehow seemed to manage to beat you at tennis.

Oskar had flown over so many English cities, yet he had no idea what any of them were like. He wondered if the houses were like these ones, with semi-circles above the doorways to let in the light. *Speisekammer, Schmelztiegel, Loge.* He could only remember their code names. He had no recollection of their real names, if he'd ever been told them in the first place. For him, they'd been crude matrices, that's all; docks, electricity installations, factories. He passed a neat network of streets radiating off behind a gasworks and it made him uneasy to think of houses like this lying snug against his targets. For the first time in days, he thought of the others, limping home without him. What did they say had happened? Had they even been punished for not having managed to stop him? And what about Mutti and Vati and Emmi? Were there repercussions for them? It was the first time it had occurred to him. The idea horrified him, and he didn't let himself explore it any further.

War over there, and here the wait for it, and just this stretch of water in between. It didn't seem much of a barricade. They would invade England once they'd softened it up and they would be here, too, soon enough. The world would keep on shrinking until there was nowhere left without a swastika on it.

There was a long shrill whistle, and he realised that the building he'd taken for a school must be a railway station. Inside, there was a scattering of people but nothing blue. The names of the destinations had been blacked out, but in the distance were Effie's two hills, one larger than the other, each a pyramid. When the train moved off in that direction, Oskar was on it.

Whitecrest

Someone for the Zoo Dance

On the second day that Oskar failed to return, Kitty pulled the heavy curtains of the Receiving Room right back and let the light stream in. It robbed the room of its mystique, and for the first time she noticed how shabby the place was. How come, after all the excitement, she found herself stuck with Effie and that Ranjit person? She couldn't imagine how Oskar would fare out there in the world, unless some other girl took a shine to him and fed him ham sandwiches and hot, sweet tea. Then again, perhaps he'd been picked up already and was locked away somewhere and she'd never clap eyes on him again. She must have stood at the window for an hour or so, watching the odd assortment of vehicles trundle down Pembroke Road, before Ranjit bustled in. He stopped dead in the daylight, then hurried to the window and pulled the drapes across.

Aunt Effie was receiving that evening. There were candles to light and charts to prepare, and every spare chair in the house was brought into the Receiving Room and arranged there in some preconceived but unfathomable order dictated by Ranjit. Effie wore her velvet turban and a long embroidered shift, and her eyes were ringed in kohl. At around seven, a trail of elderly men and women began to gather on the front steps. Kitty wasn't invited to the meeting, and when the Truthseekers were finally admitted, she made her way upstairs. Instead of going to her room, she climbed an extra storey up to the attic. She stood outside Oskar's door and listened, just in case by some chance she'd missed him coming in. She knocked, and when there was no reply, she opened the door a crack. It was clear he hadn't been back, so she stepped into the room and shut the door behind her. The bed was neatly made; the sheet turned down sharply over the blankets, the eiderdown folded at the foot of the bed.

Like those people who leave Bibles in hotel rooms, Effie had left the same book by Oskar's bed as she had by Kitty's: *The Key to Theosophy* by Madam Blavatsky. She couldn't imagine he'd get very far with that. There was also a copy of *Robinson Crusoe*, which must have come from the Receiving Room bookcase. She wondered if that's what he felt like: Robinson Crusoe. The only other thing was a little leather journal. She recognised it as the book he was forever scribbling in when he was in the shed in Dunkerin. She thought it odd that he'd left it behind him; it gave her hope that he'd be back. The pages were edged in gold and the cover was like soft, buttery caramel. You'd want to have fabulous thoughts to be using a book like that. She flicked through it. The front and back were densely packed with his angular script. The middle pages were blank. The first few entries were written in an elegant hand but some of the later pages were stained, the ink blotted. One or two were completely illegible, as though he'd spilled something over them. Although she couldn't read the German, she could just about make out dates and placenames. *Vannes, Irland*. She flicked to when *Irland* first appeared and examined each line of the first few pages for her own name.

Something that looked like Kiti appeared a number of times, and she wondered whether this could be her. The first entry was headed '*zum Frankreich*' and was dated 27 February 1941. It trailed down the page like a caterpillar. The lines were short but too long to be a list. A poem, perhaps? She ran her fingers down the reverse of the page. The indentations were deeper there than on other days and she wondered what it was he'd felt so strong about. She supposed he must have had some time to himself at Easter. She flicked to find the date. The entry was long and the handwriting curled down the page in tangles of blue. Had he flown that night? And if so, which

English city had they bombed? And then she remembered Belfast, and realised that even on Easter Sunday he'd probably been off bombing something. She liked Oskar but she hoped he had the nightmares he deserved.

Her own Easter had been a lovely one. Well, it had been a better day than most, anyway. Even though there were no children around to make it worthwhile, Mother had hardboiled some eggs after Mass and left them sitting in gorse water to turn yellow for the Monday. Later, they had afternoon tea in the Dunkerin Arms.

'We'll treat ourselves, Kitty,' Mother had said, 'for the day that's in it. We'll have a currant square for poor old Frank.'

The afternoon tea went well. Mother left off the opera cloak for once. Her dress was moderation itself: an *eau-de-nil* two-piece and a small hat. She behaved herself with the waitresses and confined herself to nodding at Doctor Russell and not once mentioning bunions. It was hard to believe that just a week later, there'd be a parachute in the lime tree.

The next morning there was still no sign of Oskar. Aunt Effie was exhausted from the Truthseekers the night before. She was on the chaise, with Ranjit feeding her tablespoons of thin soup. Down in the garden, a peacock screamed.

Kitty couldn't settle to anything. She tried to read but there didn't seem much point in reading someone else's story when she was in the middle of such a great big story of her own. There was no point in baking, either, since neither Aunt Effie nor Ranjit ever really seemed to eat. It would only make her fat and bad-tempered, and what was the sense in that? Whatever she tried, she couldn't get Oskar out of her head. Aunt Effie didn't seem the least surprised that Oskar had gone. 'Leave the boy to his quest, Kitty,' was all she said. 'He'll be back when he's ready.'

All the same, she fretted. What if he was off with those fellows Bobby mentioned, the ones in the hotel down in Wicklow?

Sure, wasn't it Wicklow he was always on about? Well, what if he was out there on the Sugarloaf right now, guiding in the planes that would blow them all to kingdom come?

She wished she could read the diary and put her mind at rest. That's when she remembered Rita. Right through school, Rita had a string of penpals. There was the Spanish girl who kept sending miraculous medals and scraps of dry skin that were supposed to be saints' relics. There was the girl from Paris who sounded very flighty altogether. She was sure there'd been a German too. She thought she remembered a photograph of a great strapping girl on a mountaintop. She didn't suppose Rita would have picked up much German from a penpal, but you never know. Anyway, she'd be glad to see Rita one way or the other. She felt so jumpy and cooped up she just had to get herself out of the house. She was beginning to feel a bit guilty about leaving Mother on her own down in Dunkerin, too. That's what happens, she thought, when you do too much sitting around. You start brooding on things. She'd go and find Rita at the Commercial College; it would be good to have somebody to talk to for a change.

Kitty walked out the gate towards Baggot Street. She was almost at the bridge when she spotted Bobby Coyle. She had a split second to make her escape but she hesitated and by then it was too late. He raised his hand to salute her. 'Well isn't this a surprise to brighten Monday morning.'

She showed him her teeth.

'I didn't think you made it up to Dublin these days. Des told me you didn't leave Dunkerin; spent your time home on the range.'

'Just a bit of a break,' she said, still moving.

'Wait till I get Des. He never breathed a word. You've an aunt this way, haven't you? Sure, you're almost a neighbour.'

'Desmond doesn't know. It was all a bit last minute. Look, Bobby, I need to get going. I'll be seeing you.'

She hoped he wouldn't follow her, and he didn't. Running into Bobby just like that made her realise it might be nearly as difficult to have a secret in Dublin as in Dunkerin. As she crossed into Merrion Square, she passed a tall, streely-looking Guard with a shock of red hair who was directing the traffic at the junction. Not for the first time, she wondered whether it was against the law to put up a German who'd jumped out of the war. The Guard looked out of place in the city, like he'd be happier behind a plough. She felt out of place herself, just looking at the country Guard. But then again, why shouldn't she be in Dublin? She was only young, wasn't she? Hadn't she a right to dances and friends like anybody else? Some days she could hardly breathe in Dunkerin, what with the dust in the hallway and the tobacco on the fire and Mother asleep in her chair. Why shouldn't she have a life of her own? At school, Kitty was the bright one. Everyone said it. So sharp she'll cut herself. Yet, somehow it was Desmond who was halfway to becoming Doctor Hennessy. At school, when they sat around whispering after lights out, it was Kitty, they all agreed, would have the adventures for everybody else.

When she reached McWilliams' Commercial College, the girls were already clattering down the front steps. Out in front was a redhead who looked like she was having a whale of a time. She was a great advertisement for Pitman's shorthand.

It was an age since Kitty had seen Rita. There were the letters, of course, but it felt like all the news came from Rita's direction. It'd been great to have the parachute in the lime tree to write about. She'd dashed off a letter to Rita that same day. Now that she'd done a flit to Dublin with the parachute man, maybe she should have kept her trap shut. The trouble with living in Dunkerin was that there was never anything much to put in a letter. She hated sounding like her entire life was a wet weekend. Kitty waited outside the college until all the girls had streamed down the steps, but there was still no Rita. In the office, they said Rita Connolly was all finished now. She'd got her cert already, they said.

It was a long time since Kitty had been on a tram. She thought of all those girls at the Commercial College, racing off into a world she knew nothing about, and for a moment she envied them, even though she'd always thought typing the dullest thing imaginable. When she reached Rita's house in Sandymount, it was reassuring that not everything was changing and rushing on without her. Everything looked exactly as it had done on her last visit. Rita's mother was wearing her blue pinny, her arms white with flour. Her father was even sitting in the same chair to the right of the fire. As soon as she spotted Kitty, Rita did a little skip and a jump. Kitty remarked to herself how nice it was to be wanted for a change.

Rita busied herself in the kitchen while Kitty stood watching her. 'We're out of tea,' she explained, 'so I've become a dab hand at the milkshakes. Strawberry?'

Rita selected one of the tiny glass bottles grouped next to the salt and pepper on the shelf above her head. 'Did you get my last letter? How did Michael Rosney strike you?'

She must have looked blank, because Rita gave her a funny look. 'Oh come on, Kitty. The fellow I've arranged for the Zoo Dance?' Rita poured out a long stream of milk then sprinkled it with dark red drops from the little bottle. She called it a milkshake, but it was all milk and no shake. 'How did he sound?'

Kitty took a sip of the flat pink liquid. No sugar either. 'He sounded fine.' Her voice came out flat, too.

'What is it, Kitty?' Rita put a hand on her shoulder. It was so long since she'd been touched that Kitty thought she might cry. 'There's something not right. What is it?'

The parachute, the diary that said God knows what; she didn't even know where to begin.

Rita was studying her. 'Did they ever find the German that came down? You wrote the morning they found the parachute but I never heard a dickybird after that. I suppose a thing like that would take it out of you: the worry of him being on the loose and that.'

Kitty shook her head, even though she'd never lied to Rita before.

'Do you think he might have been a spy? They say there's a German fellow lives up the Orwell Road who's a spy. He has three pots of geraniums on his windowsill, two red and one pink. He's forever moving them about and changing the order. Word is, if you ever see the pink one in the middle then we're all in the most shocking trouble. The invasion code, they say. A pink geranium. Did you ever hear the like? And what do you make of that Hess fellow? Imagine, second from the top, and he goes and takes himself over to Scotland. Is he astray in the head, do you think?'

'Could be, alright,' said Kitty, though she hadn't heard anything about the Hess man, and had no idea who he was.

'Did you read what the ploughman said who picked him up? He said Mr Hess's boots were as fine as a pair of gloves, imagine.'

Kitty tried another sip of the milkshake, then put it to one side.

'I do worry now, between the two of us, what kind of blackguards might be landing in the Dublin Mountains, and none of us any the wiser till they come marching past the GPO.'

'The last time I looked, it was the English we were all worried about,' said Kitty, sick of it all being one-sided. 'Aren't they the most likely ones to come traipsing across the border? Always threatening to give us a good hiding for holding on to their blasted ports.'

Rita wiped away a thin pink moustache with her hankie. 'If someone's going to invade, wouldn't you rather it was a decent person like Con Redmond than some thug of a German? Better the devil you know, that's what I say. There's enough eejits round the place thinking what's bad for the English must be good for us.'

Kitty walked home from Sandymount none the wiser about the diary. She felt dejected not to have made some progress and sad that she hadn't felt able to confide in Rita. She had barely reached her room when she heard Ranjit yelling up from the bottom of the stairs that there was someone wanting her at the front door.

She looked out of the window and there was Bobby Coyle on the front step, carrying a bunch of flowers that was just the right side of mean. He had on a pair of two-tone brogues and was constantly shifting his weight from one foot to the other, as though he was trying to cool them off. It looked very odd, until Kitty realised he was just trying to sneak a look past the door Ranjit had left ajar. When she got downstairs, she swept the door open so suddenly that Bobby almost fell forward into the hallway. Once he'd composed himself, he didn't waste any time. 'Have you an invite to the Zoo Dance?' he said, straight out.

'I have, Bobby.'

He looked put out. 'How did you swing that? There can't be too many dancing partners in Dunkerin, unless you count the fellows dropping in from above.' He laughed at his own wit.

She tried to laugh too but he was making her nervous.

'Ah come on, Kitty. We'll have a bit of a turn around the dance floor; play a few hands of whatever's going. I won't let on to Des, I promise.'

She wished he would shove off. 'I haven't a clue what you're on about, Bobby. Like I said, I already have a partner.' She made to close the door but he slid his shoe into the gap. 'And who's the lucky man?'

'His name is Michael Rosney. A friend's brother, if you must know.'

'That's very enterprising of you, Kitty, arranging that at long distance, what with the German coming down and all.'

'Would you ever stop calling him the German?'

'Well, we've no other name for him, do we?' He was watching her closely now. She felt herself get all hot and bothered, and the more she felt it, the worse it got.

'Look, it'll be a bit of gas. Tell that Rosney fellow you've had a better offer. Sure have a think about it, anyway.' He seemed happy enough as he set off down the steps but he took his flowers away with him.

*

A Fair Old Tramp

The train jerked its way along the coast, and Oskar searched every inch of it for the girl who might have been Elsa. He tramped up and down the length of the train but she wasn't there. When the train stopped, Oskar waited for it to empty, then vaulted over the station barrier. On the wall there were advertisements for things he'd never even heard of: something called Bird's, that no child could resist, and something else called Bovril. He passed a house, smelt bacon and thought of Kitty. He felt guilty, suddenly, that he hadn't said thank you, or even goodbye. He'd been so keen to get moving that he'd simply forgotten about her. Blue dress or not, he should have stuck to his plan; sold the watch, bought the map, stocked up on provisions, planned his route. Now, he was back to having no idea where he was.

He imagined Mutti and Emmi, how they would laugh if they could see him now. Typical Oskar, they'd say, haring off like that. The thought made him determined to keep going. He started to walk up the single nondescript street, though he couldn't imagine Elsa in a place like this. She hated dull things. As he walked, he peered at names on gates, at script swirling across fanlights, for something that looked like Whitecrest. He wished he'd asked the nursemaid in the park what it was about him that marked him out as a German. His own adjustments seemed to have worked but he'd have liked some confirmation that he was on the right track.

It was only when he looked for signposts that he remembered the blacked-out signs at the railway station and realised it made sense to have removed the signposts too. Unless he was to wander round in circles, he'd have to take the risk of asking for directions.

He'd noticed how the Irish seemed to lisp the Ds and Ts at the ends of words, and as he walked along he tried this out quietly.

Outside one of the houses, a couple of men, middle-aged and strangely idle for the time of day, sat smoking. He'd prepared a little speech about losing his way and was just about to deliver it, when one of them asked what he was looking for.

'Miss Alexander of Wicklow.'

The men turned to one another, as if the answer was written on the other man's forehead. Then one of them answered, 'There used to be Alexanders out Lough Reddan way.'

'And now?' Oskar asked. 'Are they still at Whitecrest?'

'I'm not even sure that's what they call the place,' he said. 'Couldn't put a name on it.'

'You'll need the boots,' said the other. 'It's a fair old tramp.'

When he asked to see a map, they disappeared together into the house, as though neither wanted the burden of making conversation with him. They came back together too, carrying a large framed map they must have taken off the wall for him. One of the men propped it up on the windowsill and ran his finger ten or so centimetres from the coast, past a lake and a little further in. 'Whitecrest,' he announced, matter-of-fact, as though this was not the miracle it seemed to Oskar. 'That's the place over beyond Lough Reddan, right enough. Once you reach the lake, head on through the village and the big house is out the other side.'

Oskar followed the main street out of town and up towards the hills. When he glanced back, the two men were still standing there watching him. Now that he'd drawn attention to himself, it made no sense to take the main road, and he turned off it as soon as he was out of sight. The road had begun to rise towards the hills and once he'd left it he found himself on little more than a track, a wide band of lush grass running down the centre. The evening drew in quickly enough, and though he passed a couple of small cottages that breathed out thin spirals of smoke, he didn't meet another soul. As darkness fell, he came across a tin-roofed shack with rough boards nailed across the windows. He drank water from a nearby stream but there was nothing to eat. Grenade throwing, trench digging, use of dugouts; the Hitler Jugend had taught him all that but he still didn't know which mushroom was which. In his imagination, there were sardines and fresh bread, and peaches straight from the tin. He inhabited the fantasy and ate hungrily, wiping his oily fingers on the lush grass. He used his knife to puncture the peach tin. He sucked the syrup through the hole, saving the fruit for later. Once the imaginary meal was eaten, though, he was left with the damp and the dark and a stomach that felt even emptier than before. His heart was on the brink; he couldn't really believe he would see Elsa tomorrow, and yet he hadn't been able to believe that he could lose her either.

It had snowed all day long and Mutti was knitting by the fire when he got home; something grey, he remembered, something she probably intended for him. Plain one, purl one, clickety-clickety-click.

'I see the Frankels have gone,' she said, without looking up from her knitting.

'They can't have done.'

'I think you'll find they have.'

When he dashed to look out the window, the tracks they'd made were still visible, but it was snowing so hard that very soon there would be no trace of them at all. Mutti laid her knitting to one side and placed another log on the fire.

'How will they manage?' He pictured Frankel, begging on Tiergartenstrasse, with his shoelaces undone.

Plain one, purl one. 'Those Jews always manage.'

The next morning was sunny, though the countryside was still drenched from the night before. Oskar tramped on through impossibly green fields edged with harsh yellow bushes, over the reddish stalks of last year's bracken, around tufts of rough grass. Here and there, sheets of corrugated metal, weathered to rust, filled gaps in fields dotted with sheep. He passed by a stream gushing with brown water and stopped to splash his face with it. Hynotised by the tramp of his own feet, he had almost ceased to notice his surroundings when he saw the beginnings of a lake. He knew then that he must be close.

The sun had retreated and the lake looked black, bottomless. He couldn't imagine picnics here or diving platforms. He couldn't imagine Elsa here either. Perhaps she would refuse to see him. When he was called up by the labour people he hadn't been home for six whole months, right when things had finally become impossible. When he returned, he'd gone round there right away, even though they all warned him not to. He marched straight up the path, still wearing his uniform. The house was shuttered from top to bottom but he could hear the faint sound of music inside. When he got to the door, he battered and battered and battered. The music stopped. He called her name. Nothing. Then the creak of a shutter from overhead. Frankel looked as if he'd just woken up. He seemed to barely recognise Oskar; just shook his head and closed the shutters again. A couple of days later, they were gone.

The sun didn't return, and soon there was a mighty downpour. As the rain eased off, he came to the edge of a village. There was no one about except for a woman in a faded housecoat who was washing down the doorstep of one of the taverns. Inside, the place was small and dark, with a cubbyhole sectioned off next to the bar. The embers still glowed orange under a layer of fine grey dust, and the ashtrays were unemptied. Using as few words as possible and lisping his Ts as he'd practised, he asked if they served breakfast.

'Seeing as you look half starved I might be able to stretch to an egg or two,' the woman said.

He sat where he was told and heard her on the other side of the door, busy with pots and pans. He walked over to the half-curtained window and looked out into the street. A youngster was driving two sturdy cows down the middle of the street but that was the only activity. Inside the bar was covered in photographs with an identical caption: Easter Rebellion, 1916. They must have succeeded in their rebellion, he thought; losers don't go on walls. He looked from face to face but he couldn't find the one they might have chosen for a Chancellor. The men looked like shopkeepers or clerks but there was one woman in white with a beautiful face. It was puzzling.

He was just wondering whether breakfast would ever arrive when the woman reappeared with two eggs, fried in brownish grease, and a slice of that terrible bread. She laid the plate in front of him but supplied no cutlery. He was ravenous, and had already started to dab at the yolks with a chunk of bread when two men entered from the direction of the kitchen. They had the air of people accustomed to receiving attention. The woman seemed flattered to have them there and stood back to let them pass.

The older man was peering at Desmond Hennessy's tweed coat. He came closer and felt the cloth between fingers and thumb. 'Did they do this for you back home?' he asked. 'Not bad.' He took a packet of cigarettes out of his pocket and flung them onto the table, as though they were credentials of some sort.

'You've done better already than the last fella,' said the younger man. 'He landed up on the Military Road in the noses of a convoy of LDF. Part-timers, alright, but not that thick they'd miss a great big lump of a German with a parachute hanging off the back of him.'

Oskar continued mopping at the congealing yolk with the bread. He tried to remember what Kitty had told him about the men who wanted to help Germany against England. He got the impression she was more frightened of them than she'd ever been of him.

'Where are you headed?'

Oskar tried to drag up a destination from one of Kitty's long monologues. When he didn't give an immediate reply, the man just asked another question. 'Do you have a transmitter?'

'Yes.' Oskar tried, watching to see if that was the right answer. 'Not with me, of course.'

'We need to get going, then. Is there a receiver as well?'

Oskar shook his head, and that answer seemed acceptable too. It wouldn't take long for them to discover there was no transmitter. They'd work out soon enough that he wasn't who they wanted him to be. For all he knew, they might shoot him then and there. He couldn't believe this was how it would end.

Then, without another word, all three disappeared behind the bar and into the back room. He could hear voices, low at first then louder, more aggressive. He thought one of them might be speaking on the telephone. He took his chance quickly, slipping silently through the front door, then darting into an alleyway that led off the main street. They would expect him to try to get clear of the village, so he hid in behind an old charabanc that looked as if it hadn't moved in decades. Minutes later, he watched them pass along the main street on a horse and cart. They were scanning right and left, and heading back in the direction of the lake. When he was sure they were gone, Oskar turned his back on the village and kept on going until he reached a point where the road began to dip. It wound its way down the mountain like a skein of dark wool around a bobbin. When he saw the house in the distance, he no longer felt the slightest bit hungry; he could go for days if he had to.

Failing to Follow

Whitecrest was a big white block of a house that resembled one of Mutti's plain iced slab cakes. The painted wooden sign was flayed and blistered by the wind and rain but he could still make out the words, 'Whitecrest Convalescent Home and Refuge for the Distressed'. The girl who answered the door looked doubtfully at him. He explained that he was looking for Elsa Frankel but the name didn't appear to mean anything to her. She looked him up and down. It was only then that he realised his boots and the legs of his trousers were caked in mud. He probably smelt dreadful. The girl bit her lip. 'Who will I say?'

She couldn't get his surname right, even though he said it for her twice. He smiled, 'Miller will do.'

She didn't smile back but told him to wait a moment. She closed the frosted glass doors behind her, capturing him in a damp space that housed an umbrella stand and some outdoor boots.

When the girl returned, she nodded and ushered him inside. She walked ahead of him down the hallway, glancing over her shoulder now and then to make sure he was following her. She led him into a drawing room of sorts, empty but for a couch with a worn brocade cover and a bony rocking chair. Miss Alexander was already occupying the couch, so he sat in the rocker opposite. The rocking made him feel foolish, so he sat forward to steady the chair, his feet planted on the floor.

She began by commenting on the weather, gesturing vaguely in the direction of the long windows behind her. Then, when the weather had been got out of the way, she focused on him. 'So, Mr Miller, how may I help?'

He found himself distracted by her hands, which seemed constantly to make precise, barely discernible movements. For all her courtesy, he could see that she was wary of him. He decided it was best to be direct. 'I am looking for Elsa Frankel.'

She raised her eyebrows. Her hands were placed lightly together now and she was watching him intently. 'A friend, Mr Miller?'

He nodded. A nurse came rushing through the door, then mumbled her apologies before backing out again.

'And why have you come here to look for your friend?' She sounded as though she had no real interest in his reply, and that angered him, though he tried not to show it.

'Your name was mentioned on the visa application. I came across it at the Irish Legation, back in Berlin.'

'They let you look through their files? Why would they do that?' She didn't sound like she believed him. He started to explain about the bribe, how the woman had assumed that he was a fellow Nazi, but she looked incredulous and he decided he was over-complicating things. He tried to start again but she shook her head. 'I didn't have a single visa granted from that Legation. Not one.' An expression rippled across the calm surface of her face for a moment and disappeared before he could name it. 'You're from Berlin, Mr Miller?'

'I'm sorry, my name is Müller.'

'You can't help your name.' She smiled, then so did he. But Miss Alexander's smiles didn't seem to last very long. 'I'm trying to understand,' she went on. 'Most Germans here have been in Ireland for years, but you're very young. Tell me more about yourself and about Berlin.'

He found himself following the little waves she made with her hand.

'I haven't been there for some time,' he said quickly.

'No, not since before the war, surely,' she said. 'Otherwise,' her hands spread.

He agreed. 'Not since then.'

'And your family?'

'Dead,' he said, feeling a combination of shame and superstitious anxiety that his lie would damn them all.

'All of them?' she asked. 'Your family are all dead?'

He nodded, trapped now.

'They died before the war? Or since?'

He could no longer look at her.

'Which?'

'They died a long time ago.'

Miss Alexander said nothing for a moment. He swept his feet back under the chair and it rocked him forward with a sudden jolt.

'Why do you want to see Miss Frankel? You can't have seen her for many years, surely. Not since she was a child. Yet you were in Berlin recently enough to check a visa application. Forgive me if I fail to follow.'

He should have told her the truth. He knew that, and so he began again. 'I jumped,' he said, his face hot now. 'I was a member of a crew of lamplighters over Belfast. Kampfgruppe 100. We were pathfinders, for the bombers that followed. But I jumped. Over a month ago, now. I jumped for her.'

When he looked at Miss Alexander, she was shaking her head. She looked insulted, then angry, then weary. The emotions flickered into life one by one.

'Please excuse me,' she said finally, standing up to indicate that the meeting was over.

He moved towards her and immediately she took a step back from him. When she spoke again, her voice was firm. 'You must go now,' she said. 'We are very busy at present.' She looked at him with at strange expression. He wondered whether it was pity or disgust.

'I jumped from a plane,' he blurted out. 'I deserted.'

She shook her head so fast it must have made her dizzy. 'Come now,' she said and took his arm, leading him towards the door.

'I came to find her. If you knew how I've tried to find her.'

'And before, when you were in Berlin, what did you do then?'

Oskar didn't stop walking until he reached the sea. He spent the night in an overgrown garden near the railway station, huddled for shelter against a wall. For hours, it seemed, he lay awake there as the sea crashed over the rocks. The air was sharp and his throat felt like it had been grated raw. At first light, he stood on the deserted station platform and waited for a train to stop. He felt hollow, defeated. Again and again he ran over things in his mind. He should have told her everything from the start instead of changing his story halfway through. He'd already decided to go back. Next time, he'd start at the beginning, with Zweibrückenstrasse. He'd bring Kitty with him too, to vouch for the parachute.

North Strand

Shabbat Moon

'They really want you to come,' said Elsa. 'Will you?'

She looked pale. Charlie wondered again if she was getting enough iron. If he brought her home to Foynes, Ma would have her fattened up in no time. He decided that when the exams were over, he would invite Elsa down to meet them all. She and Retta would have great gas together and the whole lot of them could go dancing to the Ceili in the parish hall.

He'd gone to some trouble to smarten himself up for the Shabbat eve dinner, and now he hoped he hadn't gone too far. He'd never worn a cravat before. Elsa giggled when she saw it and said that Bethel would have no peace from Hilde until he agreed to get one too.

The Kernoffs had been invited, and a little bent woman he hadn't seen before. They all sat around a large table laid with a stiff white cloth, which just about fitted into the front parlour. When no one was looking, Elsa flicked up the cloth to reveal that it was actually a door, salvaged from somewhere or other and placed on top of the dining table when there were extra guests. There was a book and candles, and two loaves of bread covered by a fringed cloth that was embroidered with symbols he'd never seen before. He became aware of a scent, dusky and sweet. The perfume had him on the edge of a sneeze but he managed to hold it back while Hilde lit the candles, slowly and with great care. Elsa was seated opposite him. He'd never sat opposite a girl by candlelight before and he couldn't take his eyes off her.

As Bethel grappled with the incantation, his complicated Dublin vowels slipped away from him. The bread was uncovered and shared, and once the meal had begun the room was alive with chatter. The conversation fell to either side of Charlie and Elsa, and nobody seemed to expect them to join in. It was as though there were only the two of them there, in the centre of the table, with the candles flickering between them.

Now that he had the opportunity of spending a whole meal with her, he couldn't help trying to squeeze in question after question. He learned that she liked the colour blue, that she adored ice-skating (though not skiing). She hated fish, but seafood was even worse. She did not approve of smoking. As for astronomy, she said she couldn't care less which star was which, but she agreed that there would one day be a colony on the moon.

'Maybe that's where we'll all end up. Maybe they'll let us have the moon if they can keep their precious world for themselves.' She looked into the candle flame and seemed lost a moment.

'Would you fancy a bit of Nelson Eddy?' he asked, keen to keep her spirits up. He had *New Moon* in mind, at the Metropole.

He was astonished to discover that she'd never even heard of him. She didn't know Charlie Chaplin either. There was so much they would have to teach each other, and the thought thrilled him. Lottie and Minnie were squealing about a spider they'd discovered that morning in the kitchen sink, and when he asked Elsa what she was afraid of, that's the kind of thing he had in mind. As soon as it was out, though, he knew it was a stupid question and wished he could bite it back.' She didn't answer at first. Then, she looked him straight in the eye. 'Can't you guess?' she said.

Now and then, he caught sight of Bethel sitting back in his chair, smiling like an indulgent father. Hilde's eyes darted anxiously between Elsa and Charlie, her eyes returning always to rest on Elsa. After the meal, they played Chinese whispers, and Elsa laughed and laughed. It was hard to believe she was the same person who'd cried such bitter tears that night by the canal. Later, when the dinner was cleared away, the table dismantled, and Lottie and Minnie sent up to bed, they all squeezed around the piano in the back parlour. Mrs Kernoff had a decent voice, and she sang a couple of light opera tunes while Elsa accompanied her. Then Elsa gave them a little medley of her own. He remembered hearing a lad from the R&R singing one of the tunes she played. He could remember some of the words, too. '*You make my darkness bright when like a star you shine on me.*' He felt too awkward to sing along because the words were too painfully precise.

That afternoon he'd been on his way to O'Neill's with some of the medical set. He walked a little apart from them, just keeping up with the conversation, as he thought of Elsa and the dinner and what little thing he might bring her. Eventually, he let the others go on, said he would catch them up. He stopped off at McCullough Pigot and asked the man in there, a reedy little fellow with a red nose, if there was anything he might bring a girl who liked Chopin.

When the Kernoffs had left and the little bent woman had been helped down the street to her own house, Charlie retrieved the sheet music from his briefcase and sat next to Elsa on the duet stool. 'Did you know it was an Irishman gave your friend Chopin the idea to write night music?'

'It's that blind harper again, isn't it?' she said, and kissed him lightly on the cheek so that his skin burned. He gave her the book, and she propped it up on the music stand and began to read aloud. 'John Field. Inventor of the Nocturne. Born Dublin, 1782. Died Moscow. After leaving Dublin at the age of eleven he never once again lived in Ireland.'

He hadn't read that bit. Hilde looked alarmed. But once Elsa began to pick out the melody, the music took over. As he watched her play, he memorised the lie of her hair, the roll of her shoulders as she used her body to give power to the music. He knew that he would be able to mark this as the moment of his falling in love and he wanted to be able to remember every detail of it. He guessed that the feeling she put into the music signalled some other love that was lost now. He wondered if she would ever feel that way for him.

After Bethel went to bed, Hilde sat nodding in her chair until Charlie realised with a start that she'd probably been acting as a sort of chaperone. He muttered his apologies and the three of them stood cluttering up the hallway while he said his goodbyes. On the other side of the street, a cherry tree strained against a garden wall. As he crossed the road, his leather soles slid slightly on the deep carpet of blossom. He looked back at the house and there she was on the first floor, waving and blowing comic kisses at him.

The moon was waiting for him at the end of the street, hung low in the sky like a lantern. He was not in the habit of noticing the moon and he smiled to himself at this confirmation that he had indeed fallen in love. As for the moon, there was something not altogether normal about it. It looked bloated, jaundiced. As he moved down towards Camden Street, he felt it bear down on him.

He looked at his watch. He'd be lucky to be home before one at this rate, and there was no way Mrs Curran would tolerate that. He decided that discretion was the better part of valour and resolved to head for Des's flat instead. He walked down to College Green, then turned the corner into D'Olier Street and over towards the Liffey. He was amazed how many people were still about at this late hour: sweethearts canoodling by the O'Connell monument, shawlies and aul' fellas all over the place. He'd been walking on air when he left Elsa, but now the moon seemed to give the night a yellowish tinge. Everything looked off-colour, unwholesome. As soon as he heard the drone of the engines high above his head he knew exactly what it was.

Kitty couldn't sleep. The moon shone straight in at her through the skylight. Desmond had been to see her that morning. He stood in the gloom of the Receiving Room and delivered his lecture. 'I'd no idea you weren't in Dunkerin,' he said, 'and Mother not well at all.'

She felt like saying to him that she was nobody's nurse-maid but not knowing how ill Mother actually was, she held her tongue.

'Dr Russell wrote to say her nerves are in an awful state. He's told her that with bed rest and good nursing she'll be right as rain, but Kitty, you should be down home at a time like this. What has you in Dublin anyway? Bobby said you were fierce cloak-and-dagger when he ran into you.'

That's when Effie cut in. 'You can be very hard, Desmond. That sister of yours is an angel of mercy to the afflicted. She brought me back from death's door.'

'But you've that Ranjit fellow to look after you, Effie. Anyway, you look in brave shape, thank God. Angel or not, it's time Kitty went home.'

With the departure of Oskar and the prospect of returning to Dunkerin, Kitty was mired in gloom. She should never have taken him in in the first place. What was she thinking? He'd just used her as a way of getting up to Dublin and then as soon as he got here he was off. She was mortified at the thought of what Con Redmond would say if he ever heard tell of it all. Maybe she should have just handed the diary over to the Guards. Maybe she still should.

After Desmond left, she went to Bewley's to meet up with some of the girls from school. Rita was there, and Mary Crosbie and her sister, and Eily Roche, who brought along a couple of the Dalkey girls. They sat under one of the great stained-glass windows, eating almond buns and drinking tea.

'But what are you doing with yourself, Kitty?' Mary kept asking. 'Have you plans?'

She felt like a right gom, saying she was just after buying her ticket home to Dunkerin.

'Aren't you great to be looking after your mother?' Eily said, a face on her like Mother Fabius. 'I suppose you'll just have to offer it up.'

After that, they got onto the subject of the Zoo Dance and what a grand job Rita had done, getting a partner for Kitty and her the other side of the country altogether.

'I couldn't be bothered with the Zoo Dance,' she said finally. There was a stunned silence.

'Ah, you must.'

'… great gas.'

'Not bothered?'

'… sure your mother wouldn't mind.'

They were all talking at once and she felt like just getting up out of her chair and leaving them to it.

'Mick Rosney's not bad looking at all,' said Rita, 'and sure looks aren't everything.' The Dalkey girls were nodding away like those little toy dogs with the wobbly heads. Rita looked sorry for her, and that was the giddy limit; that Rita Connolly should feel sorry for Kitty Hennessy, the spit of Hedy Lamarr.

When Kitty got up out of bed to go to the WC, she heard Effie padding around on the landing below. Effie was becoming ever more nocturnal. She spent the days dozing on her chaise in the Receiving Room and at night she sat up, watchful as a mouser. Kitty decided she might as well boil up some milk for them both, and see if that did the trick. When she went down to the kitchen, she found Aunt Effie already down there, a stole wrapped tightly around her thin shoulders. She had no make-up on, for once, and her eyes were small as currants. She looked so old, all of a sudden, so thin, that Kitty got a fright. She offered to make her something to eat, not expecting her to say yes. Effie never ate. To her surprise, Effie reeled out a string of instructions involving onions and cabbage and some left-over spuds. As she began chopping and dicing, Kitty wondered if Effie made a habit of visiting the kitchen at night. Maybe Ranjit cooked for her. She realised, then, that she'd no idea where Ranjit ate or slept, or even what he sounded like. It was as though he had no existence beyond Aunt Effie.

'He has the face of an angel, but his soul is all long division.' Effie had a habit of saying things out of the blue but it was hard to be quick on the uptake in the middle of the night. Kitty turned from the stove, where she was trying to keep the onion from burning on the bottom of the pan. 'Who has?'

'For the love of Isis, child, your Mr Germany. Oh, he may have fallen out of the sky, all right. But he's no dandelion clock. He's got his heart set on something and he'll not be blown off course.'

'What makes you say that?' she asked, as if Aunt Effie had ever felt the need for reasons.

'Sure it's plain as porridge,' she said. 'That boy has thrown himself out of an aeroplane. He's turned his back on the place he was born, betrayed his family and his friends. He's shut the door on everything he's ever known, and in the middle of a war, too. He's said goodbye, forever maybe, to the street where he lived. Now why did he do that?'

Kitty shrugged, not wishing to continue the conversation.

'I'll tell you why. He's on a quest, your Mr Germany. This Elsa Frankel he's looking for. She's the only one can give him what he's looking for. That's my reading of it. Whether it's love, I doubt. Forgiveness maybe. That might be more like it.' She picked a crumb from the tablecloth and brought it to the edge of the table where she flicked it onto the floor. 'He's back, by the way. Ranjit let him in this evening. Said he looked shocking, like he'd been dragged through a hedge backwards. He went straight up the stairs and not a peep out of him.'

Kitty felt her heart open out like a flower. Making Aunt Effie's supper no longer seemed a chore at all. They sat and ate together, even though by that time it was very late.

The first sounds were like the trundling of a heavy motor truck somewhere off in the distance. It was only afterwards that Kitty realised that must have been the start of it. Next, she heard Oskar's boots thunder down the flights of stairs overhead: clapping on oilcloth, muffled by carpet then scraping over the limestone flags outside the kitchen. She half raised herself from her chair, unable to contain her excitement, but when he burst in the door it was obvious that something was terribly wrong.

'Get down!' he yelled. 'Under the table, now!'

Effie raised her hands to her face, her fingers spread out around it like the petals of a daisy, but she didn't move. Oskar took her arm and guided her down off the chair. 'Come on, Miss Effie. There is no time. You must move quickly.'

Effie's knees cracked as she tipped off the edge of her chair and under the table. She was like an obedient child, still clutching her stole. Kitty was wide awake now but Effie looked like she'd gone into a trance. Her eyes were shut, her knuckles white, her red lips moving silently. Oskar's eyes were closed too but she could tell he was listening hard. Right away she realised that he was listening for planes. She gripped his arm tighter than she meant to. She started to say her prayers in her head but she didn't shut her eyes.

Dear God, don't let us be buried under here for the rats to get us. Don't let us die roaring or leave us in bits. If we have to go, make it fast, please, God. But let me see Dunkerin again, and Mother, and Con Redmond. Con Redmond? She'd no idea what made her think of him, except that he was in the war and so, now, was she. She thought of the woman in Belfast who'd just stepped into her bath when the bombs got her.

The motor truck noise grew louder and louder. She felt Oskar slide his arm around her shoulders and draw her towards him. She tried to pull away but he wouldn't let her go. As the noise reached a peak, she let her cheek fall against his shoulder, and finally she closed her eyes and clenched her fists so that her fingernails bit into the palms of her hands. She crouched there close to him as his friends prepared to do their worst.

When the explosions came, Effie let out a great wail. Her head was thrown back and she was howling away like a banshee. Suddenly, she remembered Oskar. She sat up straight and pointed a long red fingernail at him. 'They'll roast you, Mr Germany, and rightly so. Dolmens, my backside.' Then, a look of horror spread across her face. 'Ranjit!' She sucked in, hard and sharp. 'He'll be a sitting duck in the white.'

Kitty felt Oskar let go of her shoulders. He propped her up against one of the sturdy table legs, then slid out. She heard his boots retreating down the corridor and up the stairs to the front hallway. The heavy front door slammed shut.

Within minutes of the planes' retreat, the streets were full of people. Charlie decided that if he was ever to be any use as a doctor, this was the time to find out. The closer he got to the fires, the more hysterical the crowd. The LSF and the ARP had already put a cordon around the area, but Charlie managed to make his way through a side street that brought him out in front of a burning terrace where a huddle of people stared helplessly into the fire. The end house had gone, and all that remained of it was a ragged section of staircase, still precariously suspended, somehow or other, above the flames. It teetered there, before collapsing in front of him in a shower of sparks. The fire seemed too fierce and horrifying a thing to belong in the same night as the Shabbat dinner. And then a woman screamed and made it real. He was suddenly aware that people lived in these houses. The thought of that made him snap out of himself. Someone beside him pointed to a small shape standing at a window of the house next to where the flames were raging. It was hard to see what it was: a dressing table mirror, perhaps, something hanging at the window? More debris tumbled into the blaze that raged where the end house had been, and then he saw that it was a girl, a child really. She started to climb out onto the windowsill, before thinking better of it. People around him yelled at the fire, screamed for a fireman. They shouted at the girl not to panic, roaring their heads off at her, but nobody actually did anything. When Charlie declared himself a doctor, it was like a magic charm. The screaming tailed off and the onlookers stood back. It was only as someone hurried him through to the front that he realised that he was expected to be the hero.

When he got to the front wall of the building, he was not sure at first how to tackle it. From where Charlie stood, the girl looked like a small doll up there at the window, her face streaked in and out of shadow by the light of the flames. Someone gave him a leg up and he was able to hoist himself up to the first floor. He managed to inch his way along the ledge towards the tattered end wall of the house. Once he was up there, he felt like an imposter in a circus act, the top-billed high-wire act who was afraid of heights. He tried to block out the sound of the onlookers. He breathed deeply to steady himself but the dense smoke sent him spluttering as the wind changed and it billowed out in front of him. He could hardly see the girl anymore, but when he reached the window he felt her grab on to his arm. He was desperate not to lose the contact. Even if he failed at everything else – medicine, love, whatever – surely he could manage this. Slowly, slowly, he drew the girl out onto the windowsill. He looked down. Some superhuman effort had got him up here but now he felt sapped. As the direction of the smoke shifted again he could see the upturned faces of people in the crowd, like pebbles on a beach. Suddenly, he felt exhausted. Down below, some of the men had got their hands on a pinkish blanket and were shouting up at the girl to jump. She was cowering in towards the building and Charlie was on the point of trying to per-suade her to go, in two minds as to whether they wouldn't be better hanging on for the fire brigade when, suddenly, she dropped off the ledge and onto the out-stretched blanket. The men clustered around her, then one of them gathered her up and carried her off through the crowd.

Meanwhile, the men with the blanket were re-forming below Charlie. He hesitated a moment, shook his head a little, moved in against the wall. Just as the fire tender finally appeared on the scene and just as Charlie had overcome his fear of making his jump, something happened that must have distracted the men. Perhaps they moved to the side to allow the tender to pass through the cordon. Maybe they were startled by the scatter of rubble from the burning house. Whatever the reason, when Charlie leapt from the building, he landed on top of the crumpled pink blanket they had discarded on the ground in front of them.

'For the love of God,' he heard as he was falling, 'yiz all forgot about the doctor fella.'

It felt like they'd been under the kitchen table for half the night. Eventually, Kitty crept out. Aunt Effie's leg had gone to sleep and Kitty had to drag her out by the arms. She was limp as a rag doll and seemed to weigh next to nothing. She didn't say anything; just sat there where Kitty had left her. They were only out a few minutes when they heard the key in the door upstairs. Kitty had felt quite calm up until then. Suddenly, with the turn of the key in the lock, the realisation hit her that this was all part of real life. She began to shake, from fear, dread, excitement. Above all, she felt ashamed. She could hear her Mother's voice in her head. 'You see, Kitty was always herself. There was no talking to her. Mind you, even I'd have thought she'd have more sense than to harbour a German. A German, imagine, in the middle of wartime. We're not that neutral, after all.'

Ranjit rushed over to Effie. He lifted her hand and dabbed it around his cheeks and forehead as though it had powers of anointment, and then he kissed it. Kitty turned away, embarrassed, as Effie rested her head in the crook of his arm.

Where had the parachutes landed, if there were parachutes at all? In the dead tree? Along by the canal? And were there more bombs to come? She went up to the Receiving Room and sat in the window seat and looked out into the night. There was no sign of anything out of the ordinary. The moon hung unchanged over the houses opposite, a great big bladder of a thing. It was hard to believe that anything had happened at all. Well, he'd be gone for good now, she thought, now that he'd done his dirty work. She felt exhausted by everything that had happened; frustrated at her inability to work out how she felt about anything. It wasn't long after that she saw him coming through the twisted gateway. He was walking backwards, turning around, looking at the sky. Always looking at the bloody sky.

She realised then that he wasn't making for the house at all. He was walking in the direction of the Austin, still lodged in amongst the lower branches of the dead tree. She pulled up the sash and yelled out at him.

'Oskar!'

His palms were on the back of his head, his elbows joined in a point over his forehead, like he was hiding from something.

'Oskar!'

Without acknowledging her, he changed direction towards the house. She ran down the stairs to meet him. I am not dead, her head murmured: no other thought. I am not dead and neither is Oskar and one day it will all be over for both of us. He was kissing her and she was kissing him back and this was what filled the hallway.

'I am not part of the war,' he said suddenly, drawing back from her, gently pulling away a strand of hair that had become trapped in the corner of her mouth. 'Kitty, you know I am not part of the war.'

It was like if he said it often enough he could make it true. He looked like he believed it, wished it maybe. But it didn't seem to matter now, anyway. All that mattered was that he'd come back. They were both alive, whatever might happen to them in the future. When she touched him, he gave a little cry that was so tender it almost frightened her. He asked her if she had ever made love to anyone before and she felt like asking him who the hell she might have done that with in Dunkerin. He just smiled and took her in his arms and carried her up the stairs, like she was someone so precious her feet shouldn't even be let touch the floor. Each flight they climbed, the surer she was that she wanted him to be the first, and when they got to the top, to his room and the little narrow bed under the skylight, it seemed the most urgent thing she'd ever done, to make love with Oskar under the sky he'd come out of.

When she opened her eyes, she couldn't believe she was back in Dublin, after all the places she'd travelled. Oskar was lying on his back, his eyes wide open, gazing at the skylight. When he saw her watching him, he just kissed her gently on the shoulder and when she closed her eyes again, she felt him wrap the sheet tight around her like a baby and hold her as the tears tumbled out of her. She didn't know why she was crying because she'd never felt so happy and important and part of the big world that had nothing at all to do with Dunkerin. She closed her eyes and tried to separate moments from the whole so that she could keep them, boxed away like pearls.

She wasn't quite sure what a French letter was. According to a girl that Rita knew, the man would get them across the border. She didn't think Oskar had used one of them but she didn't like to ask him, and anyway he had fallen asleep. Outside, she heard a siren and felt guilty to be happy on such a terrible night. She seemed to lie awake for hours, her mind racing through everything that had happened since the parachute fell, but she must have slept because she awoke to find light streaming through the skylight overhead. She edged her elbow across the narrow bed, and when she could feel no Oskar there, she blinked her eyes open. He was gone. Of course he was. The disappointment was like a punch in the guts. It probably meant nothing at all to him. That Elsa Frankel, he'd probably done it with her dozens of times. She tucked her head into the crook of her arm. But then she heard his voice wishing her good morning. He walked across the room, and sat down on the edge of the bed beside her. She closed her eyes and breathed him in. He kissed her on the forehead, but from the look in his eyes she could tell they'd moved out of whatever world it was they'd been in last night and back into this one.

'They will put me in the camp,' he said, 'or whatever they do with German airmen.'

'Well, they haven't picked you up yet. And it's not like you've exactly kept a low profile.'

'Everything has changed now.'

She gathered the covers up around her collarbone and tried to think of something positive to say. But then she pictured Bobby Coyle and she knew he was right. 'You'll need to keep your head down for a while. No gallivanting off around town and talking to people in parks. Maybe it'll blow over, if no one's been hurt. The last time they dropped bombs, over at Donore Avenue, nobody got hurt then.'

The End of Things

The bombers were German. Four bombs had fallen, and over on the North Strand the devastation was terrible. There were reports of piles of dead people and others with horrible injuries. Kitty's heart sank. Later that morning, Effie summoned everyone to the Receiving Room. She was lying on her chaise, draped in a jumble of shawls and stoles and wearing a long white dress. Ranjit was sitting beside her and Kitty realised it was the first time she'd ever seen him sit down. No one spoke at first but it was clear that Oskar was the one who was expected to say something. 'I could wish that these things didn't happen, but they will happen anyway.' The words were not what was needed, and they hung there uselessly in the semi-dark.

'You need to get off the fence, Mr Germany. Before they blow that up too. You can't run away, you see. There's nowhere left to go.' Effie's voice softened a little, 'Have you found what you're looking for? Have you found this girl that has you tied in knots?'

He looked down at his boots and Kitty wanted to shake him. Surely he didn't need to worry about this Elsa Frankel one now. Didn't he have her? Wasn't that enough for him?

'Did you think they'd stop dropping bombs if you weren't there, Mr Germany? And as for the girl, what good did you think it would do her, you jumping out of a plane and haring across Ireland after her? Sure if she's here, she's saved already, and no thanks to you. All you've saved, Mr Germany, is your own skin.'

Oskar turned and began to walk towards the door but Effie hadn't finished yet. 'No doubt you'll last out this war, Mr

Germany. But who knows how you'll see it all later, when all you'll need to know is that you did the right thing.'

Kitty followed him out to the hallway but he was already putting on his coat: Desmond's coat. 'You need your head examined. The place'll be crawling.' She turned away from him angrily. 'Why do you have to go off again?'

When he walked out the door, he was wearing the yellow scarf. When she saw that on him, she knew he wouldn't be coming back.

Next day, mid-morning, Bobby Coyle came to the door. He was in uniform and he looked tired, older. She realised then he'd probably been called up to work round the clock on account of the bombs.

'I came to see how you were faring.'

'We're faring fine.'

'I wonder is this the start of things?'

'Isn't it the end of things, Bobby? Isn't that what it is, the end of the play acting?'

'The Guards arrested a German off Dawson Street. The blighter was wandering around like he wanted to be caught. He'd a scarf as yellow as a dandelion on him. God only knows what the fellow thought he was doing. He had some half-baked story about not being part of the war. That's what the sergeant said, anyway. Just like we're not part of the war either, I suppose.' Bobby had a funny look on his face. Almost sheepish, he looked.

Kitty didn't even try to hide her feelings. 'Where did they take him?'

'Oh, it'll be the Curragh, more than likely. Athlone, maybe, if it comes to it and he's a spy.'

'Will they hurt him?'

'They roughed him up a bit, but Kitty there's good people suffered terrible things from those bombs. And us neutral; what do they think they're doing, dropping their bombs on us?'

Bobby made his way down the steps, then stopped a moment to look at her over his shoulder. 'I suppose we'll leave the Zoo Dance then?'

When Elsa was a child, Papa had given her a picture book of dinosaurs. The one that captured her imagination was the pterodactyl. Even then, she used to consider how she might hide from it, deep in the undergrowth of some prehistoric jungle. Although it was immensely powerful – fed on the blood of its victims – it seemed almost too heavy for the air to bear it up. She imagined a time when it would fall to earth, defeated by its own inexorable growth.

Some tried to say the bombing wasn't the Germans at all; just the English trying to make it look like it was the Germans so that Ireland would join the war. Elsa dreaded the thought of that, because she clung onto the hope that Ireland might still receive refugees from Amsterdam, even now. Deep down, everyone knew it had been the Germans but no one knew why, and that was the most terrifying part of it. Elsa felt the fragility of her refuge. Then guilt that she had a refuge at all when Mama and Papa did not. Then fear for what else might come.

Before the bombing, she'd seen Charlie almost every day. Not once since. It was Bethel who said the hard thing to her, when she sat at the window at teatime and looked out to see if Charlie was on his way. 'Perhaps, Elsa, he just decided to stick to his own. You know, sometimes that's the best for everyone.'

She shut herself in Hilde's parlour and played all the Nocturnes – Chopin and Field – until she no longer knew whether she was playing them for Oskar or Charlie or just for their own sake. She tried to work out what reason there could be for Charlie's absence, then she realised she'd no idea how to contact him. She knew none of his friends; didn't even know his address. That's when it struck her that she hardly knew him at all. She was sure that something had happened between them at the Shabbat dinner, and that he cared enough to want to make her happy, but perhaps she was mistaken. Then again, perhaps he felt something that he just wasn't ready to feel. Maybe he'd frightened himself into stepping back from her for a while. Perhaps he realised she would be harder work than some girl from home. Yes, she thought, maybe Bethel was right. Maybe, like Oskar, he found in the end that he wanted to stick to his own.

Another week, and a man she didn't recognise came to the door. He was small, shabby-looking, and his glasses were bottle thick. He asked for Bethel first, then Hilde, but everyone else was out. 'Well, Missy,' he said, 'I suppose you must be Elsa Frankel.'

She said she was but when she saw the nod of his head, the small victory in him, she wished she hadn't. He said he was from the Castle, that he was some kind of government employee come to serve a notice.

'There's a letter here for Mr and Mrs Abrahamson,' he said. 'Pass it on now, Missy.'

That night, the Professor came back. Over the years, he'd become no more than a childhood bogeyman, a shadow glimpsed at the end of a very long corridor. Now he had returned, with his gaping mouth and his slurred eyes and the Party pin in his lapel. He was wearing the official's bottle-thick glasses and slavering like a dog on heat. Oskar was in the same dream, standing at the gate between their gardens. He didn't speak, seemed barely to notice her. He was holding something but she couldn't see what it was. She smelt the bonfire in the Müllers' garden, heard the clang as they hacked at her piano to add it to the flames. When she awoke, her pillow was wet. She thought of the photograph forgotten on the hall table, the lock of Oskar's hair she'd thrown away. She wished she had Herr Goldmann's spools, the ones she'd twirled and worried in her pockets until the threads became all tangled, orange, purple, pink. And then it dawned on her; Oskar had been holding the painted-over icon, the thing that had absorbed all their hatred and kept the Frankels safe. Because she hadn't got to the end of the dream, she'd never find out if he had retrieved it for her or whether he was about to add it to the fire.

The last time she'd written to Mama, just before Holland was overrun, she'd broken another spell. 'How are you really, Mama?' she'd asked. There were no more letters after that. What happened when all the magic charms had gone, when all the things that kept you safe were lost? What happened when pterodactyls could grow and grow and still stay aloft?

Charlie was used to hospitals but at first he couldn't work out why he was the one in bed. The nurse looking after him said her name was O'Neill and that she was from Monaghan. He liked Nurse O'Neill. She was very sensible, with large pink hands. She sluiced and primped him for the doctors like she was preparing him for a dog show. In spite of all her attentions, Charlie was troubled, his memory incomplete. He could still see the man who had beckoned him to jump but he could not picture the child, and it worried him to not be able to put a face on her. He'd no idea how long he'd been in the hospital but his memory of things beyond the fire had only just started to return. At first, Elsa was like a vapour for him. Something, he knew, had made him happy once. The touch of his own skin one day made him sure it was a girl and, little by little, Elsa took shape in his mind. He remembered her hiding the fish that Hilde had served up for the Shabbat dinner under a layer of mashed potato, her thick dark hair dancing on her shoulders as she turned to look at him. When Nurse O'Neill brought him his morning porridge, he asked her if he'd had many visitors.

'Droves,' she said. 'Now eat up.'

He tried again later, when she took him in a bite of lunch. She laid down the tray and stood back from the bed with her arms folded. 'Okay,' she said, 'spit it out. Did I remember?'

'Who came?'

'Well I wasn't asking for their birth certificates.' She cocked her head and sought inspiration from the long crack that ran down along the side of the wall. 'Okey dokey. Here goes. Your sister's been in here umpteen times. There was a rake of fellows from Surgeons. Another crowd who said they were from a musical society. There've been a couple of lads in sports jackets. I suppose there might have been a few girls in the musical crowd,' she looked at him shrewdly, 'but I couldn't put a name on any of them.'

'Was there a girl came on her own at all?' He tried not to sound too pathetic.

'No,' she said, straightening her belt, preparing to get on. 'Definitely not. I'd have noticed that.' She was all efficiency again but then she stopped a moment. 'Are you sure she even knows you're in here?'

He'd just assumed that all the different parts of his life would magically connect without him. The thought that Elsa mightn't have any idea what happened troubled him all night. His memory was returning in a haphazard, random fashion. By morning he had remembered Stamer Street.

It was the day for the consultant's ward round. Mr Dowling seemed to take particular exception to Charlie, perhaps because he was a medical student who therefore shouldn't also be a patient. For this reason, Charlie normally tried to keep a low profile. Now, though, he was desperate. He blurted out his question when Dowling stopped at the foot of his bed, his students trailing behind him like a streak of misery. 'Have you any idea how much longer I have to stay here?'

Dowling took off his little gold spectacles. Charlie didn't need to hear anymore. He was already an expert at reading consultant mannerisms.

'Do I have any idea?' He looked at Charlie with disdain, 'I thought Dr Kenny already told you it would be another week at least? Sister tells me that you have some medical training yourself?'

Charlie nodded.

'Then you should know better than to shop around for an opinion that suits you.'

As the last of the students trailed out of the ward, Charlie realised that compared to them, he was a free man. At the end of the day, he could do what he pleased, and he'd no intention of staying here longer than he had to. He shuffled over to the side of the bed and began to lower himself off it, gripping onto the metal bedstead and bracing himself for pain. Once he realised that he was able to hobble painlessly away from the bed, he was mad at himself for not having left days ago. He concentrated all his energy into mastering that walk from bed to wall, and back again. By the time he'd managed three trips back and forward, he had already decided that he would make his way over to Stamer Street, even if it took him all day and all night. He scribbled a message for Nurse O'Neill across the top of his medical notes and that was that. Nobody stopped him, even though he spent half an hour or so trying to negotiate the back stairs. Once he was outside and no longer had a handrail for support, his progress was very slow. Although he'd managed to grab his overcoat, he'd not been able to change out of his pyjamas. He probably looked like an escaped lunatic but he stuck his thumb out anyway, on the slim chance that someone would offer him a lift. No luck. The few vehicles on the road were already stuffed to the gills. By the time he reached Stamer Street, he was exhausted and his leg had begun to throb.

Bethel's face was solemn. Normally, he'd have thrown the door open right away but this time he only opened it a crack. Charlie tried to smile, though by now his leg was killing him. His ribs, too, had begun to hurt again, though he thought they'd healed. He held out his hand but Bethel didn't take it.

'Can I see her?'

'She's not here.'

'Don't shut the door on me, Bethel.' Charlie tried to keep his voice level, 'For God's sake, say something. What's happened to her?' He noticed that Bethel was only now beginning to take in the leg, the pyjamas. He began to try to explain but Bethel turned away. 'We've had a terrible time ourselves.'

'Just let me see her, Bethel. Please.'

'Some Jumped-up Johnny came calling on us last month. External Affairs, Justice: one or the other. Did I know it was a crime to harbour an illegal alien? Alien, if you don't mind. Like she was something dropped out of outer space. Miss Frankel, he said, your lodger, she's liable for deportation under section something or other. Deportation? I ask you, Byrne. Deportation to what?'

Charlie had begun to feel weak, and the pain in his ribs had sharpened. Bethel took his arm. 'You look like death warmed up, Byrne. Let's get you sitting down inside.'

They sat in the front parlour, as they'd done that first day. Charlie felt a little better now that he was in a place he'd been with Elsa, though his head refused to stop spinning.

'I wouldn't let the fellow in, so he had to say his piece on the doorstep there. On and on, he went. "Haven't we hungry mouths of our own to feed?" That kind of blather. "Wouldn't we be overrun if we took in every hard case?" Blah, blah, blah. Elsa said you'd know what to do. "He's so practical," she said. Then, a fortnight on, there was no show from you and one day it all got too much for her. Hilde got a terrible shock to see her. She was sitting at the piano but she wasn't playing a note. Just rocking. Back and forward. Back and forward. You just couldn't stop the rocking.'

'But where is she now?'

'She's in good hands.' For a moment it looked like that was all he was prepared to say, but then he seemed to take pity on

Charlie. 'She's being cared for down in Wicklow. They're the same people who tried to get visas for the parents and placed her with us in the first place. She'll have fresh air and a bit of peace and quiet. Esther will know how to look after her. She'll sort out those civil service Johnnies, too.' The thought seemed to cheer him up a bit, and he chuckled to himself, 'She's pull at the top, you see, Esther, and she's not afraid to use it.'

'When can I see Elsa, Bethel?'

'We have to go easy. I'll send word, and then we'll just have to wait and see. I don't want her upset.'

'You know I'd never do anything to upset her, Bethel. Surely to God, you know that by now.'

'Esther's very wary of visitors. When she came to pick Elsa up, she had a strange story. She told me that someone had come out to her, looking for Elsa. I thought it was some other penpusher, some other pain in the backside. But no, she said, not at all. The boy was a German. He wasn't one of us and yet he claimed to know Elsa. Esther was wary of the fellow, though she didn't think he could have come from the German Legation, dressed as he was. His clothes were filthy, she said, like he'd been sleeping rough. There was – how did she put it now? – a kind of desperation about him. He wouldn't give her a straight answer to anything, and she worried then that he might be someone trying to make trouble, though he seemed a gentle enough type. He did have some wild story about jumping out of a plane the night they bombed Belfast. Very strange, she said. A fantasist, I suppose. Who knows? Anyway, we decided to say nothing about it to Elsa. She'd been through enough as it was; no need to worry her any more.'

'If I saw her, I could bring her back. I know I could bring her back.'

'You're a good fellow, Byrne,' Bethel said, looking at him full-on for the first time that day, 'and you'll make a fine doctor. But, and excuse me if I sound like an old man talking down to a young one, even doctors can't fix everything. Just like love doesn't fix everything either.'

'It can't do any harm, though, can it, Sir? How can it do any harm?'

Bethel thought a moment. 'Esther's place is called Whitecrest.'

Charlie held out his hand, and this time Bethel took it. 'Good luck to you, Byrne.'

Apple Pie

Sean Galligan brought the gig to meet Kitty at the station. They sat in silence, a couple of Mother's heavy blankets spread across their laps. Kitty tried to strike up a conversation: carrots and leeks, Sean's brother over in Ballymeade who had the TB. She even resorted to raising the matter of the dampness of the summer weather, but Sean just sat there, barely moving, the whip licking at the horse's back.

When she got back to the house, Mother was waiting for her in the parlour. It was as though she hadn't moved a muscle in the weeks since Kitty had left. The only change was the black mantilla she slid down over her face as soon as Kitty appeared. 'You're back so?' she said, her breath puffing out the lace a little.

'What's the matter, Mother?'

'I got caught when the wind was on the turn. I look a fright.' She patted the mantilla down on each temple. 'You'll be grand in the old nursery, won't you pet? I had to give Bridie your room.'

'Who's Bridie?'

'Brigid Farrell. She's been helping me out this last while, since you went on your travels. The poor old stick spends that much time traipsing up and down to the house that when her sister died I thought she'd be as well with a bed here.'

Kitty said nothing, because there was nothing for her to say.

As she passed her old room on the landing, Kitty looked through the half-opened door. There were little grey rectangles on the sprigged wallpaper where her ballet prints had been. The mat had been rolled and stood upright in the corner, propped up behind the easy chair. In place of her old eiderdown, there was a crocheted blanket, and on the dressing table, little circlets of white lace and a statue of the Sacred Heart.

She was left to contemplate her comeuppance; the only daugher, so useless she had to be replaced with paid help. She stood at the window. You couldn't see the lime trees at this time of year, with all the other growth in the garden. She wasn't upstairs more than a few minutes when the rain whipped in from the sea. Down it came on the corrugated iron of the hen house, down into father's St Brendan bath. Not much of a homecoming.

In the old nursery, she lay down where Oskar had slept the night Mother was away. The bed sagged in the middle on account of all the childhoood trampolining she and Desmond had done, limbering up for the double somersaults that never were.

'From Timbuktu to Katmandu—'

'Up the Khyber—'

'And down the Orinoco—'

'The amazing—'

'The stupendous—'

'The Flying Hennessys!'

Downstairs, Brigid was standing on a chair dusting the old jam jars Mother kept on top of the dresser. Kitty greeted her usurper with elaborate friendliness. 'I hope you're finding the bed comfy, Brigid,' she said.

'The missus told me to stay put. She'll not hear of me moving.'

'Don't worry yourself. I'll be off back to Dublin in the morning. I'm only looking in, that's all.'

'There'll be no train until Monday, Missy,'

'Well, Monday it'll be then.'

Brigid crossed the room to shut the door. 'Poor Mrs Hennessy,' she said, confidentially. 'Went out in an east wind with damp hair. You can't make light of the damp.'

'Has she tried anything?'

'There's no cause to be visiting the doctor. The doctors don't understand the likes of the Bell's palsy.'

'And you do, I suppose.'

Brigid didn't miss the insult. 'I'll be here when she needs me to close up the eye at bedtime and tape it shut for the night. Even now, don't I do all her messages in the village, and there's no talking for her to do if she doesn't want to. I'm here on the spot, you see. I've no gallivanting to do.'

Later, Brigid cooked their own homegrown cabbage with some salty bacon. After dinner, she and Mother sat on either side of the fire, Brigid mending, jabbing nervously at a piece of frayed traycloth, Mother with her feet up reading *The French Huzzar*. Mother seemed to have stopped listening to the wireless. Whether that was a good or a bad thing, Kitty couldn't decide. Before she left, Brigid gave her some letters that had arrived while she was away. There was one from McWilliams' Commercial College saying she could have a place in the course that had started the previous month, one from Rita, and one with a foreign postmark, all stamped over with official markings.

Dear Kitty,

I am having a sheltered kind of a war. We have not seen much in the way of action so far but I think that is about to change. I wanted to tell you before we left here that yours is the face I took away from Ireland with me. If I'd said it then, I'd not have known if it was true, but now, each night, I think of you sitting up on a rock on Dunkerin Strand with your shells and your bits of seaweed you keep for God knows what. I would give a lot to smell that sea now and to see your dear face.

Your friend from the old days,
Con

The bombsites were on the other side of the city from Miss Effie's house, way beyond the wide boulevard with the column, but Oskar never got that far. The men who arrested him seemed to come from nowhere. They gave him a bit of a kicking, and some girls who were working at a hairdresser's on the other side of the street came out to have a look. He held onto the yellow scarf, though it was smeared with blood and oil and mud. Once he made it clear that he'd no intention of trying to escape, they let him alone. By the time they took him to the Curragh, they were almost benign. They treated his cuts and bruises and gave him thin soup to drink.

Oskar comforted himself with the thought that he had managed to find Miss Alexander and tell her his story. Even if she had not believed him then, he was sure that she would come to do so. Lots of people had witnessed his arrest, after all. There had even been a man with a camera there; he recalled the loud pop and flare of the magnesium. He felt sure that if Elsa was in Ireland, she would be told of Oskar Müller and his efforts to find her. She might even see his photograph herself in one of the newspapers that were sold on every corner. He kept telling the men who'd picked him up that he was not part of the war. He told them he'd jumped. Every day he told them, until he was blue in the face. He hoped they would write about him in their newspapers: the man who jumped out of the sky.

Back in Dublin, at the end of a long rainy summer, Kitty wondered if the whole thing had taken more out of her than she realised. She was exhausted and her stomach churned at the sight of food. Aunt Effie tried a combination of infusions but none of them worked. She sent Ranjit out to HCR for an Alpine tonic but Kitty was no better.

'You're expecting,' Aunt Effie said finally. 'That's all's the matter with you.'

By the next month, the sickness was passing, but the thought of the baby made her panic. She feared what it would make of her life. How she would live. Where she would live. She hoped it would go away. She begged it to go away. But the baby stayed put. One day she felt a little bump at the pit of her stomach. That, she supposed, was it. Aunt Effie advised her against going back to Dunkerin. 'Haven't you just come from it?' she said. 'Go back now and the fingers will be pointing, the tuts will be tutting. Dunkerin's the last place you should go. Stay here and in time you'll make your own way. Haven't you the typing now?'

It was in the middle of one more sleepless night that Kitty decided to go to the Curragh. The day before she left, she made an apple pie in Aunt Effie's kitchen. She added a bit of potato to stretch the apple and sprinkled some precious sugar on the top. She felt sick the whole way to Newbridge on the bus. To make sure nobody came and crowded her out, she put the string bag containing the apple pie on the seat next to her. The nearer she got to the camp, the more inclined she became not to see him, just to hand the apple pie in at the gate. She couldn't rely on herself not to burst into tears.

When the bus approached Newbridge, the girls around her fussed about with powder puffs and lipsticks. Someone offered her some mascara but she didn't bother with any of that. She was first off the bus and walked briskly up to the camp; she tried to get as far ahead of the others as possible so as not to have to enter into conversation.

The soldier at the gate seemed nice enough. He had a list, and when she told him who she was visiting, he ran his finger right the way down the Ms. Menten. Mollenhauer. No Müller. 'Sorry pet, he must have gave you a *nom de plume*.'

The soldier beside him sniggered, 'A bun in the oven, more like.'

'Shut up you and mind your manners.' Then he looked at her and maybe he guessed the other soldier was right. She could tell he felt sorry for her and she couldn't stand it, the look of pity on his face.

'That German shower, strutting round Newbridge like a pack of turkey cocks, they'd give you the pip. They're never done with strutting and marching and all that carry on. As for the girls round here, sure they've no sense at all. Some of the young ones we get up at the gate, weeping and wailing. Apple pies and barmbracks and God knows what. "Would you pass this on to Hans, Mister, would you? He's half starved in there." Half starved, my arse.' He checked his list one more time, running his finger down the columns. 'I'm sorry, pet, there's definitely no Müller in this lot.'

As she walked back down the road, Kitty flung the pie, bag and all, into the ditch. The girls walking in the opposite direction and chattering away like little sparrows fell silent as she passed. Maybe, they were worried the lads weren't being let out into Newbridge tonight after all, or maybe they were embarrassed for her. One or two of them called after her but she just ignored them. If she hurried, she might just be in time to catch the same bus back into town.

Ever After

Kitty

Kitty fingers the little pile of memory cards. She's not one for the creeping-Jesus kind of stuff they usually say; all she asked the printers to put on them was, 'Goodnight, Con.' The picture she chose was taken on the beach at Ownahincha the summer before. Con is smiling straight at the camera. He looks like he has a good twenty years in him yet. She's been dreading the first anniversary; just hopes she'll have enough strength in her to put a brave face on it for Clara and the boys. Then the phone rings and she rushes into the hall to answer it.

'Clara! How are you, pet? Of course I'll be there. What'll I get in? Chicken nuggets, the usual muck? Ah, you say that, but I've never seen them eat anything decent.'

Kitty rummages around in the kitchen cupboard for a tin of Horlicks. She despises the stuff, but all the same she decides it's probably what she should have in the circumstances: that and a long, bubbly bath. Time was it would have been a large brandy but after the trouble she had in the month or two after Con's death, she tries to stay clear of that now. She runs the bath, then fluffs up the bubbles with her hand and lies back, the water reaching right up to her collarbone.

She will never forget the day she first saw Con again after the war. He was demobbed sometime in 1946, when Clara was around four. Effie was still alive then, though Ranjit was long gone. The Truthseekers had tailed off and she'd taken to advertising for new recruits in *The Irish Times*. On first glance, Kitty assumed that's what Con was when she opened the door to him: someone come to Effie, looking for the Light. He was very failed that first time. His hair was more grey than sandy and he'd grown a little military moustache that perched awkwardly on his upper lip.

Right from the start, Con behaved as though they already had an understanding. She didn't realise then that war turns men soft in the head. They sat in the kitchen over a pot of tea, and he took her hand in both of his. He told her he recalled something she'd said about keeping to *terra firma*. He'd been afraid that was a bad omen when his battalion set off for Normandy on D-Day by glider but he'd got away with it all right. Afterwards, he was part of the final push through the Low Countries into Germany.

He came across such awful things in the last weeks of the war that he could never bear anything German afterwards. There was no talking to him. It was not something he was prepared to be rational about. His battalion was first into Bergen Belsen and, although he never spoke of it, she was sure that what he saw there remained always in the tiny fractures in his grey irises, in the thinness of his smile. Con was always searching for proof that innocence could be recaptured, dreams resealed. He couldn't bear unpleasantness of any kind and, when the end came, Kitty was glad he had a nice clean death. He deserved that.

All through the pregnancy, she'd been raw with the thought that the baby she was carrying was not really hers. After all, the love that made it belonged to Elsa Frankel, not to her. So it was a wonderful gift Con gave her when he lifted Clara that day he came home from the war. 'How's my little angel?' he said, and kissed her on the cheek.

It was as though Clara had been conceived at long distance, as far as Con was concerned. He never asked about the natural father at all. 'It's just one of the things that happens in a war,' he said once, 'and aren't we the lucky ones.'

She didn't look like Oskar but she wasn't a Hennessy either. Clara had eyes like a cat and loose brown curls. Kitty used to conjure up lost relatives for her from somewhere in the ruins of Berlin; people whose features she had borrowed while they did whatever they had done.

She had much to thank Effie for. Lately, there'd been a lot of hoo-ha about the Magdalene Laundries and how there were girls went into the homes to have their babies and ended up spending forty years scrubbing socks for their sins. Des made sure she was looked after on the medical side. Mother used to say he suffered for Kitty's shame when he came home to Dunkerin to make his own practice, but Des never complained.

Marrying Con was easy. It didn't seem wrong, even if it didn't seem exactly right either. Each was the other's protector. They bought a little house in a cul-de-sac in Stillorgan and Kitty counted herself lucky enough. Con worked in insurance and she had a job herself until she was able to give it up and concentrate on the amateur dramatics.

Even though she had no picture of him, no letter from him, no clear image of him in her head anymore, she sometimes thought of Oskar long after she'd got over the humiliation of landing up at the Curragh looking for a fellow who'd given her another name. Whoever he was, he wasn't Oskar Müller. She sometimes wondered what the truth of it all was, whether there was really a girl or not, whether he was really a spy or not. Not that it mattered now, anyway.

Years later, a friend who'd once worked as a clerk in the Department of Justice told her that most of the men in the Curragh didn't want to go back to Germany when the war ended. Some applied for residency, or whatever it was called, but the authorities wouldn't let them stay. Once the news came out of the camps, no one wanted a German about the place. The only way they'd let one stay on was if he was marrying an Irish girl. Did it never cross his mind, she wondered, to come looking for her as he claimed to have done for Elsa Frankel? Even just to be allowed stay on?

She was over in Dunkerin the year before last, just before Con's illness was diagnosed. It was strange to be back in the old house: one of those country house hotels now. She'd had afternoon tea there, in Mother's drawing room. It was all painted white and smothered with brash canvases with great daubs of paint on them. They'd converted a couple of the outhouses to accommodation and at the time there were a couple of Germans and French staying there for the fishing. She didn't mention that first German tourist but she thought of him all the same.

The bleakest day of her whole life was the day she went to the Curragh camp to find Oskar. She got the bus straight back to Dublin that same day, didn't register a single thing about the journey. Just couldn't wait to get away from the place. She'd had her answer from Oskar Müller or whoever he was. She remembered crying a lot. Aunt Effie had Ranjit up and down the stairs like a yo-yo with peppermint tea and nettle soup and God knows what. It didn't help that she couldn't keep anything down. Then one day she just decided to get on with it. She never tried to find him again.

Now that Con was gone, there was no need for secrets any-more. She felt fit as a fiddle. Still, there was no arguing with nature; the end would come sooner rather than later. In the year since Con's death she'd been plagued with the thought that she should tell Clara the truth. Some Christmas in the unimaginable years ahead when she might be herself again. A few glasses of sherry and out it would come.

Clara had been an unadventurous child. She never asked questions. She did, by and large, what she was told and caused very little trouble for anyone. They'd never told her that she was anything other than Con's daughter. Now and then, things cropped up that could have opened doubts in the mind of a different sort of child. The time Clara was mad keen on learn-ing German and Kitty cried herself to sleep until she settled on Spanish instead. The time there was the school trip to

Berlin and Kitty refused point blank to let her go. Maybe Clara just didn't want to know; maybe that's why she'd never asked. Still, Kitty wondered whether it was right to let her grow old without knowing the truth. She had asked herself that many times and each time she had given up the deliberations for want of a satisfactory answer. Instinct told her it was safer to do nothing than to make the wrong decision.

Clara and the children arrive in the middle of a storm of driving rain: sheets of the stuff wash over the windscreen and the wipers are powerless to cope with it. At the airport, Kitty marvels at how nowadays, every time she visits it, they seem to have added another bit on or dug a great pit in the ground or enlarged a car park. Funny, she thinks, how it seems that for years and years everything just stays the same, and then suddenly you blink and it's all changed entirely.

When Clara appears at the arrivals exit, she struggles to get through the crowds. There seem to be some footballers arriving in on the same flight because there's a clatter of young fellows dressed in red and white calling for 'Keano'. Clara looks very tired, she thinks. She's beginning to seem her age now, after years and years of looking like a schoolgirl. The two boys trail along behind her, looking bored. One of them has an earring. Kitty is glad she hasn't gone to too much trouble to find those old fishing rods; neither of them looks like the fishing type.

The boys slouch in the back seat. From the moment they arrive, she is uncomfortable with them and a bit self-conscious. In her fuss, she scrapes the door on one of the concrete pillars in the car park. She can hear one of the boys tut-tutting in the back. It makes her mad but she says nothing, and by the time they cross the East Link she has begun to relax.

'So, what about you, Mummy?' Clara asks. 'What were you up to today?'

The only things that matter are deep inside her head. None of them fits the occasion, so she says something about going through the freezer. She even mentions the visit to Superquinn, even though it has always been her policy never to descend to discussing visits to the supermarket. She hears one of the boys move about in the back seat and whisper something to his brother.

They pass the National Museum. A great big tethered flag announces the exhibition: 'Navigatio: Brendan and the Promised Land'. She opens her mouth to say something about Father and his model curragh, then remembers the boys whispering together and decides against it.

She gets home and makes the boys a supper of chicken nuggets and chips and heats up the casserole she prepared earlier for Clara and herself. The boys look sulkier than ever, until Clara explains, 'It's just, Mummy, they don't really eat that kind of thing any more. They'll just eat what we eat.'

Kitty feels for the second time that day that she's failed to match up. She and Clara stay on in the kitchen after the boys have gone into the sitting room to watch television.

'Did you think about joining something, Mummy? A charity maybe, something like that?' Clara takes her hand and squeezes it. 'You could go back to the Dramatic Society, help out behind the scenes. It must be so lonely for you now. I often think how lucky you and Daddy were to find one another, with a war between you. How lucky you were to find love at the end of the line.'

She's right, of course. Clara has always been such a sensible child, with all the right instincts. Kitty looks at the face that comes from somewhere else and realises that it's too late for German classes now. It's much too late for new things. She will let it be.

Oskar

West Cork: Summer 1999

At the airport in Frankfurt, Oskar slips away while Karl and Sophie argue over what kind of perfume to buy Ute, who doesn't wear the stuff anyway. The electrical shop isn't hard to find. Oskar has always liked gadgets; he likes them even better now they make them smaller, smoother, steelier.

He lets the Dictaphone sit snug in his palm and tries to remember the last time he used one. Not since retirement, probably. Greta? Gretl? Gisela? One of those nervy girls they employed to plough syntax into his wandering prose. The young fellow who sells him the machine is patronising, uninterested. Boredom is no excuse, and Oskar tells him so. Outside the shop, Oskar savours his acquisition. He discards the packaging, and turns the little steel machine over and back in the palm of his hand. Then he rejoins Sophie and Karl, who are waiting anxiously at the departure gate. Sophie is biting the corner of her lower lip just like her mother used to do. Karl is listening to his Tag Heuer, clapping it to his ear.

They give him the window seat. As he looks out over the cloud landscape, he thinks how some things never change. Even now he feels the catch of excitement at his throat. It was a grey day down there in Frankfurt but up here it's radiant. Sophie and Karl are still talking about the presents they've bought Ute. Oskar knows Ute will thank them, then hide the items away or give them to friends. Ute: he's looking forward to seeing her, spiky little thing. After a while, he's surprised to feel his mood change; he is melancholy all of a sudden. Then he realises that they've commenced the descent. It always had that effect on him, even back in the old days when he was cold and terrified, suspended there in the gondola. He always hated to leave the sky: things were always worse on land.

In the terminal, they stand looking blankly at the black flaps on the surface of the carousel. It starts then stops again. By the time the luggage chugs past them, Oskar is tired. He sits in the back of the rented car as they drive along winding roads flanked on either side by high hedgerows. Ute lives miles from the city, down among the ragged inlets that trail off the end of the map. When at last they arrive, he allows Sophie to help him out of the car. He declines the offer of coffee and lowers himself onto the narrow pine bed. He sleeps without dreams. In the morning, he wakes to wan light and birds. More birds than seem possible.

He gets out of bed and surveys the line of hedge on the other side of the window. There is no sound from Sophie and Karl so he does a little light unpacking. He too has bought Ute a present: a beautiful little clay pipe he bought in a Turkish shop near the station. No doubt she'll have something to smoke in it. He lays out his things on the windowsill as though he is dressing it: a scarf for his throat, a small bottle of schnapps, and the journal. He wedges his clothes between his palms and drops them onto the floor of the wardrobe.

He has already decided to give Ute the journal of his time in Ireland. If not on this holiday, then he will leave it to her when the time comes. Just before this trip he reread it for the first time in decades. He reread it with a old man's heart, knowing all the things he didn't know at twenty-odd. He realised that what it needed was a dose of retrospective realism. He couldn't change what he had written at twenty, nor would he want to, but he just had to point up the self-delusion in it, the folly.

He is past writing anything these days. It's not that there's any physical impediment; no arthritis in the hands, nothing like that. Somehow he just can't make the time to form his thoughts into sentences on a page. He can still talk, though, if it's into a little machine.

At lunchtime, they visit the pub where Ute is working part-time behind the bar. The moment she sees them she makes straight for Oskar. That's my girl, he thinks. When she speaks, he notices that her German is a little off-key. He wonders how soon that would have happened to him, had he stayed.

'How are you, you old rascal?' she says, punching him in the solar plexus.

'Careful, Ute.' Good old Sophie.

'Oh, he's solid steel,' Ute says, punching him again, not so hard this time. Her hair is purple, her skinned tanned despite the climate. She is brown and purple, peat and heather, like her pots. He catches her hand and eases the loose package into it. She rips off the paper and waves the little meerschaum at her friend behind the bar. Then she takes Oskar's face in her hands and kisses it. One. Two. Three. A man with a crumpled mouth looks up for a second, then returns to his pint.

'So, Ute, what have you planned for me?'

'I'm taking you for a walk this afternoon. I'll call for you when I finish my shift, take you up on the cliff.'

'That would be lovely,' Sophie says.

'Oh, I'm not taking you two. No offence, it's just me and the old man.'

Tape One: 14 August 1999

My name is Oskar Müller (but, of course, you know that). Born Berlin 1919, in the autumn. You told me that made me a Libran. I don't know if that is illuminating for you. It means nothing to me. I have been married twice. Generally speaking, I don't count the first time. A couple of years after the war, I married a girl from Bremen. It was short and poisonous, no more than a month or two, and I remember her no better than the others for having married her.

I met your grandmother a year or two later. Rosa would have hated your hair, by the way. She liked things to be how they should be. She was sweet, and she was my salvation. In the early days, after I decided to study architecture, there wasn't much money. She worked hard, too, at her teaching. In those days, we tried not to think too much about the past. By the time we were able to cast the occasional glance over our shoulders, it was too late really to come to terms with it. As for our own children, they showed surprisingly little curiosity about how life had been for us during the war. I think your uncle Rolf jumped to his own conclusions. He never asked me anything at all about the war, or what I did or didn't do. Perhaps he just assumed I must have done something dreadful. Sometimes I think that's why he went off to Africa: to flay himself for what he feared I might have done. Your mother, if she thought about it at all, seems to have assumed that whatever I did in the war must have been skilled, workmanlike, honourable. Sophie has always considered me beyond reproach.

With two such sensible children, I was delighted when you came along. You were always trouble, Ute. Poor Sophie was in despair most of the time. You were incomprehensible to her. No sooner had she told herself that she'd found a tree that you would never manage to climb, than you'd be stuck at the top like a wild kitten. I've always loved you for it, and I wasn't surprised when you told them you were off. What were you, six-teen? Sophie almost managed to catch up with you but then she lost you again on the edge of an autobahn as you hopped into that lorry. Poor old Karl, he didn't know what to tell the boys at that place he went riding. All their kids were thinking of sensible careers. War-proof things like physiotherapy. And there you were, off to Ireland to make pots.

My birthdays have been much marked since your grand-mother died. Each one that comes, Sophie packs everything she *can into it, in case I keel over on my next walk. She won't even let me have cream in my coffee any more, for God's sake. Which is how this visit came about. Last month, as you know, I turned eighty. Sophie suggested Ireland. Somewhere you've never been, she said, go visit Ute. I almost laughed out loud. Sophie loves so much to control and curb. Just think what she used to do to the honeysuckle! I just can't resist leaving her in the dark at times. So, here we are in Ireland and your mother has not the slightest idea that I've ever been here before.*

That evening, Ute leads them to her house, weaving all over the road on her bicycle as she rides ahead of the car. Sophie is clutching the steering wheel with her driving gloves on. Karl is asleep. The place is below the level of the road, half hidden behind a high bank of nettles. She shares it with a young man with a beard and a fisherman's sweater. She says he's a poet, and maybe the eyes do look a little mad, always flicking up to the clouds like he's lost something up there. His name is Finn and he touches her a lot. Even the sharp prickles on her head seem to relax a little when he's around. Oskar's little sparrow is in love.

Tape One, continued, 15 August 1999

I notice that paint has come into fashion in Ireland now. The pink house next to the yellow, rubbing shoulders with the green and the blue. There was none of that when I was here. I moved from hard and bright to dimly lit. Life had been so noisy, then someone switched the sound off.

Oskar is walking on the cliff road with Ute. They don't say much to one another. Just as he is wondering if she has listened to the first part of the tape yet, she leads him off the road they have walked every other day. They cut off at the crossroads and take the low road to the beach. Ute sits on a rock, skimming stones, while Oskar props himself up beside her on his shooting stick. What a strange sight they must make: Ute all cropped and dyed and himself bald as an eagle. Of course, she asks him the obvious questions. Why did you come here? Were you shot down? Were you hurt? Were you sent here, perhaps? He asks himself why it is often the wayward child who becomes interested in family history?

I was interned here for over four years in the Curragh, G-Camp. There were airmen, mariners, too. The people who picked me up were part-time soldiers and were rougher than they needed to be. The officers who brought me to the camp in the back of a car, they were fine. I was dressed in civilian clothes and it felt like a Sunday outing. When we arrived at the camp, I was shown into a room where an Irish officer with a ruddy complexion told me to sit myself down. Even though I hadn't planned to, I told him the truth: that I'd jumped.

'Good lad,' he said.

To him, it seemed a reasonable thing to do, to desert from the Luftwaffe. I wondered at the time how neutral he thought he was. He just licked his pencil and wrote down what I said.

'We'll keep that under our hats,' he said then. 'Best to keep the other German lads in the dark on that one.' They signed me in as Konrad Ritter, just in case anyone might have heard of me. So, throughout my time in the camp, I wasn't Oskar Müller at all. Losing your name has a strange effect. You start to become someone else. You realise that things are easier to change than you supposed. That helped, after the war was over. I was already more adaptable than other people. I understood that life comes in phases.

As for the camp, there was lots to eat but little variety: potatoes, meat, eggs, bacon, cabbage. Tea and sugar were in short supply, but there was milk and plenty of terrible bread. Time out, yes. Tennis tournaments, a little gardening, cinema now and then, and dances in the local towns. No shortage of girls to dance with, either.

Even so, I was never really at ease. I always worried that someone would guess the truth about me, or that someone knew all along and was waiting for the right time to pounce.

The first week I was in the camp I had a visitor: an official fellow from our Legation in Dublin. He was standing with his back to the window when they showed me into the room and I couldn't see him very well. There was just this voice, and at first I thought the game was up; it was quite the opposite, in fact. He told me it was a pity I couldn't have managed to stay out of trouble a little longer. 'No one in Berlin seems to know any-thing about you,' he said. He congratulated me on staying out of Athlone (which was where the Irish put the spies). He assumed my task must have had breathtaking significance, and I played along. He wanted to debrief me but I sent him off with his tail between his legs. He went away thinking there was something he didn't have the clearance to be told. After that, I was Konrad Ritter, the spy they didn't rumble. It gave me some kudos with the other internees and a more comfortable cover story. Better a spy than a deserter. Joachim had told me so much about Dresden that it was easy for me to talk plausibly of life there, in a super-ficial sort of a way. I lived in Joachim's house, went to his school, met my girlfriends in the same parks and cafés. I was just lucky, I suppose, that there was no one to contradict me.

Konrad Ritter or not, there was always the chance that someone would recognise me. In my nightmares, it was always a member of my own crew. I had barely given them another thought until arriving at G-camp. Perhaps it was the other men who put them in my mind, but once I was in the Curragh I thought of them every day. I was desperate to know that they made it home safely. On bad days, I examined all the worst-case scenarios. My greatest fear was that they'd been caught in a spot-

light over England, shot down because they'd missed the extra gunner. Then, twenty years on, I was on a street in Frankfurt on my way to do a site survey and I saw Willy coming towards me. He crossed the road to avoid me. I thought that was interesting, that he was the one who felt ashamed.

I formed comradely enough friendships with some of the airmen in the camp but there was always a gulf between us, because, of course, everything I pretended to be was false. They took me under their wing on the basis that, whatever else I was, at least I was better than the sailors who had to be dragged from the sea by the Irish like drowned rats. But Ute, I haven't told you the reason for all this. I haven't told you about Elsa Frankel.

He talks about Elsa: how they grew up together side by side; how they were only two years apart but it might have been ten until they reached their middle teens and fell in love; how, even then, it was impossible to be together except in the secret places they discovered by the lake, in the woods. A little uneasy at how much he is revealing, he gives the tape to Ute. That night, he sleeps badly. It's not his bad shoulder or the grinding of his heart that's disturbing him. It's that he simply cannot remember Elsa's face. The young man he once was would never have believed such a thing possible. He would have been horrified to lose that face.

The next day, Ute doesn't go to work. She has arranged for Sophie and Karl to spend a day at Ballymaloe and Oskar tries not to show how glad he is to be free of them. Ute doesn't say much at breakfast but he notices how she is gentler with him, quieter. She packs a picnic and they go off in her little car. After half an hour or so they turn inland from a little harbour. A little further on, she stops and they walk a half kilometre or so off the road through a tunnel of fuchsia. At the end of the tunnel, there is a stile, which he negotiates stiffly, and beyond that a field where wildflowers surround a stone circle. Ute seems to find in the profusion of wildflowers there evidence of some spiritual richness in the land itself. It amuses him, this faith in nature.

The fact that Elsa was Jewish is everything to Ute. It seems to absolve him of the responsibility of his generation. She refuses to believe that, when the war ended, he simply went back home to Berlin and made no further effort to find her. She cannot accept that he allowed that to happen.

'But I knew,' he says, 'that I must leave that all behind me.'

'After it all came out about the things that had happened – the camps and all the rest of it – did you not have the urge to tell people about how you tried to find her?'

'Tell them what?'

'That you didn't agree with all that. That you tried to change things.'

'Change things? How? By running away? I did nothing to change things.'

'You wanted to, though, didn't you? I mean, clearly you didn't support what they did.'

'Perhaps, if I hadn't known Elsa, I would have been the same as the others.'

'That's ridiculous.'

'Have you ever heard of a *hausjude*, Ute?'

She shakes her head, and he can see the word makes her wince.

'Even the most rabid anti-semite would have known some-one they considered not quite as bad as the others, not quite typical. A kindly shopkeeper, perhaps, or a schoolfriend. Who's to say that Elsa Frankel was not just that, my own personal *hausjude*?'

'But you stepped outside it all. You threw yourself out of a plane, for God's sake. Just after bombing Belfast. You couldn't stand being part of the regime. You were against everything they stood for, and you had to find Elsa Frankel.'

'Maybe I just didn't like war. Maybe I wanted to sleep in a

soft bed for a change, get away from the smell of men cooped up together. Don't assume that I was any better than the others. Perhaps I was just more fortunate because I knew they were wrong.'

She looks glum. 'Let's go,' she says.

For a moment he wonders, too, what explanation there could be for the profusion of wildflowers in this meadow. Flowers don't grow like this in Germany any more. They've been crowded out by supermarkets and petrol stations. Suddenly, he feels rooted to this little meadow with its ancient stones and stubborn wildflowers. It feels, for a moment, as though to step off this land would be to lose all memory of how he'd seen things when he was twenty.

Sophie and Karl are late back from their day at the cookery school. They are curious about what an old man could have to say all day to his granddaughter. Sophie seems a little nervous as to what they might have in common. That night, Oskar hears Ute tapping away on her computer. The noise of it keeps him awake, so he gives into wakefulness and takes out his little Dictaphone. He wonders if they can hear him, mumbling away to himself. They'll probably think he's finally lost his marbles.

It was just after Easter – not long after Joachim was killed. My mind was turned inside out by his death. The bus picked us up at the Hotel at about 1900 hours to bring us out to the airfield for the final briefing. We didn't know for sure until then whether it was definitely Belfast. The Etappe, we called it. Staging post. I don't think I really made my mind up to jump until the very last moment.

Years later, I was watching something on television with my grandchildren. You may even have been there yourself, Ute. It was a comedy film and they had a way of making a drink seem to pour itself back into a glass, a custard pie fly back off a face. It came back to me then, sitting on a couch in Sophie's house watching television with her children. As soon as I jumped out of that plane, I wished that I could fly upwards again and land back where I had started. I was elated to have tumbled free of the plane, but I was terrified too.

The next morning, getting out of bed is an effort. Ute is like a little current of electricity, energising them all. She has already been down at the pottery and has dropped by to leave them in some fresh bread and milk. When she finds Oskar sitting alone in the breakfast room, she closes the door behind her.

'I have such exciting news for you,' she says. 'You're not going to believe who I've tracked down.'

He knows, of course, but the girl is speaking as though it is all just a soap opera, and it irritates him.

'Why?'

'Wouldn't you love to know how her life turned out? Where she went, who she married, what she did? Were there children? Oh, a hundred questions.'

'Ute, I jumped. I didn't risk my neck in sabotage or revolt. I jumped. I don't even know now whether I did it for Elsa Frankel. Maybe I did it to get away. What had I hoped for? I hadn't even thought about it. I hadn't even done the most basic planning. No provisions, nothing. I'd deliberately left behind my emergency rations, my maps. God knows why, I can't remember now. I was pathetic, useless. I was arrested almost as soon as my feet touched the ground. I had no chance of finding her anyway.'

'I'm sure it's the same person. Got to be. Right age, in or around, German Jew, ended up in New York.'

'No,' he says. 'No more.'

She flinches and he regrets being so firm with her. 'I'd rather leave it be.'

Tape Two, 18 August 1999

When the time came to leave, they gave us next to no notice at all. Even those who had local girlfriends were marched onto the train and sent packing as soon as the war ended. I still wanted Elsa, of course, but I was too guilty and shocked by the pictures from the Nazi's own camps, the KZs, to feel worthy of her, even if I'd had the option.

It was a long way home; the boat to England, and then a sealed train through England to the coast and across to Ostend. From there, we got a train to Brussels, where they held us for a couple of weeks. Everyone said there was no point in going back to Berlin, that there was nothing there. But I had to see it again.

There was utter devastation, of course. Just little huddles of people hiding in the ruins of bomb-damaged buildings. I am so glad now that Joachim didn't live to see what happened to his beloved Dresden.

I had no idea where my family was. I did find one or two schoolfriends, girls who had stayed in the family home. Here and there, some houses were still more or less in one piece. Our own place was completely destroyed, the Frankels' too. It was a long time before there was any system set up to try and find relatives but eventually I did find Vati, sleeping rough. Mutti had been killed in an air raid, he told me. He didn't know what had happened to Emmi. The last Vati heard, she'd gone off with Reinhard on a family posting to a KZ over in the east. Vati was cagey about what he'd known of what was happening in those camps, about what Emmi must have known. I wanted to believe him, for Emmi's sake as much as for his own, but I couldn't. I saw him once or twice only after that. The last time I went to find him at his usual spot, he wasn't there.

She ran through my life like a red thread, Ute. Like a red thread. I would love to have seen her one more time. Even just once. From a distance, maybe. From the balcony in a concert hall. Through a telescope. Then closer, maybe. But not so close that she could spot me. Not until I'd decided how close I could allow her to get. All my life I've been looking for her. Running away from her pale copies, choosing the women who least resemble her. And now you find her in an evening.

It's the day of their departure and Oskar takes his final walk here. Most days, his knees give him trouble but his back is still good. Stiffly, he walks, in his green jacket, the same walk each day since he first arrived. He closes the front door quickly to keep out the wind, then walks fifteen paces to the base of the hill. A sherbet-green field angles sharply to the left, like it's propped up against the sky. Plump black and white cows clutch at its surface. To the right, long grass slopes to the sea. All around, the hedgerows are rippling with flowers. He doesn't know many of their names but one flower is everywhere. It is red with purple droplets and it spots the hedgerows like some spectacular affliction. He's been told that it's the fuchsia.

Oskar walks close enough to the edge of the cliff to see the spray tease the rocks below. The voice in his head – Sophie's – tells him to stop that now. After that, the walk loses its charm and he turns around on the pivot of his stick and heads back towards the cottage, where they will all be waiting. Sophie will flap. Karl will examine his Tag Heuer. Ute, though, will understand. She understands everything now.

Outside the rented cottage, he sees the car that Ute uses; the Irishman's little car with the battered red number plate. Ute has been to the city. She has brought something for Oskar to take back to Germany with him. It's a record, an old recording, American. She says it never came out on CD.

'It's not that she became famous or anything,' she says. 'It's a minor label, I think. It would probably never have reached Ireland only it's Field's Nocturnes. When you boil it down there aren't that many recordings. Look, Elsa Frankel plays Field. 1960. New York.' She hands him the sleeve. He can tell she's proud of herself and he tries to smile but all he can think of is how many years he has lost. He looks for a photograph but there isn't one, just a potted life story that breaks his heart.

Elsa Frankel was born in Berlin. An only child, her parents perished in the Nazi holocaust. Elsa herself escaped to Belfast thanks to the Kindertransports. She lived briefly in Dublin after the war before emigrating to the United States with her Irish husband, Dr Charles Carolan Byrne.

Ute's poet has a record player and she has brought that with her, too. She watches Oskar while she puts it on. He doesn't recognise the music; at least he doesn't think he does. It sounds like Chopin, and he closes his eyes. The music drenches his prune of a heart until the loss of her seems too much to bear. Her face is a crisp snapshot in his head and then it fades again. Can an old man cry for the young man he once was? Ute's voice is in his ear, her arm around his shoulder.

'You see, it was for her. You tried.'

Sophie is there now, too; a look of horror when she sees his face like that. She offers pills for pain, pills for the heart. Karl is checking his Tag Heuer. They will miss the flight, he says, if they don't get going.

It is Ute who puts her foot down. She shoos her parents out of the room and shuts the door behind them. Then, she sits down next to Oskar and takes his hand. 'You can't just give up now.'

Her face is full of hope and energy and he wishes, how he wishes, he was her age again. What a waste it's all been.

'Let them get their flight. You stay here. I'm sure we can find much more. Her address, maybe even her phone number.'

She leaves the room, and on the other side of the door, the voices grow louder. Karl is saying they can't hang around indefinitely. 'This is just so typical,' he says. But Oskar's head is full of Elsa. Sophie comes in, wearing her mac, with her handbag on her shoulder. She has her hands stretched out as if to catch the rain; another of those gestures that belonged to her mother.

'What do you think you're doing?' she asks.

He pats the seat beside him. 'Come, Sophie. Sit here next to me.'

'We have got to go,' she is saying. 'Now, Vati. Right now.'

He shakes his head, and she looks at him askance. 'Are you ill? Is something the matter?'

'I have unfinished business.'

'Not here, Vati, surely. In Ireland?'

Ute has come back in the room. She has his suitcase, which she wheels over into a corner.

'What is this business Vati is talking about?'

Ute waits for Oskar to say something but all he says is that he needs a little more time in Ireland. 'After all, there's no reason for me to go back to Germany. Who's waiting for me there? You don't mind, Sophie.'

It's a statement, not a question, and she doesn't argue.

'No,' she says, 'I suppose not. But you know how you like to have your things around you, everything just so. You've seen what Ute is like: chaos.'

He smiles and so does she. 'I'll be fine. Ute will find me another flight, when the time is right. With that computer of hers, she can move mountains.'

He knows he is getting ahead of himself but he is already imagining a cross-Atlantic flight, something he has only done once, at Rosa's insistence, to visit friends who lived in a terrible place in Florida with high walls and a swimming pool so blue it hurt his eyes.

Sophie knows when she's beaten. 'Well if you're sure,' she says. 'But remember to give me some notice so I can pick you up at Frankfurt.'

He can tell she thinks he'll be home in a day or two. He doubts that.

When they've gone, Ute locks up the rented house and leaves the key under a large stone by the gate. Back at her own cottage, she makes him a salad with some of that goat's cheese she likes. She puts on a lamp next to his chair and lights a little stack of peat in the grate. Her poet is with friends in the village and she says she will go and join him and they will find somewhere to connect to the internet. He wants to go with her but she shakes her head.

'Best stay here,' she says. 'You can start composing your letter. Who knows, maybe I'll have an address for you when I get back. Oh, and there's no point talking into that thing,' she points to the Dictaphone. 'How's she going to listen to those? You can use my tape recorder instead.'

When she has gone, he starts to speak to the new machine. He imagines he is talking to Elsa, though of course he is not sure who she is any more. She may be horrified by him. She may even have forgotten him. He knows, too, that it is possible he has left it too late. But he doesn't try to second-guess any of that. He just imagines the girl he knew and tells her the story as though it's something that happened to two other people, a long time ago. He talks and talks, and has filled both the tapes Ute gave him before he realises that he no longer has any doubts. There are no ifs and buts. He is face to face with the optimism of youth. He jumped for Elsa. Just for her. The realisation is an enormous relief. He pours himself a large whiskey and sits and looks into the fire. The briquettes have crumbled to powder, but here and there, hot nuggets remain. He throws on some more peat but it doesn't take, so he starts from scratch, with kindling and a pyramid of fuel, until the fire is brought back again.

When Ute returns, she joins him by the fire. The poet is there too, but he doesn't linger, just wishes them good night from the door. 'We went to the pub,' she says, 'had a word with the local GP.'

'The what?'

'Doctor. Elsa's husband was a Dr Byrne. The GP says there are places he can check. Professional bodies, things like that. If the husband's been on a register somewhere, chances are they'll still have an address of some sort. If we find him, we find Elsa.'

Oskar is not worried to hear there is a husband; he has never paid much attention to husbands. He already knows what he will say to Elsa.

Elsa

Sebastian has his own way of sitting at the piano. Not on the stool, exactly, but propped up against it, his body braced for take-off. It's their last run-through before the Pre-College audition, and Elsa has already decided to say nothing, just to let him play. In the distance, she can hear Carmela emptying the dishwasher, clashing handfuls of cutlery into the drawer, then sliding it shut. She closes the door to block out the noise, pulls her chair over to the window that overlooks the park, and sits there with her notebook on her lap.

'Play it all,' she tells him. 'The Bach first, then right through to the Khachaturian. Whatever happens, just keep on going till you reach the end.'

Even sitting with her back to him, she can sense his nerves; the deep breath she's taught him to take is gulped down. The prelude and fugue start well: bright, light but steely too. She grips the arms of the chair as he approaches the passage that always seems to trip him up. Today, though, he eases over it. She smiles out at the park. He's almost ready, she thinks. And just in time, too.

Sometimes it's hard to believe he's Maya's son. Charlie and Elsa tried Maya on piano, violin, even flute, but she'd never shown the slightest interest. It was always the dance with Maya. But then Sebastian came along and, out of the blue, they had a pianist. What was he? Two, two and a half, the day she first sat him down next to her at the piano? After he'd clashed down through the octaves with the palms of his hands, like all kids do, he stopped and listened to her picking out a melody. Very soon, he could play it back to her. It was their little game. Often he would play a single note and follow it lower and lower until the tone had completely disappeared and the side of his head was resting on the keys. And now, just fourteen, he plays baroque music with more fluency and verve than she's ever done herself. When he finishes the Bach, she has to stop herself from applauding, because, after all, no one will applaud at Juilliard. Besides, though she is quite sure it was wonderful, a grandmother can never be entirely bias-free.

He doesn't start the next piece right away, as though her silence has intimidated him. She glances over her shoulder to check that he's okay. He shuffles against the stool, fiddles with the handles. He rolls his shoulders like a boxer, cricks his neck. At last, he settles into perfect stillness. His slender back flexes as he takes on the sonata she chose for him. She went for Mozart, the C Minor, though Beethoven is always the favourite. Most kids will attempt one of the warhorses and be trampled by it. But the Mozart is so difficult to get right. Several times she's heard it played so sweet and heavy that all she could think of were those horrible Mozartkugeln a pupil gave her once at Christmas. Played badly, it was marzipan for the soul. Not Sebastian; he played with it with love and urgency and a kind of desolation. Sometimes she found it hard to believe that he was only fourteen. It was a mystery to her how someone who had hardly lived at all could play like that. Sebastian had never suffered anything worse than a bout of flu, or a girl he liked sitting next to someone else in math, and yet he seemed to understand so much.

He is just starting the second movement when Carmela opens the door and tiptoes in with the morning mail. She shakes her head, mimicking disbelief at the standard of the playing, then lays a little pile of letters on the table next to Elsa before tiptoeing out again. She recognises Maya's hand-writing on a pink envelope, James's on a white one. Of course, it's Mother's Day this weekend. They will have a family lunch in the Italian place Maya likes but James can't stand. Siblings. The rest are brown envelopes: bills or requests from charities. She resumes her concentration on the sonata and makes herself a little note. *Adagio: starts too fast. Need much more contrast with 1ˢᵗ mov.*

The door creaks open again and she feels a little stab of impatience with Carmela, who mouths, 'Sorry,' and places something else on top of the pile of letters.

This one looks more interesting; it's a little white mailer with a great splattering of stamps on its top right corner. Elsa rarely receives packages unless it's a birthday or some other celebration. Mother's Day again? She doesn't think so. The package is a little smaller than a paperback. The stamps are ones she hasn't seen before: bright blue skies, a biplane, a helicopter. Éire, they say. She looks on the back for a sender but there isn't one.

She hasn't been back to Ireland in twenty years, since Charlie died. That final visit most of the time was spent in the countryside, at his sister's house in Adare, but they'd stayed a week in Dublin too. They made a nostalgia trip to Stamer Street but there was no sign of any Abrahamsons any more. Someone said they thought the last of the family had left for Israel some years back. Portobello had changed completely. Only one Jewish bakery remained, and though they were there over Purim, there weren't even any *hamantaschen* on sale.

'No demand,' said the baker. 'It's really just bagels and pretzels these days.'

She'd been glad to get away, relieved she'd never made the trip back to Berlin.

Elsa turns the package over in her hands. The handwriting looks young, rounded, probably female. Most of Charlie's relations left Ireland long ago, in the course of one recession or another. Nowadays, they were scattered: England, Holland, even Australia. There is something odd about the package. She can't think what it is but she's sure it will come to her when Sebastian has finished. Right now, though, she needs to concentrate. She's missed most of the second movement and now he's already well into the third. He plays it beautifully, and when he dashes off the final two chords, she gets to her feet. 'Bravo!' she says. 'Bravo!' The sound of her voice makes him jump, and she realises then just how tense he is.

He smiles, a little wearily, when she touches him on the shoulder. She hopes she hasn't been pushing him too hard.

'Bubbe,' he says. 'Can I get a glass of water?'

'Take a break if you like, darling,' she says. 'Have a walk around, stretch your legs. We never really decided which one you're playing next, did we? The Chopin or the Field?' He shrugs, and next thing he's out the door and she can hear Carmela offering him a milkshake.

It's only as she's tearing open the package that she realises what's strange about it. They've used her maiden name. Miss Elsa Frankel. She draws her cashmere shawl closer around her. She changed her name to Byrne back in '48, as soon as she was married. By that time, Charlie had contacted the bureau and they'd tracked down her parents' names on a deportation list to Theresienstadt. The new name had been a comfort, a wing to shelter under. It was years before she felt strong enough to be Elsa Frankel again. It was a way of honouring Mama and Papa, to use the name professionally for the performances she gave now and then in the outer boroughs. Then, when the career ended, she put the name away.

The kids were Frankel–Byrnes: their choice, not hers. In her late teens, Maya had stood at the door of the kitchen, her hands on her hips, and announced that she wanted to go to synagogue. 'You can't stop me from being what I am.'

Charlie wasn't keen on any religion but he said nothing. As for Elsa herself, though she found it too painful to be Jewish in New York, let alone admit she was from Berlin and ally herself with the wounded and the lost, she was glad, too, that the thread had not been broken. If Maya was willing to take it on, well and good. For Elsa, it was just too hard.

She looks at the name. Elsa Frankel. She traces the curved lines of the handwriting with her fingertip. She can't imagine why she should suddenly be Elsa Frankel again. Not now, at nearly seventy-eight.

The letter is in German. She reads the opening line and at once she knows who this is. The day slips away from her, and the place, and she is back in Berlin with Oskar, as though the entire life she has lived as Elsa Byrne suddenly belongs to someone else. When she looks up, Carmela is standing over her. She is saying something about a sandwich. She recites a list of ingredients: pastrami, cheese, tuna. She talks of a little salad, maybe, if Mrs Byrne would like. But the voice in the letter is more urgent than anything Carmela has to say. Meanwhile, Sebastian has started to play the Field. It is the wrong moment for Field, and she tells him to stop. Something in her voice must have startled him. He gets up from the piano and moves towards her. 'You okay, Bubbe?' he said. 'You sure?'

She tries to keep her voice steady. 'Try the Chopin instead,' she says. 'The B flat minor. Play that.'

My dearest Elsa, the letter begins, *I have always loved you.*

While she could read the letter well enough without them, she pulls up her glasses from the chain around her neck and puts them on to hold back her tears. She reads it through, and then again, and each time more and more of it returns to her. The woods? She remembers the woods, the lake, all of it. She'd been no more than Sebastian's age when she and Oskar fell in love. She would practise for hours at the open window of the house in Zweibruckenstrasse, the music wafting over all the neighbourhood gardens that stretched right down to the tall screen of chestnut trees. How she'd loved that garden: the pale pink roses on the wall that divided them from the Müllers, the old swing, the summerhouse where Papa would drive Mama crazy with his paint spatters all over the floor. Mama and Papa. She couldn't bear to think of them. Theresienstadt, and then what? Charlie had spent years trying to find out what had happened to everyone but in the end she'd asked not to hear any more.

Through her tears, she can see that Sebastian isn't really playing any more; he's just limping through the piece while he watches her over his shoulder. Next thing, he's beside her, his arms around her. She relaxes against him. It's been so long since anyone has really held her. She tries to tell him not to worry but Carmela is there with a phone in her hand, saying something about a doctor. Sebastian picks up Oskar's envelope gingerly and examines it as if it's a suspect device. She puts her hand on his. 'It's alright, my darling,' she says. 'I'm not ill, and it's not bad news. Sometimes, we cry because we are too happy to laugh.'

He doesn't look like he entirely believes her, though he probably wants to. It takes a while to persuade them both to leave her, that she'll be fine on her own.

'Come back tomorrow, Sebastian,' she says. 'And we'll finish the rest. I just need some time to think. Your Chopin was too moving, you see.' She laughs a little, and so does he. 'Don't say anything to Mama, now, will you? There's no need for her to worry.'

Finally, they shut the door of the apartment behind them, and Elsa listens to the silence, until she realises that it isn't really a silence at all. There is the carriage clock on her desk, the longcase in the hallway, the silly ormolu frou-frou thing on the sideboard. Tick, tick, tick, tick. Before today, it hadn't bothered her too much that time was running out. Now, everything is urgent. Suddenly, there is so much to fit in. The thought that something might happen to prevent her seeing Oskar makes her heart gallop so fast she can hardly breathe.

She's been so distracted by the letter that she hasn't even looked to see what else is in the envelope: two audio tapes, strapped together with a rubber band and a yellow Post-it note.

'My story, Elsa, is in these. Our story, too, I suppose, or part of it. My granddaughter's ingenuity didn't stretch as far as your telephone number, so I have given you mine. I don't expect anything, but I hope this makes a difference.'

She panics for a moment when she realises she's thrown out the old tape deck. Then she remembers the Walkman that James gave her while she was recovering from pneumonia. She finds the right size of batteries in a kitchen drawer. Her fingers clumsy with anticipation, she slots them in. Before she presses the button, she takes a moment to look out over the park at the view that has been hers for nearly all her marriage, certain it will never be quite the same view again. Then, she puts on the headphones and waits.

It is astonishing to hear his voice. She can't remember how he sounded when young but there's something in the rhythm of his speech that seems familiar, and when he takes a breath or swallows, she feels it in her head, as though the story he tells is something she has always known but had somehow lost the ability to hear. When the story has been told, she cries. Not because she married Charlie. She loved Charlie: they were happy and it had helped that New York was a third place, new to both of them. She cries with the relief of knowing that she wasn't wrong about Oskar. It's a small thing, in the great land-scape of betrayal that was Berlin all those years ago. But it's something true, and that matters.

While she's been listening to Oskar, the day has dropped slowly down the sky. The trees are growing blacker as the sky deepens and reddens over at the far fringes of the park. The day will soon be gone, just as, soon enough, the old century will be gone too. She wonders when Maya will ring, because she knows Sebastian won't be able to keep this to himself. There will be a phone call and then there will be explanations required. How can she tell Maya about any of this? What could she say that would make any sense at all?

Far below, a long stream of traffic snarls and snakes around the edges of the park. She goes into the kitchen to make herself a cup of tea. As she waits for the kettle to boil, she struggles to recall his face, then catches her own reflection in the oven glass. They would both look so different now. They are not the same people any more. Not a single molecule of either of them remains from back then. And yet. She goes over to the piano and adjusts the stool. She still plays most days, but never Chopin.

She tries the melody on its own at first. After only a couple of bars, it gives her the answer, as she knew it would. It's nearly nightfall when she lifts the phone.

Acknowledgements

Thanks to the ZenAzzurri writers, past and present; Anne Aylor, Susan Clegg, Anita Dawood, Gavin Eyers, Aimee Hansen, Richard Hughes, Margaret Laing, Roger Levy, Steve Mullins, Sally Ratcliffe, Richard Simmons, and Elise Valmorbida. I am particularly grateful to Elise, who gave generously of her outstanding gifts – I was fortunate to have such a reader.

Thanks also to Lynn Foote, Vicky Grut, Aoi Matsushima, Kathy Page, Dallas Sealy and Novelette Stewart for their valuable input on an early draft.

I am indebted to Alan Scheckenbach, who answered some of my questions via the Luftwaffe Discussion Board and conducted an interview on my behalf with Erich Sommer, since deceased, a former member of a KGr100 crew based in Vannes.

I am also grateful to the late Margarete Fleischmann McCann whose husband, George Fleischmann, was interned in G-Camp at the Curragh and who was generous enough to lend me her only copy of his memoir, allowing it to leave Canada temporarily despite never having met me. Also, to Noel Mulvihill, who put me in touch with Margarete.

Thanks to the staff of the library of the Imperial War Museum in London for their tremendous help; to the Irish Jewish Museum, a unique window on a vanished way of life in Portobello; to the British Library newspaper archive and the London Library.

A few words about music: the piece Elsa plays at the Feis Ceoil, and again at the end of the book, is Chopin's *Nocturne in D flat Major Op. 27, No 2*; the song Charlie hears as he walks down Stamer Street is 'I dreamt I dwelt in marble halls' from *The Bohemian Girl* by Michael William Balfe; the medley Elsa plays after the Shabbat dinner is from Franz Léhar's operetta, *Das Land des Lächelns* (The Land of Smiles); and the tune Charlie recognises is 'Dein ist mein ganzes Herz'. The best-known recordings of John Field's fifteen sublime Nocturnes are by John O'Conor and Miceál O'Rourke.

One of the seeds for this book was a face in a photograph of a group of pupils at the Read School of Pianoforte in Dublin, which my aunt Nuala attended in the late 1930s. Nuala remembered the girl as a German Jewish exile and brilliant pianist and somehow, years later, she became the inspiration for Elsa.

I would like to express my gratitude to Listowel Writers' Week for awarding *Guest* the 2009 Bryan MacMahon short story award, and to Helen Carey who republished it in the brochure for that year's TULCA visual arts festival; also to Fish Publishing for awarding *Painting over Elsa* a prize in the 2009 short story competition.

Many thanks to Ronan Colgan of The History Press Ireland, and to Beth Amphlett and Maeve Convery.

Finally, the greatest thanks of all to my mother and late father, to Mike for his love and patience, and to my wonderful sons – Patrick, Conor and Rory.